DAY

OF

ICE

DAY of ICE

A
CRUSOE
ADVENTURE

ANDREW LANE

ⒶADAPTIVE BOOKS

AN IMPRINT OF ADAPTIVE STUDIOS | CULVER CITY, CA

Copyright © 2017 Adaptive Studios

Visit us on the web at www.adaptivestudios.com

Library of Congress Cataloging-in-Publication Number: 2016956283
B&N ISBN: 978-1-945293-21-4
Ebook ISBN: 978-1-945293-22-1

Printed in the United States of America

Cover design by Laz Marquez
Interior design and typesetting by Neuwirth & Associates

Adaptive Books
3578 Hayden Avenue, Suite 6
Culver City, CA 90232

10 9 8 7 6 5 4 3 2 1

Also in the Crusoe Adventure series:

DAWN OF SPIES (BOOK ONE)
BY ANDREW LANE

DAY
of
ICE

CHAPTER ONE

Friday's breath turned to vapor as soon as she exhaled, forming a plume that drifted away to join the mist that was already filling London's streets.

She was endlessly fascinated by being able to *see* when she breathed out. The island that she and Robin had been cast away on for so long had been tropical. The weather had been changeable—sometimes dry, sometimes stormy—but it had always been hot. Now that she was in England, she had experienced ice and snow for the first time—and she loved it.

She tried to blow a ring of vapor, in the same way that the men smoking pipes in the taverns and coffee shops of London would sometimes blow a ring of tobacco smoke, but she kept giggling and spoiling the effect.

Friday stood on a street overlooking the width of the Thames. On the other side were the slums, factories, and patches of waste ground that constituted the south bank; on her side were the streets, alleys, houses, shops, taverns, coffee houses, and palaces of the north. She could smell the smoke of a thousand fires: wood of all kinds, from fragrant apple and pine to the deeper pungency of oak and ash.

Of course, she was bundled up in several layers of clothes to keep out the cold. She couldn't remember ever having worn that many things at one time before. Only her head and her hands were exposed to the air, and the freezing weather caused pins and needles in her cheeks and her fingers.

Standing beside her, Robin was also bundled up in thick woolen garments and a cap. She was so used to seeing him in just something loose and light that it was difficult to reconcile the boy beside her with the one she had grown up with.

And that was another thing. He wasn't a boy anymore: he was a man. Just in the past month his body had bulked out with muscle, and it wasn't going to be long before he had to start shaving the stubble from his face. Either that or he would have to grow a beard. The thought of Robin with a beard made her giggle again: half the men in London seemed to have them, but she couldn't imagine him with dark hair hiding his cheeks and chin.

She wondered what it would be like to kiss him with a beard, then quickly suppressed the thought. She felt herself blushing, despite the cold. She knew that he had feelings for her, and she knew that she felt the same way about him, but neither of them had ever acted on it—yet. One day, perhaps, they would, but for now their lives were too complicated to add in anything more.

He turned to look at her, and raised an eyebrow. He didn't have to ask her what was going on in her mind: they had spent long enough together that each could tell what the other was thinking just from their expression or the way they held their body.

"You would look good with a beard," she said.

"My father had a beard," he said, surprising her. "I've been wondering what I might look like with one."

She reached out to touch his hand, just briefly. "You do not say very much about your family."

"I don't remember much about my mother—my father took me away to sea when I was very young. As for him—" He shrugged. "He was a good man. A dedicated man." He glanced sideways at her, and Friday could tell that he wanted to change the subject. "Of course, I can use a beard for insulation—you'll just have to wrap something around your face."

"Do you think it is going to get any colder?" she asked.

He turned and gazed out across the water again. "The Thames is going to freeze," he pointed out. "It's already getting slushy around the edges. Give it another day or two and I think we'll be able to walk all the way across to the other bank."

She looked at the river in surprise. "Are you *serious*? The river could actually freeze from this side to the other?"

"I'm serious."

"How thick?"

"Could be up to twelve inches of ice."

"How far downstream?"

He thought for a moment. "It could go all the way down past Thanet. Some of the older ferrymen and sailors say that they've known the ice to extend out into the sea and around the coast."

Friday shuddered, and it wasn't the cold that caused it: mention of Thanet reminded Friday of the time, just a few short weeks ago, when she and Robin had escaped from the fort occupied by the mysterious Circle of Thirteen, rescuing Isaac Newton and the Countess of Lichfield as they went. Isaac Newton was a friend of theirs now, and a colleague in the secret organization known as Segment W that had been set up to protect England from threats. But the countess had turned out to be an agent of the Circle. There were times during that escape when she thought she had lost Robin forever, and the terror that swept over her had made her reconsider the way she felt about him. The trouble was, she wasn't sure she was ready to act on those feelings.

She was about to broach the subject when a figure appeared out of the swirling mist. "Robin! Friday! Please accept my profuse apologies for this late arrival!"

It was Daniel Defoe—the first friend they had made when they arrived in London, and the man who had recruited them to Segment W. He was a trader and a writer of pamphlets on various subjects, which he sold for a few pence each, but he was also an undercover agent of the king, tasked with seeking out enemies of the country based on things he might overhear in the many coffee houses and taverns he frequented while conducting business.

"Daniel!" Robin extended his arm and the two men shook hands. "Are you well?"

"Passing well," he said. "My civet cats are not altogether fond of this weather, and so their production of musk for my perfume business has dropped steeply. Also, within a day or two, no ships will be able to penetrate this far up the Thames, and business will suffer. I know that ships already berthed here are trying to speed up their departures so they can get to the sea before they are trapped."

"So the river *is* going to freeze?" Friday asked. "What happens then?"

"On the minus side, a complete lack of trade for however long it takes to thaw. On the plus side, there will be booths and entertainments out on the ice, and all kinds of merriment. It will be as if London suddenly has a new road running right through its center, and people will colonize it right away. 'Frost Fairs,' they call them."

Friday grabbed at Robin's arm. "Can we go? Please?" she pleaded.

He smiled. "Of course we can. I wouldn't miss a Frost Fair for the world."

Defoe glanced from Robin to Friday and back again. "I haven't eaten in so long my stomach thinks that my throat has disowned it and has gone to look for other, more convivial, friends. Can we please find food, and quickly?"

Robin nodded, and led the way back through a maze of narrow alleys to a particular coffee house that had become a favorite of his and Friday's. The fish there was always fresh—not something that could be said of all the coffee houses in London—and the prices were fair. They did still eat in the refectory that had been set up at Segment W's temporary headquarters in what had previously been the Globe Theater—they had rooms there as well—but both of them loved exploring the various highways and byways of London. They had almost by accident assembled a collection of places they liked to rest and eat. And, of course, places they didn't. There were still many dark areas of London where it was not safe to go.

It cost a penny for each of them to enter. They took a booth to themselves: Friday and Robin on one side and Defoe spreading himself out on the other. The room was sparsely decorated: just carpeted floorboards, bare tables, and a few divans spread around. It was, however, heaving with people. A haze of tobacco smoke—or perhaps misty breath, Friday thought—hid the rafters above.

"How are the repairs coming along to the *Great Equatorial?*" Robin asked as soon as they were settled.

"Slowly," Defoe admitted. "Any work has to be done in secret, of course. Nobody knew that Segment W was based in that old wreck in the first place, so the sudden appearance of carpenters and other workmen around it would attract too much attention. We have to sneak them inside when nobody is around. As if that isn't bad enough, the water damage to the lower levels is quite bad, and the water has to be pumped out by hand before we can do anything. It's not as if we can lift the whole thing up on pillars and let the water drain naturally away—that would be too obvious." He sighed. "I am beginning to think that we might be based in the Globe for a long time—perhaps forever."

Friday found herself remembering the moment, in Sir William Lambert's study in the *Great Equatorial*, when the Circle of

Thirteen's attack ship had smashed through the large window, letting the Thames into the previously watertight hull: the crashing of the glass, the sudden rush of salty water, and the stench of rotting vegetables, burning whale fat, and worse things from the riverbanks. Leaving the island, and the threat of the pirates who occasionally used it as a base, she had thought that life would get safer for her and for Robin. It hadn't really turned out that way.

She was just about to tell Defoe that as far as she was concerned, the Globe served perfectly well as a place to live when a serving girl appeared beside the booth.

"Can I—oh! Mr. Foe, I haven't seen you for ages! What can I get you, sir?"

Defoe seemed embarrassed at being recognized, but he said: "I'll have a pie, please—beef—and ale." He looked at Robin and Friday. "What about you two?"

"A lamb pie," Robin said firmly. He'd become very fond of lamb pies since returning to England.

"And the same for me," Friday said.

"And three bowls of coffee," Defoe added.

As the girl left, Robin frowned at Defoe.

"Is Mr. *Foe* your real name?"

Defoe shrugged and looked down at the table. "I have to be honest," he said. "I was not born with the name 'Defoe.' I was christened 'Daniel James Foe' instead, of the Foe family in the parish of St. Giles' Cripplegate, London."

"Why did you change it?" Friday asked.

"Simply because 'Foe' is a very boring and common name. For a while I called myself 'Daniel *de* Foe,' in the French style—Daniel of the Foe family. Then, when I got bored of that, I told people that I was Daniel *de Beau Faux*. I've more recently settled on the simpler Daniel Defoe. It sounds interesting, and a little cosmopolitan, which is useful both in business and in the publishing of pamphlets on subjects such as politics and commerce."

The serving girl arrived back with a metal jug and three china bowls. "Food will be along shortly," she said. They drank, and when the meals arrived they ate. They discussed Defoe's early life in the village of Dorking and his move to London to make his fortune as a man of business. He also admitted to dealing in hosiery, general woolen goods, and wine, as well as attempting to manufacture perfumes.

"I'm surprised you actually have any time to work for Sir William," Robin said.

"I get bored very easily," Defoe admitted. "I need many different things going on in my life to keep me interested."

Friday smiled. "We noticed that," she said.

True to his word, Defoe quickly got tired of answering questions about his early life and changed the subject. "One of the things I am most interested in, of course," he said, "is your time on the island." He paused, thinking. "I keep calling it 'the island,' because that's the only way I have ever heard it described, but did it—*does* it—have an actual name?"

Robin frowned. "Not that I ever knew," he said.

"My father never referred to it as anything else but 'the island,'" Friday added. "In fact, the way he said it was more like '*the* island,' as if it was obvious which island he was referring to. The funny thing was, it wasn't marked on any of the nautical maps he had in his cabin. He found it by locating a small atoll a hundred miles or so away and then sailing in a particular direction until he saw seabirds circling in the sky. That's when he knew he was close."

Robin nodded his agreement. "I asked the captain of the ship that rescued us—the *Inviolate*—about it. He said that he found it by accident, and that it shouldn't have been where it was. His own charts said the ocean was empty at that point." He frowned.

"I think my father knew. He had charts in his cabin, and he would stare at them for hours, trying to work out where we were. He'd drawn an arrow on the charts pointing to where it was." Memories were flooding back to Robin as he shared them. "He had a journal as well. He was always writing in it."

"Strange." Defoe mused, "If I was of a suspicious mind I would suspect that efforts had been made to keep it off the maps." He glanced up at Robin and Friday, and his expression disquieted Friday. It was as if he was attempting to be casual while asking a question whose answer was important to him. "I mean," he pressed, "it wasn't as if the island possessed a gold mine, or a silver mine, or a quarry where jewels could be found, was it? That *could* be a reason for people to keep its location secret."

Friday took care not to look at Robin. And he didn't glance at her.

"No," he replied carefully. "Not that we ever found."

"While things are quiet," Defoe said, "I would like to question you further about your time stranded there. People in London need some distraction from the problems of their daily lives, and a series of pamphlets telling your stories would, I am sure, sell in the thousands."

"Perhaps they would," Robin said, "but we've already told you— we don't really want to talk about it. We want to put the island, and everything that happened on it, behind us. We want to move on with our lives."

Reluctantly, Defoe nodded. "Sir William has called a meeting for later this afternoon to discuss the question of the Circle of Thirteen," he told Friday and Robin. "He requested specifically that the two of you attend, given that much of what we know of the Circle is thanks to your efforts."

"Why has it taken this long for Sir William to turn his attention to the Circle?" Robin asked. "Surely something should have been done about the Countess of Lichfield much earlier?"

Defoe nodded. "I understand your concerns, but you have to remember that the countess is . . . "—he hesitated—"or at least is *alleged* to be the illegitimate daughter of the king, born of the Duchess of Cleveland, which means that any action taken against her has to be thought through very carefully. The king is very protective of her, and would need convincing that she was indeed an agent of this organization. After all, we only have Miss Friday's observations of the strange blue patterns on her shoulder—the same as the patterns on the skin of the other Circle of Thirteen agents that we have seen. It could be argued the patterns are merely similar to the others and caused by some skin disease. In addition, the Circle is not the most important thing on Sir William's mind. There is great unrest at the moment over perceived Catholic threats to the king. Some people are suggesting that other nations are conspiring together to have the king killed. Other people say they have heard the sound of digging near the House of Commons, or that they know for a fact that the French have already invaded the Isle of Purbeck, on the South Coast, and raised their flag there. All of these things have to be investigated."

"Do you believe these stories?" Friday asked.

Defoe shrugged. "There is little evidence for them," he admitted, "but that doesn't make the king feel any safer. Besides, there is obviously *something* going on. Sir Edmund Berry Godfrey of Parliament was murdered most horribly a year ago, and nobody has yet been brought to justice for his death. As if that wasn't bad enough, the Duke of Wimbourne disappeared about six months ago. Anybody even *suspected* of having Catholic sympathies has been ordered to leave London and not come within ten miles of the city. Feelings are running high."

"But these things are mainly rumors and stories," Friday pressed. "At least we know the Circle of Thirteen is real."

"Perhaps they were the ones who had Sir Godfrey killed," Robin pointed out.

Once they had finished, they left the tavern and headed for a main street where Defoe could hail a carriage. The carriage set off—not for the supposedly abandoned Globe Theater itself, as Defoe obviously didn't want to draw too much attention to the fact that it was being used again, but for a church nearby. The carriage clattered through the streets of London, headed for London Bridge. Robin and Defoe sank back into the comfortable upholstered seats, but Friday leaned forward to gaze out the window. The sight of so many people still fascinated her, even though she had been in London for several weeks now. What did they all do to occupy their time? How did they manage to earn the money to buy their food? How many of them were honest citizens and how many were parasites, stealing from the honest ones?

The streets of the city were slick and shiny with ice. Any bucketful of wastewater that was chucked out a doorway or an upstairs window froze within seconds after it hit the ground, no matter how warm it had been when the bucket was filled. People slipped on the ice and fell over, cursing the originators to high heaven. The piles of dung left by the thousands of horses that filled the streets were as hard as iron.

As the carriage turned onto the bridge, Friday's gaze passed over a group of men standing on the corner. They were dark-skinned, and their clothes were more colorful than was normal for Londoners. They wore headscarves over their hair, and Friday could see the glint of gold rings in their ears. For a long moment she thought they looked remarkably like the pirates whom she and Robin had left behind on the island. And then, with a terrible lurch, she realized: they *were* the pirates whom she and Robin had left behind on the island.

Two Years and Six Months Before the Escape

Suriya Dinajara scrubbed the deck of the Dark Nebula *with a brush whose bristles were almost all worn away. The bucket beside her contained vinegar, taken from a barrel the pirates had taken as booty in some previous attack. They had nearly thrown it over the side of the captured ship, but she had made them keep it. She had read, in some book she had rescued from another captive ship, that vinegar could be used to clean and purify a ship, and although the sharp smell made her nose itch, it was far better than the sickening stench of the ship and its crew.*

She heard muttering voices behind her but didn't turn her head. There was no point in making herself a target. Even though her father was the ship's captain, he wasn't immune to mutiny. Her position there could turn in an instant. But she kept scrubbing. Better do something than nothing.

Suriya never noticed quite how bad the horrific stench became until the ship dropped anchor at some remote island and she was allowed to go ashore. Then the fresh air and the intoxicating smell of the brightly colored blossoms made her dizzy. It felt the same way she imagined expensive wine would feel—the kind her father took from the traders whom he robbed and then either sold or quaffed directly from the bottle in his cabin, not the rough stuff that his crew drank. That stuff could bleach wood if it was spilled.

When they were in port or stationary off the coast of an island she would spend as much time ashore as possible, running across the beaches, along the rotting wooden quays of the docks, past the shanty-towns, or up and down the winding paths of the hill settlements, breathing deeply to clear her lungs of the last fumes of the ship. She imagined that she could actually see them coming out: trails of black vapor drifting from her mouth, fading and thinning the longer she spent away from the cramped, damp interior of the Dark Nebula. But then, when she went back, she could suddenly smell it all again. The stench of men who hadn't washed the dirt and sweat from their bodies for years, of rotting food and rotting teeth, of moldy wood and human waste made her throat close up and her eyes fill with stinging tears. It brought her close to vomiting. There was also an underlying odor of ancient decay, as if something had died on the ship and hadn't been thrown overboard. Something, or someone.

She had to endure it, however. It was her father's ship, and he was her protector. If she left him she would starve, or worse. He kept her safe.

She had realized, long ago, that whenever she left the ship she was followed by two of her father's pirate crew. They tried to be discreet, but it was hard to miss them. For one thing the stench of the ship clung to them like a cloud of flies. She had asked her father once why they were always there. He had smiled.

"It is not safe for you," he said. "There are people—other captains—who would take you prisoner and use you as leverage to force me to hand over some of our treasures. There are other people—traders and merchants—who would cheerfully slit your throat to punish me for taking those treasures from them in the first place." He scowled. "And men in general, especially sailors, especially pirates, cannot be trusted where girls are concerned."

"What do you mean?" she asked, confused.

"Wait until you are older," he said. "I will tell you then."

But as she grew older, she thought she knew. Or, at least, was beginning to understand. The looks she got from some of the men at port changed in some way. They became darker, more avaricious—the same expressions she saw on the faces of her father and his pirate crew when they were sailing and a merchant ship appeared as a dark dot on the horizon. In some way she had become a treasure just by growing up, but she didn't know how.

Sometimes she dreamed of leaving the Dark Nebula, just staying ashore at some port where they dropped anchor, but it was just a dream. The thought of leaving her father—the only family she had— scared her. The thought of what he might do if he found her again scared her even more.

She had other reasons for exploring, apart from the joy of fresh air and the wonders of exploration. Wherever she went, she looked for her mother.

She didn't know her mother's name, or what she looked like. Her father had told her that her mother died giving birth to her, but she didn't believe him. Her father lied often and fluently. Once, passing by a tavern window in some port, she heard her father's voice through an open window. She didn't catch the words, but the reply from whomever he was sitting with was, "You speak many languages, Red Tiberius, but the one you are most fluent in is deceit." Moments later she heard the sound of swords being drawn, and she moved on, not wanting to be discovered. And not wanting to see what she already knew—that her father was a brute.

She knew that she would know her mother, however. She knew that the moment she laid eyes on her, she would recognize her. Not only that, but the recognition would be mutual. She believed that her mother met her father while he was ashore, and for some reason Suriya had ended up with her father rather than her mother. The details were sketchy in her mind, but she knew that was the way it must have been, and for some reason her father would never talk about her mother, or explain what had happened. So she kept on looking, and hoping.

The trouble was that none of the women she saw onshore were what she imagined her mother to be. They were either drab and avoided looking at anyone, or they were buxom and bejeweled and their eyes challenged any man who crossed their path. None of them looked . . . motherly.

And then, all too quickly, they were recalled to the Dark Nebula. Sometimes it was because her father had completed his negotiations and wanted to get back to piracy rather than business; sometimes it was because of reports that the navy was about to blockade the port and everyone had to get out, or sometimes it was because he had angered someone and needed to retreat before he was attacked and his ship set fire to. But they inevitably ended up at sea, where she spent most of her time in the bow of the ship, letting the headwinds blow the stench of the pirates and their vessel away from her.

Two pirates passed by, interrupting her thoughts. One of them kicked at the bucket as he passed. She'd known he was going to do it—someone always tried—and she slid it out of the way, the brown liquid sloshing inside. The pirate stumbled and cursed. Suriya stared down at the deck, but she was aware that he was stopping and turning back toward her. His companion caught his shoulder and tried to pull him away, but he shrugged the hand off.

"What's that in the bucket?" he asked suspiciously.

Suriya's mind raced. He was obviously itching for a fight, and even if she didn't provoke him further he would probably cuff her hard on the side of her head just because he could. Her father wouldn't intervene for something that minor—he would prefer that she stood on her own two feet rather than have him protect her. She felt the spark of anger that she kept hidden inside her suddenly flare up.

"French brandy," she lied, still not meeting his gaze. "I heard it was good for cleaning decks."

"What—that booze we took from the last ship we attacked?" He was outraged. "That's for the crew, that is—not swabbing the decks!"

Suriya pushed the bucket toward him. "I'm sorry," she said quietly. "Please—have some."

He grabbed the handle of the bucket. She followed the bucket with her gaze as he lifted it to his lips. She recognized him now—Robert-shaw: a pirate whose nose had been sliced off for theft at some stage in his career. Maybe by her father, maybe by another captain.

He looked at his companion. "Cheers," he said, smirking, and swigged heartily from the bucket.

It was probably his own smell that disguised the vinegar, right up to the moment that he swallowed it. His eyes bulged as he clawed at his throat. He dropped the bucket and rushed for the side of the ship, making choking noises. Suriya grabbed the bucket before it could spill more than a few ounces of its contents.

The second pirate was looking at her. "He's going to make you pay for that, girl," he said. "And he won't think about your father until afterward."

She nodded. "I'll go below for a while," she replied quietly. Just like her father, Suriya knew when to retreat.

THE ONE IN the middle was Mohir—her father's most trusted lieu-tenant. She didn't know the name of the one to his right, but she remembered that he used to like killing the seabirds that followed the ship; luring them down to the deck with scraps of bread and then cleaving them in two with a swift stroke of his sword. It had amused him. The one to his left was new to her, but he looked equally brutal.

Her blood turned to ice. She was suddenly very aware of the thudding of her heart. How could they be here, in London of all places? Her father spent his time sailing around the Caribbean, looking for easy vessels to plunder, and besides: even if he decided to sail for colder waters this wasn't the kind of port that pirates frequented. England was implacably opposed to piracy, and the Royal Navy spent its time hunting down pirates and their ships. Docking here would be akin to walking into the middle of a pride of lions and sitting down for a rest.

Mohir was giving orders to the other pirates. He was gesticulating with his hands, trying to get his point across. They were all dressed in silk sashes and leathers, but they had removed the flintlock pistols from the ends of the sashes.

And if they were here, where was her father? Where was Vijaya Dinajara, better known as Red Tiberius? Was he in one of the nearby buildings? Was he standing just a few feet away from the carriage, staring at her the way she was staring at his men?

The thought made her tear her gaze away from the three pirates and quickly scan the rest of the crowd, but she couldn't see her father.

She sensed Robin turning his head to say something to her, but the words caught in his throat as his gaze locked on the three pirates on the corner. "That's—" he started to say.

The carriage lurched as the horses pulled it around the corner and onto the bridge. The three pirates slid out of sight behind them.

"Yes," Friday said bleakly. "It was."

"Mohir and two others!"

His thoughts struggled to catch up with his words. "But what are they doing here—in London?"

"They are looking for us," she replied. Her heart felt like it was slowly turning to ice and sinking inside her. "That's the only explanation for them being here."

Daniel Defoe glanced from Robin to her and back again. "What is it?" he asked.

Friday couldn't find the words, so Robin answered for her. "We just saw three pirates from Red Tiberius's crew. They were just standing on the corner back there."

"Are you—?" Defoe started to say, then he caught himself. "Of course you are. You two have the sharpest eyes I've ever known. But what would they be doing here, of all places?"

"My father promised me to Mohir in marriage," Friday said, and the words were like bitter ashes in her mouth. "When I ran away I not only challenged my father's authority, I insulted Mohir. Now they've come for me."

"But they won't find you," Robin promised. He put his arm across her shoulders and hugged her to him. "We'll protect you. *I'll* protect you."

Under other circumstances Friday would have nestled closer to Robin, sharing his warmth, but instead she shivered and unconsciously pulled away from him. She felt as if ants were crawling all over her skin.

"But what about you?" she pointed out. "My father bears ill will toward you as well, if only for rescuing me."

"Actually," Robin pointed out, pulling his arm back, "I think we *both* did those things."

"Yes, but I'm his daughter. He wants me for other reasons. He'll blame you for the attacks we made."

"Oh," was all he could think of to say.

As the carriage clattered across the wide bridge, between the houses and shops that lined both sides, Defoe leaned out of the window and stared at the retreating group of men. "They certainly stand out from the crowd," he said. "We should mention this to Sir William. If they are indeed in London searching for the two of you, then we ought to give you protection when you leave the Globe—one or two of John Caiaphas's men, perhaps. We should also make inquiries as to where these men are staying, how many of them are here, and what exactly they are doing in the city. If they are looking for you, then they must be asking questions."

"That's not necessary," Robin said. "I can protect Friday."

"And I can protect Robin," she added.

"That's not the point." Defoe frowned. "You are both working for Segment W now. You are in our employ. We pay you for your time and your service, but we also have an obligation to protect you. If anything happens to either of you, then our investment is wasted."

"Investment?" Robin questioned, affronted. "Is that all we are to you?"

"I consider you my friends, over and above everything," Defoe clarified, "but remember that an organization like Segment W has no feelings, no emotions. Everything is business—a tally of profit and loss, assets and debts, prospects and threats." His expression was serious. "In the end, does it matter *why* we are offering protection? The important thing is that we *are*."

Friday slumped back against the seat. "Where my father and his crew are concerned," she said bleakly, "I think that distance is the only protection. If they are here, then perhaps we should not be."

CHAPTER TWO

D uring the rest of the journey to the Globe Theater—
now the interim headquarters of Segment W—Crusoe
sat staring out the window. He scanned every face they
passed in case he recognized them, every headscarf and jacket in
case they indicated the wearer was a pirate. Nothing. As far as he
could tell, everyone he could see was a genuine inhabitant of the
city.

Glancing sideways, he saw that Friday's face—usually so open
and expressive—was withdrawn and worried. She caught his eye.
Although her expression didn't change, he knew what she was
thinking. It was what *he* was thinking. Were Red Tiberius's pirates
there by accident, or were they really looking for the two of them?

Friday had once told him that her father never forgot an insult
or a slight. He could wait for years before he took his revenge on
someone—and when he did take that revenge, the scope and se-
verity of it was multiplied by the passing time.

By the time they got to Southwark, and the circular bulk of the
Globe, he was in a dark mood.

Defoe led them straight in, past John Caiaphas's guards, discreetly disguised as beggars grouped around a fire beside the
main entrance.

Crusoe noticed that one of the guards appeared to be roasting a dead rat on a stick. That, as far as Crusoe was concerned, was taking authenticity a bit too far. He'd eaten rats on the island, but he wouldn't choose to do it again in a hurry. Their meat was tough, and tasted rank.

Despite the fact that Segment W was small enough that Defoe, Crusoe, and Friday were instantly recognized, Defoe still surreptitiously showed the guards the ring on the little finger of his left hand—the one with the symbol of Segment W incised on it. Neither Crusoe nor Friday had been given such a ring yet—perhaps there was some kind of initiation ritual they had to go through, or oath they had to swear.

The sight of Defoe's ring dislodged a thought in Crusoe's mind—a memory of a similar ring that his father had worn when they were on the *Rigel*. Similar, or identical? Enough time had passed that he wasn't sure, and the ring was on the bottom of the sea now.

He shook his head. No point in thinking about that now—they had more important things to worry about.

Fires had also been lit in the central area of the building, where the theater audience would have previously stood. They provided some warmth, but the ground itself was frozen hard in between where the fires were placed.

Sir William Lambert was using one of the audience boxes overlooking the stage for his office. The box next to it functioned as a meeting area, with a circular table and several chairs. A platter of meats and sweetmeats had been placed in its center, along with a pitcher of beer and a set of tankards. Building a fire would have been risky, considering that the box was made entirely of wood and was ten feet or so above the ground. Instead, oil lamps on the floor and the table provided some illusion of warmth. Even so, their breath misted in front of their faces as they talked, leaving a haze above the table to join with the smoke from the lamps and the fires below.

Sir William nodded his welcome to them as they took their seats. His powdered wig made him seem taller than he actually was. Moments later John Caiaphas entered the box and waited, with his hand on the back of an empty chair, for Sir William to give him permission to sit. Despite his position as Head of Security, which effectively made him, along with Defoe, one of Sir William's immediate deputies, he deferred to Sir William in a very military way—something that Crusoe noticed Daniel Defoe did not.

"Welcome," Sir William said as they settled. "I realize that we let the matter of the Circle of Thirteen lay fallow while we dealt with other, more pressing threats, but it is now time to take active measures against them. John—have your investigations uncovered any information that might be useful to us?"

Caiaphas shook his head reluctantly. "Every piece of evidence that my men have followed up has finished in a dead end. Nobody will admit to having heard of them, or knowing what it is they want. We have even spread rumors that a member of the king's outer circle came into possession of a scrying orb he was willing to sell, if the price was right, but apart from the usual set of eccentric collectors, nobody expressed any interest."

"I think you will find that at least one of those eccentric collectors was working for the Circle," Defoe pointed out.

Caiaphas nodded. "Indeed, but negotiations ended nowhere. I think they became suspicious, and we could never establish a link between any of them and the Circle."

Sir William turned to Defoe. "Daniel—did you establish any link between the Circle and that great empire in China, given their use of balloons and apparently Asiatic weapons?"

"I made contact with a number of travelers and explorers who have been to China," Defoe said. "I didn't explain why I was asking, on the basis that one or more of them might have been working for the Circle, but none of them provided me with any useful information." He smiled. "Actually, that's not true. I have enough material now to write several pamphlets on the wonders and terrors of the Orient, from which I expect to make a significant amount of money, but I have no useful leads for Segment W to use."

"In the absence of any usable facts," Sir William said decisively, "I wish to pursue a more active plan." He looked around the table. "We believe, based on the markings that Miss Friday saw during their escape from the fort, that the Countess of Lichfield is associated with the Circle of Thirteen. She does not, as far as we're aware, know that we have penetrated her secret. This gives us an opportunity."

"Have you notified the king?" Defoe asked immediately. The same question had been on Crusoe's mind.

Sir William shook his head. "It is more than my life is worth to make unfounded accusations about someone who enjoys the king's favor to the extent that she does. I will need more evidence, but I intend to get it. What I propose is that we allow the countess to 'accidentally' overhear something concerning our operations against the Circle. She will want to get that information to her employers as soon as possible. We will follow her, in secret, and discover who her contact is. That will then give us a way of finding out more about them and the way that they operate."

John Caiaphas nodded slowly. "We could tell His Royal Majesty that our attempt to sell a scrying orb actually *has* identified an intermediary," he said. "That is what we intended to do, of course, and the Circle has no way of knowing that we failed. We can say that we traced that intermediary's contacts, and we will be raiding them shortly. If we are ambiguous enough, then there will be no way they can disprove the information."

"The occasion will have to be carefully chosen," Defoe pointed out, "in order to avoid suspicion. The overheard conversation will have to appear natural."

Sir William nodded. "I think we should choose an entertainment at which the king is present. I will take him to one side and brief him on our supposed plans." He thought for a moment. "I have seen the king's diary, and I believe there is one tomorrow afternoon, at the Drury Lane Theater. We can do it there."

"From what I know of the king," Defoe murmured, "it would be difficult to find a day on which he was *not* attending an entertainment."

Sir William glanced darkly at him. "Let us remember that the king is our patron, our lord, and our master. I will countenance no disrespect."

Defoe nodded, abashed.

"The difficulty," Caiaphas pointed out, "will be making sure that the countess is close enough to overhear."

Crusoe leaned forward. "Remember," he said, "she *is* supposed to know about the Circle of Thirteen. As far as the king is concerned, her kidnap was real. If you choose a moment when she is alone with the king, you can brief him on your supposed raid while she is there. Neither she nor the king would think it was strange that you spoke of the Circle in her presence."

"Her being there with the king actually gives you a reason to raise the subject in the first place," Friday added. "All you have to do is say that you want to reassure her and the king that you are taking action against her kidnappers."

"Very good." Sir William nodded. He glanced at Crusoe and Friday. "You will need formal clothes. Fortunately, I believe there are still some costumes stored backstage. Daniel will take you there and get you fitted with something more suited to a royal entertainment. Now, is there anything else to discuss before we adjourn?"

Crusoe glanced at Friday. She glanced back, and nodded slightly.

"Actually," he said, "there is. Both Friday and I saw three of Red Tiberius's pirates on the street as we came here. The coach went by too fast for us to do anything, and I'm not sure what we could have done, but you ought to know—there is a good chance that Red Tiberius is here in London, and that he is looking for us."

Sir William leaned back in his chair, his fingers steepled in front of him. "Interesting," he said. "If true."

"More than interesting," Defoe added. "It indicates that two of our newest but most trusted agents, two agents we have come to rely on, may have to go into hiding. That could weaken our attempts to fight back against the Circle of Thirteen just at the wrong time."

"If it is true," Sir William repeated.

Friday frowned at him. "You do not believe us," she said quietly.

"It isn't that I disbelieve you. I do wonder how sure you can be that three men, glimpsed briefly through the window of a moving carriage, were the same three men you saw on an island many thousands of miles away and several months ago."

Friday opened her mouth to respond. Crusoe could see she was in danger of losing her temper, so he reached out with his right hand to squeeze her leg warningly while he interrupted: "You must remember that Friday grew up on her father's ship. She knew every one of the crew. If *I* am confident that the men we saw were members of his crew, then *she* is much more certain."

"One of them wanted to marry me," she said, staring at the table. "Mohir, he was called. A beast of a man. The marriage would have been a pirate ceremony rather than a Christian one, but it would have been just as binding. My father was going to give me to him. That is why I ran away from his ship, and that is how I came to meet Robin, and eventually to end up here."

Sir William looked over at Daniel Defoe and raised an eyebrow.

"I believe them," Defoe said firmly. "I saw their reactions when they caught sight of these men."

"And how long did this take?" Sir William queried.

"Long enough," Defoe countered. "We had slowed and were going around a corner at the time. The three men were standing on the corner. There was more than enough time for our friends here to recognize them." He shrugged. "And frankly, they looked like pirates to me."

Crusoe smiled inwardly at Defoe's use of the words "our friends." He was subtly reminding Sir William that Crusoe and Friday were a part of the team, and deserved to be taken seriously.

Sir William turned his attention to John Caiaphas. "Have there been any reports of people asking questions about Robinson Crusoe and Miss Friday?"

"Not that I have heard," Caiaphas said. He glanced over at Crusoe and added: "It's not that we've been checking on you, lad, but any unusual attention paid to Segment W's agents needs to be followed up, and quickly."

Crusoe nodded his understanding.

"Make some inquiries of your own," Sir William said to Caiaphas. "See if any ships matching the description of Red Tiberius's vessel have docked anywhere within reach of London. Find out if anyone matching the description of Red Tiberius has been seen. Rumors of a man such as him would quickly spread through the criminal underworld." He frowned. "I confess, Miss Friday, that I don't even know the name of your father's ship. I should have asked that long ago."

Friday opened her mouth to answer, but it was Defoe who spoke first. "It is called the *Dark Nebula*."

Both Friday and Crusoe stared at him, surprised. Crusoe was fairly sure that neither of them had ever told him the name.

Defoe shrugged. "I did some research," he said defensively. "After all, I still want to write about your adventures. It turns out that the Royal Navy has been interested in Red Tiberius for some years now. They have quite an extensive file on his operations and habits."

"Whatever they think they know, it is nowhere near the truth." Friday glowered.

"Perhaps so." Sir William straightened up and placed his hands flat on the table. "John Caiaphas will investigate whether anyone in London has been asking questions about you. If your father is here, Miss Friday, then we will find out, and quickly. In the meantime, let us operate as normal. We will meet here tomorrow after breakfast to decide on the details of our story, to make ready for the entertainment, and"—he looked directly at John Caiaphas here—"to ensure that we have our resources in place to follow the countess, if she takes our bait, and to attack whatever Circle of Thirteen base she goes to with overwhelming force."

John Caiaphas nodded. Crusoe knew that, in his mind, he was running through the details of how many men he would need, how they would be armed, and where they would be stationed.

Crusoe and Friday spent the afternoon at the Globe, picking out more formal clothes for the next day. Neither of them wanted to head into the streets of London. They didn't know what they might find there—or what might find them. Instead, they stayed in the theater, talking to Daniel Defoe and watching John Caiaphas train his men. They had dinner at the Globe's refectory and went to bed early.

Crusoe found sleep difficult to achieve. This was partly because his body was warm beneath several blankets, though his face, exposed to the air, was cold; but it was partly because of the possible presence of the pirates in London. He kept trying to remember the exact details of the three men whom he and Friday had seen on the street corner and comparing them with the men he had seen on the island or on the deck of the *Dark Nebula*. Friday had known these men a lot better than he had. She had lived in close proximity to them. If she was sure, then he was sure, but the more he tried to compare the various blurred faces in his memory, the more confused he got.

He could hear Friday shifting around in the small room next door to his. He could sense her, just a few inches away on the other side of the wooden wall.

Knowing she was there reassured him. The bond between them was unspoken but real nonetheless. He knew that he had strong feelings for her. What he didn't know was what to do about them.

As the hours passed, sleep continued to evade him. He kept flipping between the certain belief that the pirates were there by accident, that they were there to kill both him and Friday for what they had done to Red Tiberius's pride, or that they were there to kill Crusoe but to take Friday back to her father—and to Mohir.

The thought of the bestial first mate of the *Dark Nebula* wanting to marry Friday made Crusoe's hands clench into fists and his face twist into a scowl. He would do anything to stop that from happening. Anything. Even kill the man.

Several times he started to get out of bed so he could go check that Friday was all right. Perhaps to put his arms around her and hold her close to reassure her. Each time he pulled the blankets back over himself and cursed himself for being stupid. Friday wouldn't thank him for waking her up with his worries.

He must have fallen into a disturbed slumber at some point, because when he awoke the sun was shining through his window and his feet were sticking out of the blankets at the end of the bed and were freezing. His head hurt, and he felt like he hadn't slept at all. Knowing that he wasn't going to go back to sleep, he threw the blankets off, dressed, and stumbled down to the refectory, where the heat of the ovens and the fires was enough to drive the chill from his bones.

Friday was already there, halfway through a plate of bacon, eggs, and fried potatoes. She looked like she had somehow managed to siphon off all the sleep that he had missed and added it to her own. She looked . . . beautiful.

After breakfast they attended another long meeting with Sir William and Daniel Defoe at which the fake story was agreed upon. The only point of contention came when John Caiaphas said: "Sir William—I have been drawing up plans for this operation over-night, and I believe I have identified a problem."

"What is it?" Sir William asked.

He nodded. "In short, you have asked that I set a small number of my men to follow the countess once she leaves to share our false story with the Circle of Thirteen."

"Indeed," Sir William said, nodding.

"We are, of course, assuming that the Circle has a base in London itself, and that rather than send a letter to them the countess will go in person."

Defoe, sitting beside Sir William, leaned forward. "London is the greatest and most important city in the world. If the Circle does not have at least one representative here, then they aren't the threat we believe them to be. And as for the countess—I cannot believe that she would entrust such important information to a letter that might get lost or delayed."

"Indeed," Caiaphas agreed. "The problem is that none of my men have ever met the countess, and I am not aware of any paint-ings of her in London that they could look at—even granting that such a painting was lifelike rather than flattering."

"It would be difficult to flatter the countess in a painting," Crusoe said without thinking. "She *is* very attractive."

Somehow, Friday's foot hit his ankle as she changed position. He winced as the pain shot through his leg.

"So sorry," she murmured, but she didn't sound it.

"Even so," Caiaphas continued, "my men would be trying to follow her based on a description. They might end up following someone else by accident. The countess might even try to disguise herself. I believe there is a strong chance that they might lose her completely." He shrugged. "My apologies, Sir William, but even with the best planning there is a chance that something might go wrong, and it is my duty to point these things out."

"Indeed," Sir William mused. He turned to Daniel Defoe. "Suggestions?"

Defoe thought for a moment. "The solution is obvious—either I, Mr. Crusoe, or Miss Friday should follow her, as we have had the closest acquaintance with her. This means that we would recognize her under a range of circumstances, but it has the disadvantage that *she* would also recognize *us*."

"We could stay as far back as possible," Crusoe said, "hiding in the crowd or in doorways."

Defoe shook his head. "Even a single glimpse of either of us would serve to warn the countess that she was being followed, and that we knew about her membership in the Circle."

Friday laid a hand on the table. "I should be the one to do it," she said firmly. As all four of them opened their mouths to argue, she went on: "The countess paid far more attention to Daniel and Robin than she did to me. She is an attractive woman, and she knows it. She is always looking to see what effect her beauty has on the men around her. The only time we were together for more than a few seconds was when we were hanging beneath a balloon, escaping from Lord Sebastos's fortress, and she spent most of that time with her eyes closed, praying." She hesitated, and looked away.

"Then there is the color of my skin," she went on in a quieter, more controlled tone. "I have realized, since arriving in London, that many people believe that people from the West Indies and from Africa all look the same."

"Not to me," Crusoe said quickly.

"Or to any of us," Defoe added, "but you make a very good point, Miss Friday. The countess has undoubtedly spent less time looking at you than she has at either me or Crusoe, whereas you are well aware of her looks." He turned to Sir William. "I do believe that she has put her finger on the solution."

Crusoe was about to object when Sir William raised a hand to quiet him. "I agree. Mr. Crusoe, I am sure that you will protest, based on your desire not to put your friend in danger, but she has demonstrated an amazing aptitude for survival and I am confident that following one woman through London will pose no challenge for her. Miss Friday—you will follow the countess, wherever this might lead. Mr. Crusoe—you will join John Caiaphas in the attack on the Circle base, when it is identified."

Crusoe felt a curdled mixture of concern and anger bubbling within him, but he kept quiet.

Friday raised a hand. "What do I do once I have followed the countess to her Circle of Thirteen contacts? Should I return here to tell you where their base is?"

"If you do that," John Caiaphas said, "then the Circle might have enough time to evacuate and disappear."

Friday nodded. "That's what I was thinking."

It was Defoe who suggested the solution. "What if, when you begin to follow the countess, two of John's men start following *you*? For as long as you keep the countess in sight, they will in turn keep *you* in sight. When it seems as if she has arrived in the right place, then you can signal to John's men. One of them will get a signal back to us while the other stays with you. If the Circle is quicker than we expect, and manages to get out, then you can follow them to wherever their replacement base is and John's other man can get the new location to us."

Sir William glanced at John Caiaphas, who nodded slowly.

"That works," Sir William said decisively. "Now—is there anything else we need to worry about?"

Yes, Crusoe thought, Friday's safety! but he kept his mouth shut. He knew he wasn't going to change her mind, or anybody else's, but it didn't stop him from worrying about her.

The meeting broke up soon after that. After lunch—a rabbit-and-oyster stew—Crusoe and Friday wandered out of the Globe and across the patch of weeds and wild grass that separated it from the riverbank. Their breath misted in front of their mouths and trailed behind them like scarves as they walked.

Crusoe gazed out across the Thames in wonder. It had frozen overnight. He'd sailed on that river—both when he and Friday had first arrived in London, and then later when the two of them traveled down to the Isle of Thanet to rescue the Countess of Lichfield from Lord Sebastos's fortress—and he knew it as a wide, turbulent, dangerous river, full of strange undercurrents. He wasn't used to it being a nearly flat surface of hard ice. He wasn't used to seeing people *walking* on it.

The edges had been pushed up into what looked like small mountain ranges, but closer to the middle it was completely flat and dusted with powdery snow.

Boats that had been tied up to the bank were now imprisoned: locked fast in the grip of the ice. The boatmen who used to take people back and forth, from one bank to the other for a few pennies, now couldn't practice their trade. On the other hand, it was now possible to walk from one bank to the other, if you were careful. Enterprising Londoners—including those boatmen who weren't making any money—immediately set up stalls on the ice, selling all manner of goods from woolen hats, scarves, and gloves to hot food—carved from pig carcasses on spits over roaring fires—and mulled wine or spiced beer. There were tents as well, constructed from oars lashed together and covered with sailcloth. The Thames had become London's High Street—a wide concourse running through the heart of the city. The stalls and tents were decked out in colorful bunting, giving the whole thing the appearance of a carnival. There were even swings and roundabouts set up for children—and some adults—to play on—again, for a few pence a time. If there was one thing Londoners were good at, it was making money from whatever fortunes or misfortunes life delivered to their doors.

Crusoe looked at the several fires burning on the surface of the river and decided not to go anywhere near them. Surely the heat must be melting its way through the ice, and eventually a hole would be formed through to the freezing waters beneath.

Maybe it didn't matter. Maybe if a hole formed, then it would just be below the fire, and wouldn't spread to where people were standing. Maybe, once the fire dropped through into the water and was extinguished, the cold air would start freezing the water again.

Some people had deliberately cut holes in the ice, using axes or circular saw blades, and were dangling hooked fishing lines into the water. Crusoe wasn't sure what kind of fish could survive the low temperatures, but he supposed the fishermen knew what they were doing. Several of the fishermen already had piles of fish by their holes.

As he and Friday watched, he was amazed to see people *gliding* across the surface of the river, children and adults alike. His memories of living in London before sailing with his father to the island were sketchy, but he was sure he'd never seen anything like this before. For a few minutes he thought they were just slipping on the ice, but when one of them came closer he saw iron blades strapped to their boots. The edge of the blades sliced through the ice, leaving trails behind them. Not only were they controlling it, they were laughing and joking as if it was *fun*.

People were strange.

Friday gazed out at the scene as if she couldn't believe what she was seeing. Crusoe smiled at the expression of wonder on her face. On the island she had been the one to show him odd, strange, and surprising things. Now that they were back in London it was his turn, and he was enjoying every minute of it. He moved closer and slipped an arm around her shoulders.

"What do you think is happening to the ships down past London Bridge?" she asked.

"The clever captains will have moved their ships farther down toward Gravesend," he replied. "The rest will probably have woken up to find themselves caught in the ice, unable to move."

"And the birds? There are always ducks and geese and swans on the river. Where have they gone?"

He shrugged. "I think it's the same as the captains—either they've moved somewhere safer while the cold spell lasts or ice has formed around them—although in their case they won't just lose some trade—they'll die."

"I still can't believe what I'm seeing."

"I know."

A sudden chill seemed to strike her, and she shivered beneath the weight of his arm.

"What's the matter?" he asked instantly.

"I was just thinking about the Circle of Thirteen," she said. "They knew where Segment W's last base was, even though it was supposed to be secret, and they must know where this one is. The Countess of Lichfield was brought here after we rescued her, re-member? Before the river froze, John Caiaphas's men just had to guard against attacks from the land, but now an army could make it across the ice quite easily."

Crusoe glanced along the banks at the men fishing through holes in the ice. Could some of them—maybe all of them—be enemies of Segment W?

He shivered, and it wasn't because of the cold. Would there ever be a time when he and Friday could live their lives without threat?

CHAPTER THREE

Sir William, Crusoe, and Friday headed off in a large formal carriage. The entertainment—one of many that London had to offer—was at Drury Lane, on the north side of the Thames. The theater was an ornate-fronted building set in the middle of a wide road of shops and houses. The carriage dropped them outside and Sir William led them straight in, pushing through a crowd of well-dressed attendees who, when they saw who Sir William was, moved apart to give him a path through. They in turn were surrounded by a crowd of less well-dressed locals who were jeering or cheering the gentry in equal measure. It was, from what Crusoe had seen over the past few weeks, just another afternoon in London.

They emerged past a hall that served the dual purpose of ticket office and bar into the entrance of the auditorium itself. It was similar to the Globe, only smaller and shaped more like a fan than a circle, with the stage at the narrowest point of the fan. The only illumination was the weak sunlight shining in through the large windows in the ceiling. Boxes lined the walls on each side of the stage, occupied by small groups of well-dressed men and women, but the majority of the audience milled around on the wooden floor, talking and mixing with vendors who were selling fruit and hot chestnuts all while a woman onstage was singing, accompanied by a small orchestra in front of her. It was difficult to hear her over the sound of shouting, laughing, and cheering coming from the audience and calls from the vendors. Watching the hubbub, Crusoe couldn't help wonder what the point of being there was if people were just going to wander around, talking and eating.

Several boxes nearest to the stage were more ornate than the rest, and curtains cast shadows over them so that it was difficult to see who was inside. Crusoe guessed that the king and his retinue would either be sitting in there now or would be arriving later. The shadows made it difficult to tell, and the audience didn't seem to be paying much attention to the royal boxes.

Sir William turned and led the way up a narrow stairway to the first story. A curved corridor led the way around the back of the boxes. Curtains blocked their entrances. Crusoe could hear laughter and the sound of conversation from inside many of them.

The final boxes had liveried footmen standing outside, along with a huddle of finely dressed courtiers who were probably anticipating orders from the king and a clutch of uniformed soldiers preventing access to anyone who wasn't supposed to be there.

Sir William nodded to one of the courtiers. The man nodded back and gestured toward the entrance to a nearby box. He then slipped through the brocaded curtains into the king's box. Crusoe held open the curtain of the box to which they had been directed, and Sir William led the way in.

They all sat down to wait. Crusoe and Friday gazed down in interest at the stage, where the poor singer and her accompanying orchestra were doing their best to compete with the noise of the crowd. Once in a while, someone would throw an orange or a chestnut from one side of the auditorium to the other. It was chaos. Crusoe wondered how the singer could keep going.

Interestingly, he noticed that despite the crowd's apparent indifference to the presence of the king, many of them would quickly glance up at the king's box every now and then, and then look away. They knew he was there, but they also knew, apparently, that he didn't like to be acknowledged. Certainly, none of the thrown fruit and nuts went anywhere near him. King Charles II was, by all accounts, a very tolerant ruler, but there were limits. Hitting the king with a piece of fruit would probably be counted as an act of treachery, punishable by death.

Crusoe found himself scanning the faces of the crowd to see if Mohir or the other pirates whom he and Friday had seen were in the audience. Or, he thought with a spasm of concern, if Red Tiberius himself was there. He didn't see anyone whom he recognized, but half the audience had their backs to him. Any one of them could have been a pirate.

The singer left the stage to scattered applause and some cat-calls. Several men and women in white costumes and pale makeup came on and took up positions as if they were in the middle of some activity and had suddenly been frozen. The orchestra played a little fanfare. While Crusoe and Friday watched, entranced, the performers held their positions for a long moment, hardly even breathing. They were obviously meant to look like statues re-creating some moment from mythology or history that Crusoe didn't recognize. The orchestra finished their fanfare, and the performers quickly shuffled around to take up a different set of positions before the next one.

The curtain behind them opened and the courtier who had acknowledged them earlier slipped through. "His Majesty is pleased to see you now, Sir William," he murmured.

Sir William glanced at Friday. "You stay here, and wait for the countess to come out. Follow her, see where she goes, and get a signal back to John Caiaphas when she gets there."

Friday caught Crusoe's eye as he was about to leave. "Don't let her turn your head," she said quietly.

"Already turned, and not by her," he replied, and left before the blush could spread across his face.

Sir William and Crusoe followed the courtier out, along the curved corridor, and into the final box.

There, in an ornate chair larger than any of the others, sat King Charles the Second. He was leaning forward, elbow on his knee and chin resting in his hand, as he watched the entertainment onstage. On his left sat a beautiful woman probably half his age, dressed in fine clothes and with curly brown hair caught up in clusters on either side of her face. On his right was the Countess of Lichfield.

Neither the king nor his female companion turned to see who had come in, but the countess did. She nodded politely at Sir William Lambert, but when she saw Crusoe her full red lips curved into what looked like a smile of genuine pleasure.

Crusoe bowed his head toward her and smiled back. Sir William had been right—she did recognize him and certainly would have spotted him following her.

Without turning around, the king waved a regal hand, indicating that they should sit in the row of chairs behind him.

Sir William did as the king had indicated and gestured to Crusoe to sit beside him. They sat quietly, watching the performers onstage take up one classical position after another. The drapery being used to shield the box from prying eyes cut off some of the view, but it was still possible for them to see what was going on if they craned their necks.

Eventually, the performance ended, to the usual cheers and abuse from the audience. The king half-turned and said: "Sir William, we have not had the pleasure of seeing you at Court these past few weeks."

"An unfortunate side effect of the fact that . . . we . . . have been working hard on Your Majesty's behalf, following up on the events on the Isle of Thanet."

Crusoe noticed that Sir William had deliberately avoided saying the words *Segment W*, probably because of the lady on the king's right. The Countess of Lichfield already knew about the secret organization, of course.

The king noticed as well. "I don't believe you have had the pleasure of being introduced to the Duchess of Cleveland," he said. As the lady nodded, the king continued: "The duchess is a close friend of mine, and privy to all kinds of secrets—including many that are not even known at Court. She is aware of Segment W and the excellent work that you and your people carry out to protect this great nation. You can speak of these matters in her presence." He patted the lady's knee. "She can be trusted: I assure you of that."

Crusoe could see only part of Sir William's face from where he sat, but he could tell that the head of Segment W noticeably flinched at the suggestion that the king was telling his friends about the organization. Crusoe himself had been surprised that the lady in question wasn't the queen but was instead some other female friend and companion of His Majesty. He supposed that the queen didn't enjoy entertainments of this kind, whereas the duchess apparently did.

"The Countess of Lichfield, of course, is already well aware of the work you do," the king went on, "and you have my gratitude for the quiet and efficient way that you went about rescuing her from the hands of that scurrilous organization—what did you say they were called?"

"We believe they refer to themselves as the Circle of Thirteen," Sir William murmured.

"Indeed. Should they have harmed the countess in any way, then I would have mobilized any and every resource at my disposal, but you managed to retrieve her unharmed—you and your people." He half-turned and glanced at Crusoe. "I believe you have introduced this gentleman to me before, have you not? I recognize his face."

"Indeed I have," Sir William replied. "Mr. Crusoe was instrumental in organizing the escape of the countess—who demonstrated great courage and resilience herself," he added diplomatically.

"Mr. Crusoe risked his life several times to save mine," the countess said breathlessly. Her smile made Crusoe feel uncomfortable.

"Then Mr. Crusoe also has my particular thanks," the king said. "Now, I believe you have something in particular you wish to tell me."

"Indeed I do, and I appreciate the opportunity to brief you on our progress." Sir William took a deep breath, preparing to tell the story that had been concocted in Segment W's headquarters that morning. "You are aware, of course, that the countess was taken by this Circle of Thirteen in order to force us to bring out of hiding a particular *object* that is in our possession—an object which we know they covet, and which they attempted to steal from us."

"And succeeded," the king murmured.

"Ah, yes—for a time. We retrieved the *object*, of course, along with the countess, and we have recently been circulating rumors that another object, identical to the one in our possession, has recently been found. We have offered this supposed treasure for sale in various"—he coughed—"unlawful places, and—"

"And someone from the Circle of Thirteen has shown interest?" the king exclaimed, sounding intrigued for the first time. "That is excellent news."

"They backed away after some initial discussions," Sir William expanded, "but we have had our agents following them, and we know where they are based. Our forces are poised to attack in the next day or two."

"Very good." The king nodded. "You have my permission to proceed."

Sir William's shoulders twitched slightly. Crusoe knew that Sir William believed he had full authority to proceed with any such mission already, without having to seek it from the king, but diplomatically he said nothing.

The countess leaned forward. "Where *is* this base?" she asked intently. "Is it nearby? In London?"

"Alas, for operational reasons I cannot divulge that information," Sir William said, holding his hands out, palms up, and shrugging in a gesture of apology. "Everyone here is above suspicion, of course, but I cannot rule out the possibility of hidden listeners."

"But you will be attacking in force?" the countess pressed. "With all of your troops?"

"It will be a large-scale operation," Sir William confirmed. "We fully expect to suppress any defenders rapidly, and press home the attack to those who lead this terrible organization."

"Including this 'Lord Sebastos' whom I have been told about?" the king asked. "I find it offensive that this man pretends to be a noble of this country. For that alone he should be punished."

Remembering all the many evils that Lord Sebastos was responsible for, Crusoe thought that impersonating a member of the nobility was probably the least of them.

"Do you know any more about the identity of this 'Sebastos'?" the king asked.

Sir William shook his head. "The name is an alias, of course, but we have yet to identify him."

"Keep me informed," the king said, turning away and focusing on the stage again, where a troupe of female dancers had arrived to general cheers from the audience. "I wish you success in your endeavors."

"As Your Majesty instructs," Sir William said. He stood and bowed.

Crusoe copied Sir William's example and followed him out of the box. As they moved down the hall, Sir William murmured, without turning his head, "And so it begins."

* * *

FRIDAY WAS WAITING alone in the box when Sir William and Robin reentered.

"What happened?" Friday asked as Sir William let the curtain fall behind him.

"She has taken the bait," Sir William said quietly. "Stand here, by the curtain, and watch for the countess to leave."

Friday moved to look through the narrow gap between the curtain and the wall. All she could see was the corridor, curving away out of sight. She stood there, breathing shallowly, trying to keep her mind as calm as the surface of a pool of water rather than let random thoughts disturb its tranquillity. It was how she had been taught to wait when hunting animals, and the way she had taught Crusoe to hunt. Thoughts could be distracting; the perfect hunter should be simultaneously ready for action and yet completely calm.

People came and went—courtiers delivering messages to the king, vendors trying to get the king to try their fruit or their pies, soldiers changing shift. She didn't react to any of them. Behind her, Sir William and Crusoe were silent and still, aware that she needed to concentrate on what was going on outside.

And then, something different. A female figure—small and well-dressed, with a cloak over her shoulders—visible only for a few seconds as she half-walked and half-ran along the corridor, away from the king's box. Friday slipped out to follow before her mind had fully registered that something had happened.

Friday stayed out of sight, relying on her sense of hearing to tell where the countess was. She could hear delicate footsteps heading away from her. The rhythm of the footsteps changed when the countess got to the stairway, and Friday quickened her pace, knowing that if the countess was on the stairs, then she couldn't look over her shoulder and catch sight of Friday in the corridor.

When she reached the door that led onto the stairs she paused, listening. The countess's footsteps were distinctive on the wooden steps, but their sound changed when she reached the ground floor. Friday moved into the stairway and quickly downward.

Friday emerged into the main part of the theater. It was still crowded, still chaotic, but she could see from the movement of people's heads that someone too small to see properly was moving in a straight line toward the exit. Whoever it was must have looked aristocratic enough that individuals in the crowd moved to one side to let her pass, rather than stay where they were and have her push her way through. It was almost certainly the Countess of Lichfield.

Friday moved through the crowd quietly, slipping sideways and around people in the same way she had avoided trees and bushes on the island when following an animal. It meant her course was longer, but she moved faster and didn't leave any trace of herself in her surroundings. As she moved, she raised her hood to shield her features.

When Friday got to the exit from the auditorium, the countess had just moved into Drury Lane outside. She turned around, checking if anyone was following her. Friday ducked her head to one side, avoiding eye contact. Her skin was dark enough that the shadows of her hood would hide her features. The countess was unlikely to recognize her, she knew, but if she saw Friday too often during her journey, then she would become suspicious.

Even though Friday wasn't looking directly at the countess, she could still take in details of how the woman was dressed. Her pale pink bodice matched a skirt of the same color beneath her cloak. As Friday watched, she pulled her own hood up to cover her face and vanished outside, turning right.

Friday slipped across the foyer and out the main doors. It was still afternoon outside, and the sun was shining from a sharp blue sky. The countess was walking quickly away from her. Her shoes, Friday noticed, were hardly suitable for walking long distances. If she hit a patch of ice she was likely to slip and hurt herself. Obviously, she hadn't been intending to go on a long walk. This was a panic reaction, which meant that the plan was working.

Looking to her left, Friday tried to spot the Increment personnel whom John Caiaphas had promised would be there to support her. For a moment all she saw was a mass of humanity, everyone from nobles to beggars, all pressed together, but then details started to come through. She saw one man, in ragged clothes with a scarf wrapped around his neck, slipping his hand beneath the doublet of a well-dressed noble. It emerged a few seconds later clutching a purse that bulged with coins. She smiled slightly. Wherever she went there were predators, and there were prey.

Another man caught her eye, and nodded slightly. He was dressed in simple, anonymous clothes, but Friday noticed that his boots seemed more expensive than his clothes suggested he could afford. Beside him, another man—similarly dressed—turned his head. He was younger than his companion, maybe no older than Friday or Robin, with fair hair and strikingly blue eyes. He also nodded and smiled. John Caiaphas's troops—members of the Increment.

They both moved their left hands so that Friday could see the identical rings they wore.

She tilted her head slightly in acknowledgment, then set off after the countess.

The woman had a good twenty-yard lead, but Friday had memorized not only the color of her hood but also the particular way she walked. Everyone had their own distinct gait. Animals moved in different ways as well. Back on the island, Friday had amazed

Crusoe by being able to tell not only whether a wild boar or a deer had gone down a particular path, but also which one of the herd or group it was.

The countess abruptly stopped and raised her arm. A two-wheeled carriage swerved toward her and stopped. She said something to the driver seated up top and then climbed into the carriage. As she settled back, the driver flicked his whip and his horse trotted off again.

Friday cursed under her breath. She had known this might happen, but she had hoped it wouldn't. She could catch up with the carriage and climb on the back, but with only two wheels and one axle, her weight would pull the whole thing backward and the driver might well spot that someone was trying to get a free ride. Fortunately, there were lots of carriages and carts on Drury Lane, along with people crossing from one side to the other, oblivious of the risk of getting run over. Friday broke into a run, weaving in and out of the crowd. She managed to keep the carriage in sight as it moved along the road. Every time the carriage would get too far ahead, something delayed it and she caught up.

A man she was passing suddenly took a step backward, crashing into her. She was knocked sideways, almost falling into the road.

"Oy!" the man shouted, thinking he was being robbed. He frantically patted his pockets, glaring murderously at Friday.

"Sorry!" she called as she caught her balance and kept running.

The man continued to shout behind her, but he was already fading into the general noise of the crowd. She couldn't see the carriage with the countess inside. Desperately, she swerved into the middle of the road, trying to separate the one she was chasing from all the others.

She had noticed a scratch in the painted wood at the back of the countess's carriage. She scanned all of the vehicles moving away from her, looking for that particular mark. Most of them were battered in one way or another, but . . .

There! The carriage had broken out into a relatively open space and sped up. As Friday watched, it came to a corner and began to turn.

This wasn't working.

Friday sprinted along the center of Drury Lane, regardless of the massive horses and the rolling wheels that were only a few inches away from her. Horses snorted at her and shied away, while drivers yelled and flicked their whips to drive her off.

The countess's carriage was completing its turn up ahead. Friday came up behind a four-wheeled cart that carried bales of straw and was also maneuvering to turn. She jumped for the back of the cart, scrambling up onto the wooden boards. She stuck her head out sideways, keeping the countess's carriage in her sight.

"This is *my* straw!" a voice hissed in her ear.

She almost let go and fell off in surprise, but managed to hang on by her fingertips. A young urchin pushed his head out of the nearest bale. He was glaring angrily at Friday. A hand emerged from the bale beside his head. It was holding a knife.

"You can keep it," she said. "I'm just along for the ride."

"If you try and take it, I'll cut you bad," the kid said. He pulled his head back into the straw, but Friday could see his eyes glittering in the darkness.

The carriage abruptly lurched to the right, readying itself to make another turn. Leaning out perilously, Friday could see the countess's carriage up ahead. It was keeping in a straight line.

"Good luck with the straw," she called, and dropped off the back of the cart.

It swung away from her, wheels trundling and leaving ruts in the frozen dirt and manure that covered the street, but she hit the ground running and managed to catch up with a four-wheeled carriage that was just in front of it. She scrambled up onto the empty luggage rack on the back. John Caiaphas's men followed—not appearing to hurry but still moving fast through the crowded streets.

She grabbed at the edge of the carriage and twisted in her seat to look around the side. Her carriage was going faster than the countess's. Another few seconds and the countess would be able to look out of her window and see Friday. Friday was fairly sure that the countess wouldn't recognize her, but she wasn't about to take the chance. She quickly looked around, weighing her options.

As her carriage passed the countess's, she turned away. Urchins hitching rides on the backs of carts and carriages were a constant feature of London's streets, despite the attempts of the drivers to stop it. If the countess happened to glance sideways and see her, then she probably wouldn't think twice—as long as Friday hid her face.

It only took a minute before Friday was far enough ahead that the countess wouldn't be able to see her without leaning out the window. Friday straightened up and looked back along the street. She had lost track of where they were in London, but she could see that the countess's driver was pulling on his reins, getting his horses to slow and to veer to the left. He was turning a corner, and Friday was pulling away ahead of him.

Reacting instinctively, she jumped off the back of her carriage without thinking it through. This time she was facing backward, and she couldn't hit the ground running. Instead, her feet hit the frozen ground and she slipped, falling backward before she could get out of the way of the carriage behind her. She felt the ice and stones of the street ripping the clothes on her back.

The driver of the following carriage shouted something as the horses reared up in front of her. Either he didn't have time to brake or he didn't want to: either way, the carriage kept on coming.

Two horses and wheels on either side. If she lay completely straight and flat, then the whole lot might just go over the top of her—assuming its underneath wasn't so close to the road that it would scrape her along the ground. It would be like the old pirate punishment of keelhauling, which she had seen once and never forgotten.

She had to try. It was her only option if she wanted to survive.

Two Years and Six Months Before the Escape

Robertshaw made his move three days after Suriya tricked him into drinking a bucket of vinegar instead of the French brandy he'd been expecting.

She'd known he was looking for revenge. She'd stayed belowdecks or in her small personal cabin—a converted storage cupboard near her father's cabin—as much as possible, but there were times she had to come out for food, or for fresh air—and each time she'd felt the heat of his gaze on her skin. It felt like the prickling of sunburn. Once or twice he'd started to approach her but someone near him would stop him. But this time they were alone.

He was waiting in her cabin when she came back from the galley with a plate of salmagundi—the mixture of cooked onions, cooked garlic, and bread that was the basic staple of sailors at sea—in her hands. She had some smoked meat hidden in a hole in the side of her cabin that she'd stolen from the kitchen, and she was going to tear it into shreds and add it to the food.

It made her smile when she thought about it—the gaps between planks on a ship were usually caulked with rope fibers, but she used smoked meat instead.

Before she could get to her hammock, his dirty, blistered hand was around her face, covering her mouth.

"You an' me, we've got unfinished business," he snarled in her ear. His voice was whiny and nasal—the result of the fact that his nose had been sliced off at some time in the past.

She lashed back with her booted foot, but he was expecting that. He turned his leg so that he took the blow from her heel on the leather side of his own boots. Before she could twist away, he wrenched her backward until her feet were hanging in the air.

"You made me look foolish," he growled. His breath smelled like there was something dead and decaying inside him. She could almost imagine it blistering the skin behind her ear.

She bit his finger. The taste almost made her vomit, but she swallowed hard as he let go of her.

"You don't need me for that!" she said.

As he lunged for her, she proved it by throwing the plate of salmagundi in his face.

He cried out as the hot food hit him and tried to claw the sticky, steaming mixture from his skin. His body still blocked the door, so she ducked down and scrambled between his legs. She was almost through the narrow gap when his hand came down on the back of her blouse to haul her back.

She threw her weight onto her hands and lashed backward with her feet. One heel connected with an eye; the other with his cheek. The force propelled her forward, and she exited the cabin in a forward roll.

By the time she got to her feet and turned around, hand dropping to the small knife at her belt, he was emerging into daylight himself. His right eye was rapidly swelling closed, and he was spitting blood and teeth onto the deck. His single remaining eye blazed with uncontrolled rage.

"You little—"

"What's going on?" a voice shouted from the quarterdeck. It was Mohir—her father's first mate. He was a fierce West Indian with earrings and a gold tooth.

Friday was faced with an instant decision—try to use her father's position to shield her, or fight back? The pirates wouldn't respect her if she tried the former course of action, and neither would her father. She had no choice.

"He's been stealing!" she cried before Robertshaw could say anything. "I caught him doing it. He's been taking things from the booty every time a ship is taken!"

The roar of outrage from the nearby crew drowned out Robertshaw's shouted denial. There were strict rules about how booty was distributed among a pirate crew, even on a ship like her father's. Pirates broke those rules at their own risk, and Robertshaw already had form in that regard—his missing nose was the penalty for a previous attempt at taking more than he was entitled to.

"I ain't!" he finally managed to shout, but too late. The pirate crew was gathering around, and they weren't happy.

"How do you know this thing?" Mohir rumbled, looking at Suriya.

"I saw him!" she said. "He's got a secret stash. It's in a hole just outside the door to the cannon deck. I saw him down there, looking at it, but he chased me away. It's covered with a rotten bit of wood."

"It ain't true!" Robertshaw protested.

"We will find out," Mohir said calmly, but in a tone of voice that carried across the deck. He nodded at one of the pirates, who quickly moved to one of the hatches that led below and vanished out of sight.

"There ain't nothing there, I tell yer!" Robertshaw said, angrily but nervously.

In fact, Suriya knew that there was. She had put a silver necklace and three doubloons into that hole two days before. She'd known that Robertshaw would want revenge. If he had chosen to do nothing, then the stolen booty would have stayed part of her own haul—hidden in secret places all over the Dark Nebula, *for when she eventually left the ship. If he had chosen to attack her, then so be it*—knives and cutlasses weren't the only weapons a person could use. *Suriya's mind was a weapon, and it was far sharper than anything else on that ship.*

CHAPTER FOUR

Crusoe watched with mixed feelings as Friday slipped away through the curtain. Part of him wanted to go with her, help her, *protect* her, but another part knew that she would hate that. She didn't need protection. She was a survivor.

He turned away to gaze across the audience—wondering if he would be able to see either Friday or the countess as they passed toward the exit.

He leaned forward, hands resting on the edge of the box, as he caught sight of the countess's blond hair heading through the crowd. She was unmistakably aristocratic. People moved to one side to let her pass without even realizing they were doing it. A few seconds later he saw Friday following, but much more discreetly.

"Be careful," Sir William warned from behind him. "Don't give away the fact that we're interested in the countess, or Miss Friday. Let them do their jobs properly."

Crusoe nodded and deliberately let his gaze wander around the auditorium as if he was fascinated by what was going on. Which he actually was. The audience themselves looked more like people crammed into a tavern than people in a theater.

A man in the audience with his back to Crusoe turned around, and Crusoe felt his heart jump. His hands automatically clenched on the side of the box.

It was Mohir.

"Sir William!" he hissed. "Quickly—come here and look!"

Sir William moved to his side. "What is it? No—don't point. Tell me."

"Do you see that man over near the stage? He's taller than everyone around him, his skin is heavily tanned, and he has a gold earring."

Sir William's gaze drifted over the crowd. "Yes, I see the man. What of him? Have you seen him before?"

"That's Mohir!" Crusoe said darkly. "He's the first mate on Red Tiberius's ship."

"Are you sure?"

"Perfectly sure." Crusoe felt a grim determination welling up within him. "I'm going to follow him—see where he goes."

"You will do no such thing!" Sir William's face was like granite. "I expect you to support the operation against the Circle of Thirteen. You can worry about Red Tiberius and his men when that has been concluded successfully."

"But—"

Sir William shook his head. "No more discussion." His voice was firm. "For as long as you work for me you will do as you are told!"

Crusoe glanced at the exit from the theater to the foyer. The countess and Friday had vanished. His gaze returned to where Mohir was standing. Abruptly, the pirate began to move toward the foyer, pushing through the crowd like a heavily armed warship pushing smaller boats out of its way.

"He might be going after Friday," Crusoe said. "I have to stop him."

Sir William started to say something, but Crusoe wasn't listening. He knew he didn't have enough time to head out of the box, along the corridor, and down the stairs, so he quickly scrambled over the edge and hung there, hands clutching the rail and feet balanced precariously on the gilded ledge that ran around the bottom. He glanced down, looking for a gap in the crowd. He sensed Sir William moving toward him, extending a hand toward his shoulder. Before it could take hold he swung himself sideways and grabbed one of the decorative draperies that hung between the boxes. He half-climbed and half-slid down the drapery, falling the last couple of feet to the floor. His ankle twisted as it hit the ground and he stumbled into a well-dressed man who stood below. The man fell sideways, hitting the woman beside him. As the effect rippled out through the closely packed crowd, Crusoe ducked down and pushed his way through the people turning to see what was going on.

He couldn't see Mohir from his half-crouched position, but he already knew how fast the first mate was moving, and he got to the doorway a few seconds after him. As he moved out of the crowd and into the emptier foyer, he spotted the burly man heading out the door and into Drury Lane. Crusoe followed.

Part of him wondered if Mohir would recognize him. He'd been thinking, the night before, about whether he and Friday had been correct in their identification of the big pirate, but he realized that it worked both ways. It had been nearly a year since Mohir had last seen them. They had both grown. True, he had spent more time with Friday than with Crusoe, but would he actually be able to recognize them?

Crusoe got to the door to the street and glanced around it. Mohir was close by, talking to another man—probably a pirate as well, although he wasn't one of the men Crusoe and Friday had seen earlier. The other man was shaking his head. It seemed that neither of them had spotted Crusoe or Friday, even though they were clearly looking.

But why were they here, in the theater? How had they known that Crusoe and Friday were there?

That was a question for another time. Crusoe knew that his task now was to follow Mohir and see where he went.

The two pirates set off away from the theater, and Crusoe slipped through the crowd behind them. He was pretty sure that they would walk wherever they were going rather than take a carriage. They were athletic men, used to physical exercise, and they would rather reserve their money for important things, like beer and women.

He followed them along several main streets through the center of London. They walked in a straight line, with people either getting out of their way or being *pushed* aside. Mostly it was the former. There was something about the way the men swaggered around that meant people didn't want to annoy them.

As the buildings began to change from places of commerce and entertainment to houses, and then to tenement blocks, the pirates crossed to the other side of the road and took a side street. They were heading gradually downhill, toward the Thames.

Were they heading for the *Dark Nebula*? Had Red Tiberius been so bold as to sail his ship up the Thames and dock it where everyone—including captains and merchants whom he might have robbed in the past—could see it? Was he cursing the fact that the ice had formed, preventing him from leaving?

Crusoe doubted it. He knew, from things that Friday had told him, that Red Tiberius was no fool. If he was going to bring the *Dark Nebula* to England, then he would have docked at some remote port where nobody would ask questions—not in the heart of London.

Crusoe stayed well back. Every now and then one of the pirates would turn around to check whether they were being followed. Sometimes, if he had enough warning, Crusoe would duck into a doorway or an alley before he was seen. At other times, he would change his appearance after the pirate's attention had turned back to what was in front of him: taking his jacket off, turning it inside out so that the lining was displayed, rolling his sleeves up—anything to look different from the last time he was seen. He managed to snatch a scarf from one unconscious drinker slumped against the wall of a tavern, and a cap from another, and he wore these in various combinations. He even tried to walk differently—sometimes slouching, sometimes striding along, sometimes limping.

Crusoe's mind was racing as he followed the men. He had gone against the direct orders of Sir William Lambert! What had he been thinking? Sir William had given him and Friday somewhere to live, food, a job, and money since they had arrived in London. The two of them owed Sir William everything. He hated to think about what might have happened to them if they hadn't joined Segment W, and yet he had deliberately disobeyed his instructions. Would there be a place for him when he returned?

Crusoe decided that it didn't matter. He was doing what he had to do to protect both Friday and himself. There was no choice.

Eventually, just when he thought the pirates might leave the city entirely, he glimpsed the icy surface of the Thames ahead. The pirates turned left at the end of an alley, and Crusoe took the opportunity to sprint ahead to the corner.

The three pirates were crossing the wide and frozen path, lined with wooden piers, steps, and quays, which led along the side of the Thames. They appeared to be heading for a stone bridge that crossed the Thames to the south bank. Somewhere over there, Crusoe reflected, was the Globe Theater. It would be ironic if they were heading in that direction.

The pirates turned off the path when they reached the crossroads that led onto the bridge itself. Its many arches supported a bustling collection of houses, shops, and other places of business. It was like a small town in its own right.

A group of men stood around a fire at the entrance to the bridge. They were warming their hands and roasting bits of meat on skewers. As the pirates approached, Crusoe noticed something odd. At the same moment, each of the pirates made a circle with his thumb and forefinger. It just lasted a second, and Crusoe might have wondered if it had been an accident, or some strange religious gesture like making the sign of the cross, if the men standing around the fire hadn't made exactly the same sign.

They knew one another. Or at the very least they all knew the same sign, which suggested they were part of the same group.

Were the men standing around the fire pirates as well? Crusoe didn't recognize them, but that didn't mean much. They might have been from a different ship. Crusoe knew, from what Friday had told him, that all pirates considered themselves members of a community, despite the fact that they were all competing to attack the same ships. There were even safe harbors where they could gather together, to swap crew and information. Maybe this bridge was like those safe harbors, but in this case set right in the middle of London.

That was probably something that Segment W would want to know.

Crusoe found himself torn. Part of him wanted to turn around, go back to the theater, and make things right with Sir William by telling him that there appeared to be a nest of pirates directly in the center of London, but another part of him wanted to follow Mohir and the others onto the bridge and see exactly where they went.

The second part won. As soon as they were out of sight, hidden by the shop on the nearest corner of the bridge, Crusoe crossed the road after them.

* * *

FRIDAY PULLED HER arms in, scrunching her shoulders up to minimize her width. Looking up she could see a narrow blue slice of sky above her, between the sides of the two horses. Her view was crisscrossed by the web of leather straps and harnesses that linked the horses and carriage together. A hoof came down beside her head. She could feel dirt splatter on her cheek. Another hoof hit the ground by her shoulder, so close that it trapped the cloth of her jacket, preventing her from moving. Not that she had anywhere to move to. She was helpless.

Then the horses were past, and the dark bulk of the carriage itself replaced the blue sky. She could have reached up and touched it. Wheels cut through the ground to her left and to her right, creating deep ruts and pushing the dirt, manure, and ice on the ground toward her from both sides.

And then the carriage had passed. She grabbed a rail at the back and hauled herself up, letting it pull her along. She twisted her body around, swapping hands so that she was facing down rather than up, and her feet were pulled along the icy street. Glancing around hurriedly, she saw that there was a gap between vehicles. She let go of the carriage and ran sideways, avoiding two carts that were passing by.

The countess's carriage was still visible, heading off down a wide thoroughfare. Friday ran after it, wondering momentarily what John Caiaphas's men had made of her gymnastics.

Somewhere in her head, during the past few minutes, Friday had decided that she was going to grab hold of the back of the countess's carriage and haul herself up, and damn the consequences. If she timed it correctly, just as the carriage was going over a bump in the road perhaps, then the driver might not even notice. The problem was that her current technique for following left a lot to be desired.

Before she could attempt it, the countess's carriage slowed down and began to edge toward the side of the road. She had arrived to where she was going.

Or she had seen Friday and was going to get out and confront her.

Either way, Friday dashed across the road and onto the pavement. She hid herself in the shelter of a closed door, set back in a recess of the brick building in front of her.

Her pulse was racing, and she could feel the blood pounding through her body. This had not gone as planned.

But she still had the countess in sight. At least that was something.

She watched as the driver quickly dismounted to help the countess down. The countess waited until he had gone and then started walking along the road, pulling her cloak up to hide her face.

Friday followed, crossing the street so that she was on the other side as the countess.

The street ended in a crossroads, and Friday realized that the other side was a bridge. It was lined with shops and houses to a height of three or four stories. They completely blocked the view of the river from the bridge itself. The only way to see the river was to stand on the bank, before the bridge started, or to be in one of the buildings and look out of a window.

Friday waited until the countess got to the other side of the intersection and then followed.

Wooden stairways led down the banks of the river on either side to the icy surface below. Normally, they would finish in a wooden quay, but now the people climbing down the steps could just step onto the ice.

On each side of the bridge, where the pavement continued on, small groups of men were standing around improvised fires. They were feeding the fires with bits of wood pulled off crates and other boxes. For a moment Friday just assumed they were the kind of loungers who gathered on any street corner in the city, but as the countess approached them something interesting happened. Several of the men turned around and glanced at her, and she quickly brought her hands together in front of her, making a circle with her fingers. The gesture was gone as soon as it was formed, but one of the men gave the same sign back. He glanced at a second man, who pulled a scrap of paper from his pocket and made a mark on it with a stick of charcoal.

A chill ran down Friday's back. The Circle of Thirteen base must be on the bridge, and these men were guarding its entrance.

She hesitated for a moment, wondering whether to cross after the countess and give the same sign or to avoid the risk and just wait here until John Caiaphas's men arrived, but a second's thought made her keep walking. The Circle of Thirteen couldn't keep an entire bridge isolated from the rest of London. People would notice, and object. The fact that they had a base *on* the bridge didn't stop other people from crossing it, or visiting the shops on it. The guards on the corner were noting who was with the Circle and who wasn't, not actually preventing anyone who didn't show the correct sign from stepping off the bank and onto the bridge. She would be okay if she continued—just another Londoner out for a stroll.

She supposed that she *could* make the sign of the circle with her fingers, but that would only serve to draw attention to her—attention that she didn't need.

Friday crossed the road and walked past the men with the bonfires, deliberately looking at the ground to avoid eye contact. One of them turned toward her and held out a hand. For a heart-stopping moment she thought she had misread the situation, and he was going to stop her, but he was reaching for a piece of wood being handed to him. Without looking at Friday he chucked it on the fire and continued to warm himself.

The countess was still in sight up ahead. The surface of the bridge was raised in the middle—higher than where it touched the banks. Friday assumed that was so boats with masts could get beneath more easily. Certainly nothing as large as a ship could pass under—they were constrained to stay farther downriver by the docks. The rise and fall of the bridge was mirrored by the houses, giving them a strange, distorted appearance.

Friday watched as the countess reached a shop with a grid of wooden spars across it, making a series of little glass-filled windows. Icicles hung from each wooden spar. As she got closer, Friday thought she could see hats through the glass. The countess gazed through the window as if choosing what she wanted, then went inside. A bell above the door tinkled as it opened and closed behind her.

Friday moved to the window and pretended to look at the hats. In actuality, she let her gaze focus beyond the glass, at the inside of the shop.

The countess stopped at the counter. Instead of saying anything, she made the same sign of the circle as she had before. The shop's proprietor made the sign back. He nodded toward a door at the back of the shop. The countess quickly pushed it open and vanished into the darkness on the other side.

This must be where the Circle of Thirteen was based.

Two shadows appeared, one on either side of Friday. She tensed, ready to defend herself, but a voice from her left asked: "Is this the right place?"

"It is," she said firmly.

"Good work." He looked over to the man on the right. "I'll carry the word back," he said. "You stay here with the lady."

* * *

CRUSOE WATCHED THE pirates leave the road and start out across the bridge. Possibly they were intending to stop at some tavern or a house where they had based themselves, or possibly they were crossing the river to some location on the south bank of the city. He sighed. He would have to follow them to find out, and that meant disobeying Sir William's orders for even longer.

Maybe this hadn't been the best idea in the world.

He was just stepping out into the road when a hand came down on his shoulder and pulled him back.

"It's Robinson Crusoe, isn't it?"

He turned around quickly—not toward where the hand was tightening on his shoulder but in the opposite direction, breaking the contact. At the same time he stepped backward, hands raised ready for a fight.

The man standing in the shadows of a doorway behind him wasn't a pirate as far as he could tell. He wasn't wearing bright colors, scarves, or gold jewelry, and his skin wasn't roughened by years of sun and salt water. He was tanned, yes, but he was anonymous. Unremarkable. He was bundled up against the cold, but Crusoe could see that his clothes, bulky as they were, still allowed him significant freedom of movement.

Did pirates go undercover, or was he working for the Circle of Thirteen? Crusoe clenched his fists, waiting for the man to make some sudden move, but even as he did so it occurred to him that a member of the Circle wouldn't make polite conversation. He would be more likely to stab Crusoe in the back.

One of John Caiaphas's men, then. One of the Increment.

Crusoe nodded, still wary. "Do I know you?"

"I've seen you around," the man said, his breath misting in the cold. He briefly held his hand out, showing Crusoe the ring on his little finger. He glanced past Crusoe, toward the bridge. "Lookin' for your girl? She's already on the bridge. Been there about ten minutes now. One of my lads is with her."

Crusoe felt as if a large hole had opened beneath his feet and he was about to drop into it. "Friday? She's on the bridge?"

The man nodded. His gaze flickered everywhere except Crusoe's face. He was constantly checking for threats or opportunities, and Crusoe was neither. "She followed that countess lady on there." He smiled—a brief change of expression that lit his face up, showing the personality beneath the mask of professionalism. "Clever girl, that one. The way she can move through a crowd, an' keep up with 'er target—I dunno where she got 'er training, but she could teach us a thing or two. It was 'ard keepin' up with 'er."

Crusoe's mind raced. What was the countess doing on the same bridge as Red Tiberius's pirates? Was it a coincidence—the kind of thing that happened in a city like London, where there were only a few ways across the river, or was there some kind of connection between them?

A dark thought welled up, obscuring the rest of his thoughts. "The attack—when's it taking place? She needs to get off the bridge!"

The man shook his head. "The word's been sent back to Mr. Caiaphas. I was told a minute ago to prepare for action. The boss is goin' in mob-'anded."

"But Friday!" Crusoe protested.

The man shrugged. "She'll 'ave to take 'er chances, lad. Mr. Caiaphas don't want any of the villains on that bridge to slip away." He smiled again—something he seemed to do when he admired someone or something. "Clever idea, basin' yourself on a bridge. People don't think of bridges as places, even if they got shops an' 'ouses on them. Bridges are things you cross, not stay on." He shrugged, the motion nearly invisible beneath his thick coat. "Of course, there's only two ways on an' off. That's the down side. Means you're vulnerable to attack. Mr. Caiaphas is goin' to mount 'is attack from both ends—bottle the villains up, like rats in a drainpipe."

Crusoe turned around and stared at the bridge. Abruptly, he took a step toward it.

The hand came down on his shoulder again. "Can't let you do that, son. The lads, they know that the girl is on the bridge an' they'll watch out for her. They don't know about you. If you go on there, they'll treat you like a member of the Circle. Might be nasty. Besides—with you an' the girl on the bridge together, you might do somethin' or say somethin' that'll give the game away too early, an' allow the villains to escape."

Crusoe reached up, took the man's hand, and lifted it away. "Are you going to stop me if I try?"

The man nodded. "Better me deliberately 'ittin' you a little bit now than the lads cuttin' you with a sword later by accident— that's my thinkin' on the matter."

"I need to talk to Sir William," Crusoe said hurriedly. "Where is he?"

The man indicated, with a slight flick of his head, a nearby corner. Several carriages were drawn together, the breath of their horses forming a mist around them. "'E's in the middle one. Said 'e wants you to join 'im anyway. Good view of the action, 'e said."

Crusoe sprinted across the road toward the carriage. Opening the door, he pulled himself up inside, where Sir William Lambert was busy taking a pinch of snuff from a small enameled box.

"Ah, Crusoe—our plan is going even better than we had anticipated. Identifying a major Circle base here in the center of London—that is something that will impress the king! I may even ask for our stipend to be increased so that Segment W might grow."

"Is the attack going ahead?" Crusoe asked urgently.

Sir William abruptly breathed in the snuff, then tucked the box away inside his coat. "Of course it is. That was, and still is, the plan."

"But Friday is there! She followed the countess!"

Sir William nodded. "Yes, so I understand. Worry not—John Caiaphas's men have been informed. They all know her by sight. She will be protected."

Crusoe took a breath, trying to calm himself. "But if there's a fight, then anything might happen. There might be a riot. She might get injured by accident. The Circle's people might realize who she is and kill her. You've got to give her time to get clear."

"That will not happen," Sir William replied calmly. "We have a critical few moments here to seize the initiative. If we miss our chance, then the Circle might be alerted and might be able to prepare for our attack. We need to catch this tide at its flood to succeed."

Before he could stop himself, Crusoe said angrily: "You cannot do that."

Sir William raised a slow eyebrow. His face remained calm, but there was a glint in his eye that suggested he was reining in his temper. "You misunderstand your place in the scheme of things, Master Crusoe," he said. "Because you are new to London, and to civilization, I have granted you certain leniencies, but you cannot forbid me to do anything. I am a noble of this country. You are a servant. That is the way things are. I give the orders and you carry them out."

Crusoe bit back his response—words that might have severed forever his connection to Segment W. Instead, he thought for a moment, then nodded, trying to look as if he was reluctantly agreeing. "I apologize." He sighed. "I am overwrought. You're right, of course. I'll sit this one out. I'll watch from over there, if that's all right?" He nodded toward the bank of the river, where wooden quays and piers blurred the boundary between land and ice.

Sir William nodded coolly. "It should be quite a sight."

Crusoe set off diagonally across the road, away from the bridge. He could feel the man's gaze on him all the way, but then he could feel the sensation of relief, of released pressure, as Sir William turned his attention back to the bridge.

Crusoe knew he couldn't walk across to the bridge's entrance without being seen and probably stopped again, so he looked around. The surface of the ice was covered with people, animals, and stalls. He could even see an ox being roasted. Some of the people had cloth tied around their shoes to stop them from slipping. The arches of the bridge swept above it all, remote and incurious.

He turned and looked back. The man in the doorway had been joined by several others. They were all dressed anonymously, but they all held themselves the same way. Like soldiers. They weren't talking—just standing there, in a group, relaxed but ready for action.

As Crusoe watched, another man walked up. It was John Caiaphas. The group all straightened up as he approached. They didn't salute, but it looked as though they were stopping themselves from doing so.

He didn't have much time. The attack was about to take place.

Crusoe descended a set of wooden steps to the quay. A man was standing on the bottom step, and as Crusoe approached he held out a hand and said: "That's a penny."

"For what?"

"To get on the ice."

Crusoe stared at the man. "A penny, just to get on the ice? Are you serious?"

The man nodded. "I'm a waterman, see? When the river's flowing, I charge people like you a penny to cross it. Now it's frozen

I'm not earning anything, so it's a penny if you want to step on the ice. My river, my rules."

Crusoe debated pushing past the man without paying, but he didn't want to draw any undue attention to himself. He paid with bad grace and stepped off the stairs.

"It's another penny when you want to come off," the man called after him. "Any stairway, you'll find one of us on it, collecting our dues."

Crusoe's intention—as much as he had one—was to get close to the bridge and then cross the ice. If he got to the other side, he might be able to get onto the bridge there without being seen. If he was lucky, then one of the arches might have steps leading up to the roadway. Or he might find a rope. Or something.

He suddenly heard shouting and the sound of whistles up on the bank. Down on the ice, heads turned to see what the commotion was. Across the ice, people were suddenly running toward the entrance to the bridge. Some of them were carrying wooden benches, which they used to block the road.

He was too late.

Crusoe was about to step out onto the ice, desperately scanning the bridge for some kind of way up, when he saw a dark opening at the point where the nearest arch met the north bank. He moved closer, trying to make out what it was. It almost looked like—it was!—a doorway set into the stonework, and with a mossy stone platform in front of it that might, in better weather, have been a place for boats to come to rest unseen.

And it was unguarded.

He started running, aware of two thoughts running simultaneously through his mind—it might be a way for him to get onto the bridge, but it might also be a way for the members of the Circle of Thirteen—if they were actually on the bridge—to escape.

He could hear more shouting from up above—angry this time, not giving orders. Women were screaming as well. Suddenly, there was the noise of metal clashing against metal. Swords? It sounded as if John Caiaphas's blockade and search was already meeting resistance.

He had to get up onto the bridge and find Friday—quickly. Once he'd done that he could warn John Caiaphas about the hidden exit.

The doorway was deeply shadowed, but Crusoe could just make out a wooden door inside. It was studded with metal, and secured with three padlocks. He obviously wasn't going to get through there in a hurry.

Crusoe was about to turn away when he noticed something strange. The wood around the large upper hinge, on the side opposite the padlocks, was scratched. It looked as if years of people accidentally scraping against it with their fingernails had worn the wood away, but why would people be touching the hinge? Surely, if they were trying to open the door they would be concentrating on the padlocks.

And why would the hinges be on the outside of the door? It would be safer to have them on the inside, with the door opening inward, so that they couldn't be interfered with.

Unless . . .

On a hunch, Crusoe reached up to the cylinder of the top hinge. He tried pushing it—up, down, sideways. It didn't budge.

As a last option, he tried turning it.

The whole cylinder rotated through ninety degrees. It wasn't a hinge at all—it was a lock!

Quickly, he tried the other two sets of hinges. They all rotated.

The door creaked open on hinges that were hidden inside the door frame. This lock was designed for anyone to open, but only if they knew the trick. It must be a secret entrance—or exit—for the Circle of Thirteen.

The weak sunlight barely illuminated the gloom within, but Crusoe could just make out steep stone steps leading upward.

At the top of the steps, another opening gave out onto a long, brick-lined tunnel. In one direction it went along the bridge, beneath the road, like a hidden backbone. There must be access points along the corridor to get up to hidden entrances in the buildings above. Thin diagonal beams of light illuminated it, coming from holes drilled into the bricks. The holes led all the way up to the top of the bridge. In the weak sunlight that somehow found its way along them and into the tunnel, Crusoe could see moss and fungus making a patchwork of green and orange on the dark surfaces along the bricks.

The tunnel continued in the other direction as well, penetrating into the north bank of the Thames. Maybe it connected up with the cellars of some of the houses, providing a way on and off the bridge without being observed.

Crusoe was about to step out into the tunnel when he heard movement. He drew back, into the shadows.

A few seconds later, flickering orange light splashed across the brickwork. People were down there with him, and they were carrying lanterns.

The sounds of movement got closer. Crusoe wondered whether he should go back down the stairs. It obviously depended on whether whoever was coming along the corridor planned to leave the bridge by the ice or along the corridor leading into the city. He was torn, but burning curiosity won out over prudence. He wanted to see who it was.

Maybe he could tell John Caiaphas about it. Maybe it would help him with Sir William.

A few seconds later a group of people rushed past where he was hiding. They all had long robes, with the hoods pulled over their faces, so he couldn't tell if they were men or women, but the bizarre thing was that the robes were all different colors—red, blue, green, purple, yellow . . . He lost count of how many of them rushed past. In the unstable light it was like some phantasmagorical carnival, like something he might see on the stage of the Drury Lane The-ater, not in a dark tunnel beneath a bridge.

One of them—a figure in long red robes—turned to look back along the tunnel. The figure pulled the scarlet hood back in order to see better, and Crusoe stifled a gasp.

It was Red Tiberius! His sharp-bearded, swarthy face was unmistakable!

Friday's father gazed into the distance, a scowl on the face that Crusoe had only ever seen from a distance but which he would—could—never forget. Crusoe's heart was hammering so loudly he was sure Red Tiberius would hear it. His hands were suddenly slick with sweat. This made it certain—the pirates were here, and their master was with them. But what were they doing at a Circle of Thirteen base?

A figure in white robes reached out and tugged at Red Tiberius's sleeve. The dark-skinned pirate nodded, pulled his hood back up, and followed the rest of his companions.

And then they were gone. The flickering light receded ahead of Crusoe, leaving blackness in its wake. He stepped out into the tunnel and watched them go.

He was about to turn around to head back toward the bridge when he heard a noise behind him. Someone else had entered the tunnel!

CHAPTER FIVE

From the shadows of her doorway, Friday and her Increment companion kept watch over the shop the Countess of Lichfield had entered. It was the blond-haired, blue-eyed lad who had been left behind with her, and she was very conscious of his nearness.

"I'm Paul," he said softly. She could feel his breath on her ear. "Paul Shadrach."

"I'm Friday," she murmured back.

"I know. Everybody in the Increment knows who you are." He paused for a moment. "So—what's the plan? What are we waiting for?"

Friday wasn't actually sure. Should she follow the countess inside, or stay where she was? If she followed, then she might be spotted, but if she stayed where she was, then the countess might get away through some hidden passage and Segment W wouldn't be able to tell who was with the Circle and who wasn't.

The decision was taken out of her hands. A sudden cacophony of whistles, rattles, and shouts echoed between the walls. People on the bridge stopped what they were doing, but there were two separate types of reaction. Some people looked puzzled and slightly wary. Others moved their hands to their weapons, making eye contact with one another.

The innocent and the guilty.

She saw men hauling wooden barricades across the entrance to the bridge. Segment W, obviously. They would be doing the same at the other end as well.

"You should get behind the lines," Paul Shadrach said. He took her arm, pulling her away from the doorway. "I'll be in for it if any harm comes to you during the attack."

"I need to stay here," she replied forcefully.

He glanced along the road. "I might be needed," he said.

"Then leave me here. If the countess leaves, then I need to follow her."

After a few seconds of consideration, her shadow nodded and slipped away.

From her position in the doorway, Friday watched the progress of events. Having blockaded the road, John Caiaphas's men started moving along the bridge. They were herding people into lines so that they could be searched, questioned, identified. Friday wasn't sure how they were going to tell a Circle adherent from anybody else without getting them to strip and look for blue shapes on their skin, but presumably John had some ideas. She wasn't actually sure that he had any authority to do this— Segment W was a secret organization, after all. It wasn't like they could show any identification. Maybe he was relying on shock to make people compliant.

And then it all became very simple, very clear. As John Caiaphas's men began to direct people to lines, some of them drew swords or daggers and resisted. Brutal fights broke out in both directions. The clashing of blades competed with the shouts and cries of the fighters. Meanwhile, although a few people just stood where they were, looking concerned, many began to walk purposefully toward the fronts of the shops and taverns, obviously getting to safety while they could. There must be other ways off the bridge!

It was immediately clear to Friday that there were far more Circle adherents on the bridge than there were ordinary Londoners. Segment W had made a serious miscalculation. It wasn't that a Circle base was on the bridge—the bridge *was* the Circle's base!

A man sidled along the wall toward her. She prepared to fight, but he made a calming gesture. She suddenly recognized him as another of the Segment W personnel. He was the other man who had followed her from the theater.

"Where's the countess?" he asked, looking grim.

Friday nodded toward the shop. "In there."

He followed her glance. "You'd better get off the bridge," he said. "This is goin' to go down worse than we thought. We were only expectin' a handful of them. This—it's going to be like clearin' rats out of a basement!"

Friday nodded. She stepped out of the doorway and started back toward the entrance to the bridge, expecting the man to follow her, but he just stood where he was, looking around.

"Are you coming?" she asked.

"You'll be okay," he said. "The men know your face. They'll let you through. I've got to stay and look for your friend."

"Robin? He's here?"

He nodded. "Spoke to 'im myself. Told 'im not to come onto the bridge, but one of my men down on the ice saw 'im."

"But—!" She turned to stare at the carnage that was occurring everywhere. Fights were going on across the whole of the bridge. "He might get hurt!"

"Serves 'im right, if you ask me," the man said. "'E disobeyed Sir William's direct orders. 'E's in trouble whether I find 'im or not!"

"But—where *is* he?" she asked. "How did he get onto the bridge?" Her brain caught up with something she'd heard the man say, and she added: "Did you say he was down on the *ice*? What was he doing?"

"There's an 'idden doorway down there. Looks like there's tunnels built into the structure of the bridge. Probably accessible through secret entrances in the 'ouses and such. We're tryin' to locate all the doors and block 'em off, but we might be too late. Mister Caiaphas reckons that some of the rats 'ave already escaped." He shrugged. "I s'pose we ought to thank your friend. If it 'adn't been for 'im we might not have known about those secret doors and the tunnels until it was too late."

Friday considered her options. If Robin was here, on the bridge, then he was right in the middle of a small war. She didn't know *why* he was there—perhaps he was looking for her—but she had to find him, make sure he was all right.

And if there were secret ways off the bridge, then the nearest entrance was probably in the shop that the countess had entered.

Before her Increment companion could stop her, she ran across the road and pushed open the door of the shop.

She had been right—it *was* a hat shop. It was deserted now, but she went straight through the doorway behind the counter. She found herself in a small hallway. Stairs led upward, and a second doorway led into a back room. There was no sign of the shop's owner, or of the countess.

There was no point going *up*stairs looking for a way to go *down*, so she started to move toward the back room, but she suddenly noticed a length of carpet, rolled up and carelessly left to one side. She glanced down and saw that the joins between the floorboards marked out a rectangular shape just in front of her. It looked like it might be a trapdoor. She knelt down and felt around the edges. There was just enough space for her to get purchase with her fingertips. Thankfully, she had small fingers. Grimacing at the pain, she tried to pull the trapdoor upward. It shifted slightly, enabling her to get a better grip. With an effort, she pulled it open and let it fall backward onto the floorboards, revealing a shadowed opening rimmed with stones.

The dank, unpleasant smell of the river rose up and made her nose wrinkle. In the small amount of light she could see the top rung of a ladder. Swinging her legs into the hole, she quickly scrambled down into the darkness.

Just as her head cleared the flagstones beneath the floorboards, her feet touched ground. She was in a small antechamber with a wet floor and stone walls covered in fungus that looked like long green hair. An opening led into a tunnel that appeared to run exactly underneath the length of the bridge.

Which way? She listened for a moment. To her left there was silence, but to her right she could hear the distant sound of footsteps. They seemed to be getting quieter as she listened—Circle of Thirteen members trying to escape? Perhaps even the Countess of Lichfield. If Robin entered the corridor from the north bank of the Thames, then he would be approaching from that direction. Decision made, she ran to her right.

As her eyes adjusted to the darkness, she thought she could see the glow of candles or lanterns up ahead. She slowed down, trying to make as little noise as possible. Black openings flashed by her on either side—ways up to the buildings lining the bridge. Fortunately, nobody was using them—either everyone who knew about the secret tunnel had already used it or John Caiaphas's men had caught the majority of people up on the surface by surprise.

Fixated on the orange glow from up ahead, Friday almost ran into the back of someone who was standing half in and half out of one of the openings. Her foot scuffed the stone floor of the tunnel, and the person whirled around.

"Friday!"

She felt relief rush through her like a warm tide. "Robin—what are you doing here?"

He grabbed her shoulders and pulled her into a hug. "I wasn't sure what had happened to you," he said. Pushing her away slightly, but still keeping hold of her, he stared into her eyes. "Listen— there's no easy way of saying this, but I'm pretty sure I saw your father pass by. He's up ahead. It looks like he's with the Circle of Thirteen!"

The warmth that had washed through her body was suddenly replaced with fear. "My *father?*" She felt her heart clench. "With the Circle?"

Robin nodded gravely. "We need to get out and tell Sir William."

"You're going nowhere."

The voice was grim and determined. They both turned.

Two men were standing in the darkness just ahead of them. They had knives, held ready to thrust or slice. They weren't pirates—or if they were, then they were disguised as ordinary Londoners. One of them had a blue rash covering his left cheek and extending down his neck—the characteristic sign of a Circle of Thirteen member.

"Sound echoes down these tunnels," the second man said. He grinned, revealing several broken and missing teeth. "I'd say you should remember that, but you'll never get the chance. You're not with us, which means you must be against us."

"Which means you die," the one with the blue rash said.

Two men, with knives, in a confined space. There were times to fight, and times to run. This, Friday knew, was a time to run.

Robin had come to the same conclusion at the same time—as she knew he would. He released his grip on her shoulders, and they both ran back the way that she had come—back toward the center of the bridge.

Two Years and One Month Before the Escape

The salt spray stung her lips and her eyes. Through half-closed lids she could see the deep blue of the sky and the slightly darker blue of the sea ahead of her. The wood of the ship's bow was slippery under her hands, and the sun shone down hard from high above. If she let her mind drift, then she could forget she was the only woman on a pirate ship with a crew of nearly fifty violent men. If she let her mind drift, then she could imagine that she was a bird, skimming freely above the waves, catching the breeze beneath her wings. Or a dolphin just emerging briefly from the sea and hovering above her own shadow before plunging back into the calm depths of the ocean.

Imagination only kept her going for so long, however. Soon enough there was the reality of the ship. The fights. The sickening stench. The long stretches of boredom tinged with nervousness as she waited for the next burst of violence. Already since the last time they dropped anchor there had been two attempts to oust her father from his position as captain; attempts met with a terrible retaliation. As her father had told her many times: a captain cannot be soft. Your crew must respect you, but that respect must be based on fear, and that fear must be reinforced by examples of what you are capable of doing. When she was younger, Suriya had taken her father's words at face value, but as she got older, she started to wonder if he sometimes deliberately showed weakness in order to manipulate the more unstable members of his crew into mutiny. Then he could torture and kill them in the most horrible ways and so keep the others in line.

She turned and gazed up into the maze of sails above. Barely visible, hanging from a spar on the main mast, was the body of John

Robertshaw. He hadn't been a mutineer. He hadn't even been a thief, which was the supposed reason for his hanging. In fact, he had tried to attack Suriya a while back, and she manipulated the crew into believing that he was stealing from them. He had been hanging there for a while; alive at first and then dead, although nobody was quite sure at what point the one had changed to the other. His body was now gaunt and leathery, tanned by the sun and the salt breeze. Just bones and tendons and thin fingers clutched in perpetual agony around the ropes that held him. And Suriya didn't feel any guilt. Not one shred.

Maybe, she thought darkly, she was more like her father than she wished.

The most recent mutineer was still alive, but that probably wouldn't last for long. Her father was at the stern of the ship, standing directly above his cabin, ready to pronounce his sentence. The crew gathered on the quarterdeck beneath him, waiting to see what he would decide. Looking at them, Suriya lost count of the number of hands, eyes, ears, and other bits of their bodies that were missing. She wasn't sure there was a whole man among them. Life as a pirate was hard.

The mutineer—a dark-skinned man named Petitfleur who spoke with a French accent and who hadn't been with the crew for long, stood in front of the crew alone, bound in chains.

"What's going to happen to him?" a nervous voice asked.

Shaking the moisture from her face, she turned and glanced over her shoulder. A boy stood behind her. She had noticed him a couple of times since their last landfall. His skin and his eyes were both a dark shade of brown, and his hair was black. She thought that her father had traded a barrel of wine for him and two other crewmembers with another captain. He was the new cabin boy. They'd lost the last one during a battle with a merchantman, when a badly aimed charge of chain shot had swept across the Dark Nebula's deck. The two cannonballs linked by a few feet of chain had missed the mast but hit the cabin boy and several other pirates. The spinning scythe of metal links had cut them in half and kept going, taking a chunk out of the rail before it vanished.

"What's your name?" she asked.

"Diran," the boy replied. "You're Red Tiberius's daughter, aren't you?"

She raised an eyebrow.

"I used to be a prince, once," he continued quietly. "That was three ships ago now."

"You were taken during a raid?"

"From my father's ship." He clamped his lips together, then said: "He's looking for me. He'll find me soon."

Suriya thought about her mother, then quickly thought about something else.

"They'll probably keelhaul him," she said.

"What's that mean?"

She glanced over to where her father was addressing his crew. "It means they keep hold of both ends of a rope and throw it over the bow here. Then they let it drift back until it passes directly underneath the middle of the ship. They'll tie Petitfleur's arms to one end of the rope and his legs to the other end, then they'll throw him over the side with an oiled rag in his mouth so he doesn't drown. They'll pull on the rope, dragging him underneath the hull until he comes up on the other side, then they'll pull him up to the deck."

Diran frowned. "So he just has to hold his breath for a while, otherwise he drowns. That's not much of a punishment for mutiny."

"Have you ever seen the underside of a ship's hull?" Suriya asked. He shook his head.

"It's covered with barnacles. They're like little blisters made of rock, but they're alive. The longer a ship's at sea, the more barnacles it gets. If you get keelhauled, then you get scraped underwater along

*those sharp barnacles." She shuddered suddenly, despite the heat.
"If you're lucky, then it just rips your flesh off. If you're unlucky, then
when you get pulled up on deck again there's hardly anything left of
you."*

A shout came from the crew, back on the quarterdeck. Diran
turned to look at Red Tiberius. Suriya's father was pointing at the
rail. Petifleur shouted incoherently, and struggled to escape, but the
crew dragged him over to the edge of the ship.

"Take my advice," Suriya said. "Don't look. Just go back into my
father's cabin and prepare a bottle of wine for him." She grimaced.
"He always gets thirsty after carrying out a punishment like this."

POOLS OF WATER on the stone floor had turned to ice, and Crusoe
felt his feet slipping as he ran. He reached out for Friday's hand,
grabbing it and holding on tight, as much to stop her from falling as
to prevent him from the same fate. Strands of moss hung down like
cobwebs, brushing their cold, wet fingers over his face as he passed
beneath them. The sound of their footsteps echoed back and forth
from the stones, multiplying the number of hunters and the number
of hunted until it sounded like a crowd of people were running.

Black doorways whipped past them every few feet. Crusoe felt
an almost overwhelming urge to swerve into one of them and push
Friday up the ladder, but that would leave him defenseless against
two men with knives. He could cope with that if he thought that
Friday would escape, but he knew in his heart that he would be cut
down within moments, and they would just grab Friday's feet and
pull her off the ladder. No, running was the only option.

But where were they running *to*? They had no goal, no destination in mind. They were running blindly.

He heard a *swish* and something sharp touched the back of his neck. A prickle of pain was immediately replaced by the warm trickle of blood. The men chasing them were lashing out with their blades, trying to cause some wound that would incapacitate them and force them to stop.

Crusoe heard a sudden cry from behind, and then a clatter as one of the men slipped and fell. Without thinking, he skidded to a halt, crouched down, and threw himself backward. His shoulders hit the knees of the remaining pursuer. The man shouted in pain as Crusoe straightened up, flipping the man over. He tumbled forward, past Crusoe. His outstretched arms took most of the impact with the floor, but before he could pick himself up, Friday had turned around and kicked him in the jaw. His head snapped sideways, and he fell forward onto the moss and the ice.

Crusoe was now more concerned with the second pursuer—the one who had slipped on the ice. In the darkness it was difficult to see what had happened to him. Crusoe took a step back along the tunnel, looking for the man, but he seemed to have vanished.

As Crusoe came level with one of the shadowed arches, the man leaped out at him, knife slashing viciously downward. It cut through Crusoe's leather jacket but didn't catch his skin. He whirled around, grabbing the man's arms to stop any more knife blows, and brought his knee up abruptly. The knee connected with the man's groin; he screamed, and doubled up in agony. Crusoe chopped at the back of his neck as he fell to his knees. The man fell to the floor, stunned. His knife clattered against the stone, and Crusoe snatched it up.

When he turned, Friday stood above the unconscious body of the other man. She held *his* knife.

"Which way?" she asked. She gazed back along the tunnel. "Can we catch up with my father, do you think?"

"Do we want to?" Crusoe shook his head. "They're guarded, they're too far ahead of us, and they've almost certainly found their way to the surface. We need to get back to Sir William and tell him what's happened."

Friday nodded. She indicated the nearest black archway. "Up there."

He nodded. "Why not?"

Crusoe expected the ladder to lead to the interior of a house or a shop on the bridge, but as they kept climbing he realized that they were going past the level of the bridge. The ladder finally ended in a room on the first or second story of one of the bridge's buildings. A window, too narrow to climb through, gave a view out onto the ice of the Thames far below. A single door was the only way out, apart from the hole in the floor from which they had emerged.

Friday moved across to the door and pushed it open. Crusoe heard her gasp.

He moved to look over her shoulder.

The room on the other side of the doorway had many sides. Each side seemed to be paneled with polished stone of a different color—red, blue, green, yellow, and all the possibilities in between. A rectangular patch of blackness that Crusoe initially thought was a doorway was, in fact, an entirely black wall. Light spilled in from a skylight high above.

A table in the center of the room was piled high with manuscripts, papers, and books.

"This," Friday said, "has to be some kind of conference room, like the one Sir William has back at the Globe. Do you think this is where the Circle of Thirteen actually *meets?*"

Crusoe nodded slowly. He followed Friday into the room. The doorway they had entered through was paneled in white stone on the inside.

That made him think. He moved around the room in a clockwise direction, pushing at each stone panel to see if any of them concealed hidden doors. Friday, seeing what he was doing, did the same in the other direction. None of the walls moved apart from the one paneled in white stone.

"I'll check the other doorway in the next room," she said. She left the multicolored room, and Crusoe heard her footsteps as she crossed the anteroom where the shaft from the tunnels ended.

"There's a hallway through here," she said. "I can see stairs. It's a way out, I think."

"*I* think," Crusoe said slowly, "that we may have found something useful. . . ."

FRIDAY WALKED BACK to see Robin examining the various papers scattered across the table. "It looks like they were holding some kind of planning meeting," he said. "These documents are written in different languages, but they look like reports from agents whom the Circle has scattered in the royal courts of Europe." He grabbed the corner of a larger sheet of parchment and pulled it clear. "*This* one is really interesting. It's some kind of map, I think, but I don't know what it's a map *of*. There are lines, and circles, and words in code." He laughed suddenly. "It's the kind of thing that Isaac Newton would have in his study, I think."

Friday was just about to enter the room when she heard a noise from behind her. She spun around. Someone was climbing up the ladder!

She opened her mouth to call to Robin, but before she could say anything a hand appeared on the top rung. Robin couldn't get out of the stone-paneled room and across the anteroom to the hallway before whoever it was climbed up. They were going to have to fight.

She saw the top of someone's head emerging from the hole. If she moved fast, she could kick them back down the shaft, or stamp on their hands, or something.

Before she could do anything, the door to the hallway opened and a man came through. He was black-skinned, like her, dressed in colorful silks and wearing a scarf knotted around his hair.

She didn't recognize his face, but she knew with a despairing lurch in her heart who he was: one of her father's crew.

He saw Friday and grinned widely. "Wए सेअर्च्ह हल्fा थे चतिय्, अन्द् हेरे योउ अरे—इन् ओउर् ओwn बसे!" he said. It took her a few seconds to translate the Sanskrit words into English—it had been so long since she heard her native language spoken. *"We search half the city, and here you are—in our own base!"*

The man climbing up from the tunnel below was halfway into the anteroom now. His jaw was swollen, and he had a nasty bruise forming across the lower half of his face. "She's one of Lambert's people!" he snarled in English. "She kicked me in the face, down in the tunnels! I'll slice her up for that!" He clambered out into the anteroom, glowering. Behind him, his companion from the tunnel started up from the shaft as well.

"She's Red Tiberius's daughter," the pirate said in a warning tone. "He'll want to talk to her—before he has her killed."

"Doctor Mors will have something to say about that," warned the second man from the tunnels.

The name surprised her. She had heard of Doctor Mors before, but where?

"Where's the other one? He hurt me bad, he did. When Doctor Mors gets to see him, there's going to be bits missing. Nothing important, but enough to make him scream. At least, until they pull 'is tongue out. Then he'll just gurgle."

Friday hadn't thought her heart could sink any further, but it did. There was no way out.

Out in the hallway she could see a fourth man's face. Four of the Circle against two of the Segment. The result was a foregone conclusion.

Friday knew that Robin was still in the stone-lined room, just a moment from discovery. She knew he would be preparing himself to run into the room and start fighting, but she had to protect him. Whatever they had discovered here was important. Sir William had to know about it before the evidence could be taken away.

And if she had to sacrifice her life, or even just her freedom, for the boy she cared so much for, then so be it. She would do that happily.

Before any of the men could get to her, she ran across the anteroom and thrust her head out the window. The chill wind outside made her gasp for a second. Below she could see the icy surface of the Thames. She yelled, "Robin—they've got me, but you have to get away! Tell the Segment what's happened! Get Sir William to send men up here as quickly as he can!"

Someone grabbed her and pulled her back into the room. It was the black-skinned pirate. He put a sweaty, rough hand across her mouth. "Just be quiet, like a good girl."

The man she had kicked in the face, down in the tunnels, ran to the window. His head barely fit through the narrow gap.

"'E's gone!" he snarled. "The tyke! She's warned 'im off."

"You heard what she said," the man's companion added. "He's going to come back with reinforcements. We've got her, at least. Let's get out of here."

The second pirate pulled the door from the hall shut behind him. Friday vaguely recognized his face from the days when she lived on the *Dark Nebula* with her father and his crew. He hadn't spoken much English then, and didn't now. He just pointed at her, pointed at the hole in the floor, and raised his eyebrows in a question.

The pirate holding her fast nodded. She could feel the movement of his jaw against her head. "You're right—we need to get out of here quickly."

The second man from the tunnel glanced at the stone-walled meeting room, frowning. "What about the stuff? Doctor Mors isn't going to be pleased that we left it."

That name again. Where *had* she heard it before?

"If it's that important 'e should've come back for it 'imself," his friend said. "We ain't got the time." He glanced at Friday. "She's a wild one. She's goin' to fight us every step of the way. That'll slow us down."

"Not necessarily," the pirate holding Friday said. She felt his grip loosen, and she prepared to wriggle free and bring her elbow back hard into his stomach, but he was only shifting her weight so that he could get his right hand free. Just as she realized what he was doing, he brought his fist down hard on the back of her head.

Everything went black.

CRUSOE'S HEART THUMPED so loudly in his chest that he was sure all four of the ruffians in the anteroom could hear it. He was torn between running into the room and fighting to free Friday— and almost certainly losing—and staying where he was.

Like a coward, a little voice in the back of his mind kept repeating, but he knew what he had to do. He knew what *Friday* would do if their positions were reversed—rather than fruitlessly getting both of them captured or killed, she would bide her time, follow them, and look for a better chance to intervene. That's why she had fooled them into thinking he had already escaped through the window.

So that's what *he* would do: wait, and look for his chance to save her.

He hid himself behind the white stone panel, listening. When he heard the pirate holding Friday knock her out, he had to stop himself from launching into the room and tackling the man. Now, more than ever, he had to wait, because now Friday couldn't join in the fight.

He heard a degree of scuffling from the room as the men tried to work out how to get an unconscious Friday down the ladder, but eventually everything went quiet.

He moved silently out into the open. It was empty. Glancing cautiously down the ladder, he couldn't see anyone standing down there waiting.

Quickly, he slipped down and into the tunnel.

The group had headed in the opposite direction to the way he and Friday had come. One of them had slung Friday over his shoulder like a sack of coal. Fortunately, he was bringing up the rear, which meant that the ones in front would have problems looking past him to see Crusoe.

They walked, and Crusoe quietly followed for a few minutes until they moved out of the tunnel and into a side area. Flickering orange light from lanterns outlined their silhouettes. From the change in the echoing of their voices and footsteps it was a much larger area, but still built out of stone.

Crusoe slowed down, listening. He heard a lot of scuffling, and the sounds of wood and metal objects being dragged around, as well as a lot of cursing. A sudden *swishing* sound made Crusoe frown, but then there was silence.

He ran down the tunnel and into an area of brick and stone about the size of a typical dockside tavern. Lanterns were hanging from hooks all around its damp walls. The heat from them wasn't enough to melt the icicles that hung from the brick roof. The room was large enough that it must have been past the end of the bridge, actually underneath the south bank of the Thames itself.

It was some kind of hidden dock: five small boats were stored, hull-up, but the strangest thing was a wide slipway leading down from the boats to an opening onto the Thames. A big canvas sheet had been pulled to one side, exposing the ice. The outside had probably been painted to look like stonework, or earth, but it was a hidden entrance—or exit!

Marks on the frosted stone indicated to Crusoe that a boat had already been dragged to the slipway and launched onto the Thames—but how? The river was completely frozen!

And then he noticed that the upturned hulls had been modified. They had been fitted with wooden crossbeams, on which thick bits of metal like sword blades had been fastened. When the boats were the right way up the blades would be touching the ground.

He remembered earlier seeing people out on the ice with metal blades strapped to their boots. They had been sliding across the frozen river without a care in the world. *Skating*—that was the word he had heard.

That's what these hulls had been turned into—boats that could *skate* along the ice. That's how the pirates and the Circle of Thirteen ruffians were making their escape.

And he had to follow.

Crusoe rushed across to the nearest boat and, using all of his strength, pulled it over so that it was resting on its metal skates. Fortunately, the mast and furled sail were inside the hull.

He pushed the boat over to the slipway, feeling and hearing the blades grating on the stone. The surface of the slipway was covered with ice—someone had melted buckets of water and thrown them on the stone, letting them freeze to make an easy way out for the boats.

Grooves in the ice, running from the top of the slipway to the bottom, showed where the men had left, taking Friday with them.

Crusoe heaved against the back of the boat. Just as it began to topple forward he jumped inside. His weight toppled it even far-ther, and it began to slide down the ice toward the hard surface of the river.

Crusoe ducked his head as the boat *swish*ed beneath the stone roof of the hidden dock, past the canvas screen, and onto the river.

Snowdrifts lined the slipway where it entered the ice, forming a gradual curve so that the boat slid easily out onto the river rather than grinding nose-first into the hard ice. As soon as it was clear, Crusoe heaved the mast upright and slotted it into place. Quickly, with well-practiced hands, he unfurled the single mainsail while glancing back and forth to see which direction the ruffians had taken Friday. To his right, heading downstream toward the sea, the revelers were enjoying themselves unaffected, but upstream Crusoe could see that the crowds had parted to let something through. People were still shaking their fists, and some had fallen down onto the ice.

And there were white lines etched into the ice, like a sign pointing him in the right direction.

That way!

He let the wind fill the sail. The boat surged ahead like a wild animal let loose. He knelt in the back, one hand on the tiller and the other hand holding the sheet rope that ran to the corner of the sail.

Crusoe aimed squarely at the gap in the crowd he had noticed. Just as people were moving back or climbing to their feet, they had to throw themselves out of the way again as he came past.

Tiny fragments of ice the size of grains of sand lashed his face as the boat raced along. He had to keep his eyes nearly shut so that his eyeballs didn't freeze solid.

How had John Caiaphas missed all this? he wondered. Not just a secret base actually built into one of London's bridges, but a whole secret dock as well!

Up ahead, through the thinning crowd, he caught a glimpse of the other boat racing away from him, sail billowing. There were several dark shapes inside. The blades on the bottom of the boat were carving white channels into the ice, like the wake of a boat in water but more permanent.

Smells of cooking meat from the various hogs and cattle being roasted on the ice kept assailing his nostrils. Sometimes people didn't notice his approach, and he had to shout at them to get out of the way. Sometimes they didn't hear him, and he felt the boat shudder as they were knocked to the ice and slid away.

As his own sail filled with wind, Crusoe began to catch up with the boat in front. There were five people in it, compared to just him, which must have been weighing it down. The question was— did he want to catch up and do something or did he want to keep his distance and discover where they were going? At least, in the latter case, he would have information to give to Sir William in apology for having disobeyed orders.

Was he chasing, or was he just following? He wasn't sure.

His boat skimmed too close to a stall selling woolen garments and hats. It clipped the edge, and the stall toppled over as he raced away from it, spreading its contents all over the ice. People shouted curses after him, shaking their fists.

By now he could see four dark heads in the boat in front. No sign of Friday—she was almost certainly lying in the bottom of the boat, either unconscious or pretending to be.

Buildings flashed past on each side of the Thames—the Palace of Westminster, St. James's Palace, various churches and big houses.

Aware that he was getting too close to the boat ahead, he started to release the tension on the sheet rope he was holding, allowing the wind to escape from the sail and slow him down. He didn't want them to see him—after all, they were the only two skating boats on the surface of the Thames, and they would know instantly that they were being followed—but he was too late. One of the heads turned around to look behind and then turned again to stare at him.

They had spotted him. That meant he was definitely in a chase now.

The boat ahead slid beneath another bridge, passing briefly into shadow before emerging again into sunlight. Crusoe followed, once again allowing the wind to fill his sail and push him forward faster. He still had no idea what he was going to do when he caught up with the boat—ram it, maybe?—but he would think of something. He always did.

The men in the boat seemed to be talking. Their heads were closer together, and there was a lot of arm-waving and gesticulation. What could they do? They were moving, he was moving, and it wasn't as if there was anywhere else they could go apart from upriver. Yes, he knew that there were rivers that joined the Thames even in the center of the city—the Walbrook, the Fleet, the Tyburn—but he couldn't see how they were going to be able to turn their boat and navigate up what, in most cases, were even narrower channels without allowing him to catch up.

His cheeks burned with the cold now, and he couldn't feel his nose. His hands were so numb they were almost losing their grip on the sheet rope. With a flash of humor he wished he'd had enough time to snatch a pair of gloves from the stall he had knocked over.

One of the heads in the boat in front vanished for a moment, as the man ducked down. Within a moment he was back. He fiddled with something in his hands, then turned and threw the object backward, directly at Crusoe's boat.

It was round, and from the way it hit the ice Crusoe thought it was probably made of metal. People on the ice moved closer, curious. Crusoe tried to wave them away before his boat hit them. He frowned as he watched the object on the ice get closer. What was it?

The object suddenly vanished, replaced by a rapidly expanding ball of smoke and flame and a loud *bang*.

Some kind of firework? Crusoe thought as people fell backward in shock, but then the ice beneath him jerked like a rumpled blanket whose corners had been abruptly pulled, and his boat left the ice entirely.

CHAPTER SIX

For a long moment the boat hung in the air, still traveling forward but not touching the hard surface of the river, and then it crashed and slid sideways. Crusoe could hear the metal blades grating against the ice, and he was convinced that at least one of them was going to come off, but then the wind caught the sail again and the boat was snatched forward, almost pitching Crusoe out onto the surface of the Thames. By the time he caught hold of the side and the tiller, the blades were slicing their way through the ice as they had before. Crusoe caught a glimpse of a cracked hole in the ice, big enough to bury a body in and with water in the bottom.

The other people on the river had all turned to stare, trying to work out what had made the noise. Those closest to the hole were backing away fast in case it cracked open beneath them, dumping them into the freezing depths of the river.

The man who had thrown the device bent down again. Crusoe knew what was coming. Tugging on the tiller, he tried to steer sideways, but his blades were cutting their own grooves in the ice and they didn't want to be shifted. Eventually, he felt the boat creak reluctantly as he persuaded it to adjust course, bumping as it crossed the grooves made by the boat in front, but he was too late. The man in the boat was close enough now that Crusoe could see his sneer as he threw the second object.

This one bounced twice on the ice before sliding to rest. Crusoe's boat would miss it by about ten feet. Maybe it wouldn't go off until he was past it.

He was wrong. Just as he came alongside, the object exploded in an eye-searing flash of red and yellow. Fragments of metal peppered his sail with tiny holes. The force of the blast added to the wind to make the sail billow outward to the point where it almost tore, pulling the boat so that only two of the three metal blades were in contact with the frozen river. Despite its holes, the sail was so taut that Crusoe feared it would drag the entire boat sideways and spill him out. Glancing to where the explosion had happened, he saw that an entire slab of ice had been dislodged and was sticking up at a crazy angle. Beneath it he could see the murky waters of the Thames, rolling like dark oil.

It took every last ounce of his strength to balance the tiller and the sheet rope until his boat lurched back onto the blades with a *thud* that echoed through his entire body.

Some kind of struggle seemed to be going on in the boat in front. The man who had thrown the metal objects was fighting with someone. Friday? It looked like she was trying to stop him from throwing another device, but Crusoe felt a flash of horror when he saw the man punch down hard with his fist, then turn around with a third device in his hands.

There was nothing Crusoe could do apart from let go of the sheet rope and let the wind out of his sails, slowing his boat down—and that was the last thing he intended doing. If he did that he might lose Friday forever.

The problem was that nobody in Segment W knew he was here. If something happened to him—if he died, or was seriously injured—then Friday would be lost.

Whatever happened, Crusoe had to succeed.

The man threw the third object. Either his aim was better or Crusoe was getting closer, because this time the metal object bounced twice on the ice before dropping into the bow of Crusoe's boat.

It was a metal ball about the size of a grapefruit. A seam ran around its middle. It looked like it had been made in two halves and then riveted together. A small tube stuck out of it, and something like a piece of string poked out of the tube.

It was on fire.

It only took a fraction of a second for Crusoe to realize that he couldn't get to the sphere and throw it out of the boat before the flame vanished inside the shell and the thing exploded. Even if he tried, he would have to let go of the tiller and the sheet rope, and that meant his boat would veer sideways and possibly hit something.

There was only one thing he could do.

He scrambled backward and rolled out of the boat. The wooden tiller flashed past his head as he fell. He hit the ice hard, knocking the breath from his body, but he was still moving, sliding along the ice behind the boat. If the sphere exploded now, then the fragments of wood and the metal blades beneath it would form a cloud of dangerous shrapnel that he would slide right into.

He rolled over, onto his stomach, and dug his fingers into the ice. Within seconds his fingertips were numb—probably a good thing because otherwise the pain would have been unbearable. It worked: he began to slow, and the gap between him and the boat stretched to five, ten, fifteen feet.

He turned over, onto his back, just as the sphere exploded. The boat suddenly vanished—replaced with smoke, flame, wood, and metal. A wave of heat passed over Crusoe, replaced instantly by more of the freezing cold. He felt his face stinging, and he wasn't sure if it was shards of ice that were hitting him or splinters of wood.

He slid gradually to a halt. His boat had just . . . ceased to exist. Meanwhile, far ahead, the boat in which Friday was being held captive was getting smaller and smaller as it sped up the frozen river. Eventually, he saw it tilt around a bend in the river, and then it was gone.

THE LAST THING Friday remembered clearly was struggling in the bottom of a boat that was sliding across the ice. She had been keeping quiet, lying under a piece of canvas sacking and wiggling a nail loose from the wood beneath her—the closest thing to a weapon she could find. Once she had worked it loose, she slipped it beneath the collar of her jacket so that it wouldn't be found and turned her attention back to what her captors were saying.

They were talking about someone following them along the icy river. She knew, with a warm feeling inside her chest, that it had to be Robin. Despite her instinctive sacrifice in getting captured so that he could get away, he had obviously come after her, hoping to rescue her. It was what she would have done if their positions had been reversed.

It was when her captors decided to throw exploding devices at Robin that she knew she had to act. She grabbed the leg of one of the ruffians and bit down, hard, into the muscle of his calf. His skin was dirty and sweaty, and she almost gagged, but he pulled his leg back with a curse, leaving a chunk of his flesh and some of his blood in her mouth. Instead of throwing one of his explosive devices at Robin, he hit her, hard, in the side of her head. Everything went black.

She woke up with a throbbing headache. At first she thought she was in the same place as before—the boat. It took a couple of minutes before she realized that she was in a cart, but still under the same piece of canvas sacking. The rocking motion was similar, but every few minutes the wheels went over a stone, jerking the cart into the air.

She couldn't see anything from under the sack, but her cheek rested on a pair of hobnailed boots that kept shifting, so she knew she wasn't alone. She tried to tell what was outside the cart by smell alone, but the stench of the feet inside the boots, combined with the musty odor of whatever had been in the sack, covered up everything else. Instead, she tried listening for distinctive sounds—church bells, the cries of street sellers, the barking of dogs—but there was nothing. That probably meant they had left London behind and were somewhere out in the countryside.

After a long period of uncomfortable travel, the cart turned sharply and slowed down. They had arrived somewhere.

Instead of being allowed to get up and walk, Friday found herself picked up in strong arms while she was still wrapped in the canvas. She was flung across a man's shoulder and carried across something that crunched underfoot—small stones, perhaps. Maybe it was the front area of a large house.

She was dropped like a sack of potatoes on a hard floor, knocking the breath from her body. Footsteps walked away, and a door slammed shut. The sound echoed in a large space.

Friday pushed the sacking away and stood up.

She found herself in a circular hall. White flagstones covered the floor. Two corridors with white stone walls led away from the hall, left and right. They were tall and narrow, and from what she could see the windows lining them were all covered in bars. The glass in the windows was colored, like the stained glass in church windows. The light shining through them cast diagonal beams of red, blue, and green through the dust that hung in the air.

Sounds echoed down the polished length of each corridor: strange cries that sounded like animals calling out to one another, repeating the same noises again and again. They seemed to be just on the edge of forming words, but not quite.

A door ahead of her, directly between the two corridors, softly opened. A woman emerged. She was small, and her face was wrinkled like an apple left lying in the sun. She wore the kind of odd cloth headdress that Friday had come to associate with nuns. It covered her hair and her neck completely and then curved upward on each side of her face like the edges of some ornate roof. Her robes and headdress were white, but what started Friday's heart beating faster was that the bottom half of the woman's robes were covered in blood.

What *was* this place? What went on here?

"Welcome," the woman said. "My name is Sister Berenice."

"I am—" Friday started to say, but the woman held up a hand.

"I don't care what your name is," she interrupted. "Patients come, and patients go. Only the Sisters and the Brothers keep on. And Doctor Mors, of course."

Friday glanced again at the spots of blood on Sister Berenice's robes and felt a chill run through her.

Over Sister Berenice's shoulder Friday could see little of what was in the room—a desk, illuminated by light from another of the colored windows, with a man sitting behind it. He seemed to be wearing white robes as well, along with a white mask. Was this Doctor Mors? She didn't recognize him, but she was certain she knew the name from somewhere.

The sight was suddenly blocked by two men who came to stand behind Sister Berenice's shoulders. They wore white jackets and white trousers, but instead of blood, the cloth was covered in stains and dirt.

"These men are Brothers Jegudiel and Eremiel," she said. She put her hands together and stared down at Friday. "Now, child, the rules here are very simple: obey all instructions, ask no questions, stay in your assigned room or bed, and never try to leave. Do you understand?"

Friday paused just long enough to make it clear that she understood but she didn't necessarily agree. "I understand," she said.

"Good, then we should have no problems." Sister Berenice glanced left and right, down the corridors. "We're a bit full at the moment, due to recent events, but Doctor Mors has specifically instructed that you must have your own room. Follow me, and I'll show you where you will be staying."

"How long do you intend—" Friday started to ask, but Sister Berenice stepped forward and swept her right fist around in a sweeping arc, catching Friday on her cheek. A flash of crimson and a wave of pain went through her as the blow sent her sprawling on the floor. The woman was much, much stronger than she looked, Friday thought, through what sounded like a bell ringing inside her head. She could taste blood in her mouth from where her teeth had caught the inside of her cheek.

"I did say, quite clearly, that we *ask no questions*. Do you remember that? Each time you break a rule there will be a consequence, and the consequence will become more severe each time." She paused, and her eyes gleamed. "Do you understand *now?*"

Friday climbed to her feet and glared at Sister Berenice. She nodded slightly.

"Good." Sister Berenice indicated the two men behind her with a slight twitch of her head. "Our Brothers here will enforce the rules when I am not around. Now, follow me and don't dawdle."

She swept off down the left-hand corridor, the hem of her robes dragging against the floor.

Friday followed, with her two angels bringing up the rear.

The light from the stained glass windows cast glowing pools of color onto the tiled floor. Sister Berenice's heels clicked on the hard surface as she walked, like the sound of a clock running far too fast.

The wide stone corridor was lined with thick wooden doors, and the animal-like noises seemed to be coming from behind them. They had passed three of the doors when one opened just ahead of them. Another woman in white robes, splattered with blood, and a white headdress emerged and nodded to Sister Berenice. Curious, Friday turned her head to look into the room as they passed by.

And gazed into hell.

The room was long and lined with beds. There were people in the beds: men, women, and children, all mixed up. Some of them were lying still, as if they were asleep—or dead—but others were struggling to get up. The problem was that tight leather straps across their chests and their legs were holding them down.

The animal-like sounds that Friday had heard were louder now. They were coming from the strapped-down people—cries of pain, cries of anguish, and low moans of despair, all mixed together into an aural miasma that made Friday's skin crawl.

There was blood on the patients, blood on the walls, and blood on the floor.

A smell drifted out behind the gruesome sights and sounds. It was a smell Friday was familiar with from her time on her father's ship. It was the smell of wounds that had been left to fester, of blood that had spilled and not been cleaned up, and of human waste.

Before the Sister closed the door again, Friday saw that the closest bed was occupied by a man. His arm was missing from the elbow down. The stump had been bound with cloth soaked through with his blood—some old and dried, but some vividly fresh. He was writhing about in agony. Another Sister was standing beside his bed. She had a bottle in her hand, and she was trying to pour the contents into his mouth. The trouble was that he kept turning his head and coughing, sending the liquid spraying everywhere. Friday could smell it, above the stink of infection and old blood. It was brandy. Cheap brandy. The thought triggered a sudden memory of cleaning the planks with brandy to get rid of the disease that infested every ship. She shook her head to dislodge it.

"There was a fight," Sister Berenice said as the door slammed shut. "Swords were used, and knives, and razors. There were many injuries. The ones who survived are here, being looked after, but there will be more deaths before the day is out, I fear."

Friday opened her mouth to ask if the fight had taken place on a bridge, but she closed it again. She knew what the answer would be: another blow to the head. She also knew that the answer was obvious—these *were* casualties from the battle between the Increment and the Circle of Thirteen, and these weren't John Caiaphas's men. No, these were the Circle's casualties.

"Come," Sister Berenice said. "I have other things to do."

They passed several other large doors, and Friday felt sure that behind each of them was a similar room of injured and dying patients. The ones in the greatest pain would be given brandy or gin to keep them quiet and to dull the pain, but there wasn't enough strong drink in the world to stop *all* of them from feeling the pain of their wounds.

Sister Berenice led Friday past door after door, to the end of the corridor. The two Brothers followed: lurking, silent presences. Behind most of the doors Friday could hear the sound of people moaning, screaming, shouting, and crying. Behind some of the doors there was only silence, and strangely that disturbed Friday more than the sounds of people in pain. In her mind she pictured rows of beds containing people so weak or in so much agony that they couldn't make a sound, and people who had died of their injuries or illnesses but who hadn't been taken away yet.

One of the doors was open as they came alongside it. Friday tried not to look, but she couldn't help herself. She had expected more patients with cuts or missing limbs, but this ward was different. Many of the beds were unoccupied, and the patients inside lay motionless in bed, staring at the ceiling. All Friday could hear was a wet rattling noise as they tried to breathe through the congestion in their lungs. One of them—the patient closest to the door—coughed. It was a horrible wet noise, as though bits of him were coming loose inside his chest. He turned his head and stared at Friday. Vivid red spots covered his face. There was despair in his eyes, and the knowledge that he was probably never leaving that bed—not alive, at any rate.

Sister Berenice stopped and cleared her throat. Another Sister, who had been hidden by the open door, tending to another patient, appeared in the doorway. Nodding her head in apology, she closed the door, cutting off the view.

Friday found herself missing Robin very much, and the knowledge that she didn't even know if he'd made it off the river in one piece pierced her like a knife. What, she thought, if he was in one of these beds, or the beds of another hospital? What then?

She didn't think she could bear it.

Sister Berenice started walking again. She didn't check that Friday and the two Brothers were following—she knew they would be, otherwise there would be consequences, and she had already demonstrated what form those consequences would take.

At the corridor's end was an open door leading onto a spiral stone stairway. Sister Berenice led the way up.

The stairs continued up to higher levels, but Sister Berenice left them at the next floor. She headed down a corridor directly above the one they had already traversed. The doors here were closer to-gether, suggesting that the rooms were smaller. She stopped at an open doorway and motioned for Friday to enter.

Friday didn't know what to expect, but the room was empty apart from an iron bed that was bolted to the floor. Halfway to the window, a doorless opening separated the room into two. The floor was tiled—easy to wipe clean, Friday thought unhappily.

"Through there are a table and chair," Sister Berenice said, nod-ding toward the opening, "and a bucket for you to use when you need it. This is where you will stay until Doctor Mors wishes to see you. Do I have to chain you to the bed, or will you be a good girl?"

"You don't have to chain me to the bed," Friday said carefully. She was desperate to ask what she was doing there, what the Circle wanted with her, whether her father knew she was there or not, but she knew what would happen if she did ask. Sister Berenice had made that very clear.

"Good." The woman smiled. "You will be fed . . . well, when-ever we decide that you will be fed. Try to get some sleep—you will need it." She turned away and gestured to one of the Brothers. He stepped forward and hauled the door shut. The noise it made echoed along the corridor outside. Friday heard the sound of a bolt being slid, and then she listened to three sets of footsteps as they retreated until there was silence.

Three sets of footsteps. That meant no one had been left on guard. She was alone in the room. The *locked* room, she reminded herself.

Friday closed her eyes and thought for a moment, working out her best course of action. She knew that the best times to escape from imprisonment were either just after you'd been imprisoned, when your captors were relaxing slightly and congratulating them-selves, or a long time afterward, when your captors assumed you'd given up all hope. Friday had no intention of waiting that long, so she had to make an attempt right now. The big question on her mind was—did she really *want* to escape? Well, obviously she did, but if she got completely away, then all she would know was where she had been taken. If she took the opportunity to look around this place instead, then she might be able to get some information that she could pass on to Segment W when she *did* finally escape.

Added, of course, to the fact that she was sure Robin would be looking for her—if he was all right. If she got away now, then she would have to find her way to safety by herself, but if she waited, then the forces of Segment W might eventually arrive to help.

She glanced around the room, but quickly realized that escaping to the outside was not an option. The window was too securely barred and the walls too thick to get through, even if she could find something to scrape the mortar from between the bricks. The door was her only option, so she concentrated her attention on that.

The door opened inward, which meant that the hinges were on her side, and there was a gap of about an inch between the top of the door and the frame. She smiled. That gave her a chance.

She reached up under her collar and removed the nail that she had hidden there while she was in the boat. She moved closer to the door and examined the hinges, feeling the sharpness of the nail against her palm. The flat parts were hidden between the door and the door frame, of course, but the central tube that held the two sides together was exposed. It looked like the tube was in two halves, with one half attached to the top part of the hinge and the other half attached to the bottom. The two halves were secured by a metal shaft running down the center of the tubes. If these hinges were like others she had seen, then the shaft would be fixed to the top half of the tube but it just slid into the bottom half, quite snugly. All she had to do was to push that shaft out and the hinge would come apart. Hopefully.

There was nothing in the room that she could use as a hammer, so she slipped her right boot off. The heel was solid—she could use that.

She placed the point of the nail beneath the top hinge with its point resting against the metal shaft. She let the hand holding her shoe drop to her side, then abruptly swung it up. The heel hit against the underside of the nail with a *clink* that she hoped couldn't be heard too far away. There was no obvious movement, but she hoped that at least she'd loosened it.

It was tempting to keep hitting that hinge, but she had to get the entire door to move up. She knelt and placed the point of the nail against the shaft inside the lower hinge. She didn't have as much room to swing the boot down near the floor, but she managed to bring it around in an arc. Again, the heel hit the nail with a loud *clink*.

Top and bottom. Top and bottom. She kept alternating, trying to force the shafts out of the embrace of the tubes they were held in.

It took ten minutes before there was any movement, but eventually Friday noticed a growing gap where the top half of each hinge was being pushed away from the bottom half. Nobody came to check what the noise was. Fortunately, there was enough of a space above the door for it to move up, and the metal shafts were held securely enough by the bottom parts of the hinges that the weight of the door didn't cause it to slide back down every time she managed to knock it up a fraction.

She halted for a while to catch her breath and let the burning in her muscles subside, then started again.

Another ten minutes of hammering and the hinges were perhaps an inch apart. There couldn't be much more of the shaft left inside the bottom part of each hinge.

She looked up at the top of the door, worried. There wasn't a lot of space left there. She had shifted the door up so much, bit by bit, that there was hardly any room left for it to move. If the shafts didn't come loose soon, then she'd be out of options.

Two more taps, bottom and top, and the bottom hinge suddenly came apart. The lower part of the door shifted abruptly toward her. There was enough space beneath it now that she could get her fingers in, scraping against the tiled floor, and heave upward.

The top hinge resisted for a moment, and then the door jerked upward to hit against the top of the door frame. Friday was suddenly taking the entire weight of the door on her fingers—which were in danger of being squashed against the tiles. Quickly, she pulled the door inward, using the bolt as a makeshift hinge. Once the door was open wide enough for her to get through, she pulled her fingers out and let it rest on the floor.

She felt breathless and slightly nauseous, but she couldn't afford to rest. She had to get out of the room—the cell—and look around.

She peered around the edge of the door. The corridor was empty and silent. She slipped out of her cell and pulled the door closed behind her. To the casual observer it would look as if it was still closed and locked. All she had to do when she got back was to heave the door up from the inside and slide the shafts back into their tubes again.

She smiled to herself. How easily that phrase—"*all* she had to do"—came to mind. None of this was easy.

Keeping to the side of the corridor, she started her reconnaissance, remembering her father's advice that information was more valuable than jewels or gold.

She suddenly cursed under her breath. Thinking about her father, and his advice, had recalled a memory. She knew where she had heard the name of Doctor Mors before!

One Year and Six Months Before the Escape

Suriya and Diran were gazing over the stern of the Dark Nebula *toward the strange island that lay behind them.*

The Dark Nebula had dropped anchor at night, when all that could be seen of their destination was a series of flickering lights stretching out into the darkness until they faded into nothingness. It was only when the sun came up that the island could be seen—if it was an island. It looked like a vast collection of ships tied together with cables and linked with wooden walkways to form something like a wooden city moored in the ocean. Some of the ships looked like things she had seen plying the high seas, but others—especially those farther away from the edge—were older, like things she had seen drawings of in books. She could see people moving around on the ships, crossing from one to the next. Several of the ships seemed to house markets filled with stalls covered with cloth, once brightly colored but now faded by the strength of the sun. Others appeared to be floating taverns, or places where tents and shacks had been set up for occupation. Right in the middle was a tall structure, built across several ships and rising three or four stories in the air. It looked like a cathedral, but one that was made of dark and twisted wood.

"Have you ever seen this place before?" Diran asked.

Suriya shook her head. "Never. I would have remembered."

"It's called 'Lemuria,'" he continued. "I saw a map on your father's desk when I was delivering his dinner. He covered it over when I came in, but I could see the name."

"Lemuria?" Suriya thought for a moment. "I've heard the word before, but never said by anyone who had been there. It was more *like a legend. Lemuria." She turned the word over in her mouth. "Who would have thought?"*

"Do you think it's some kind of, I don't know, special place where pirates go that nobody else knows about? Somewhere that isn't known, and so can't be attacked?"

"I suppose," she said, but her attention was distracted by a boat as it emerged from a dark channel in the floating island and pulled toward them, rowed by ten men who were naked to the waist and heavily muscled. It was narrow, with a stern that rose up high and curled to form a cover over the passengers. There were three of them. Two were dark-skinned, dressed in black robes and black turbans, with black cloth pulled across the lower parts of their faces. The third man was extremely old, with a white beard and sparse white hair beneath a black skullcap. He too was wearing black robes.

The boat was obviously heading for the Dark Nebula, and a reception party of pirates had already formed. The pirates had even made some attempt to clean themselves up, although Suriya knew there wasn't much they could do in that regard.

"Is my father expecting visitors?"

Diran nodded. "Yes. He asked me to set his table with wine and fruit. He didn't say who they were, though. Usually, he'd want me to stay to serve them, but he just told me to get out, and then he hit me when I wasn't fast enough leaving."

The boat had vanished around the stern of the Dark Nebula now, and Suriya watched as the reception party threw a rope ladder over the side. A few moments later the three dark-robed men climbed on board. They gave the impression of men who didn't usually climb anywhere. They weren't happy.

Suriya gestured to Diran to come with her to the front of the poop deck, where they crouched behind a barrel and looked down at the quarterdeck immediately below, and the main deck beyond and below that.

"What are we doing?" Diran asked nervously.

"Collecting information," Suriya murmured. "It's more valuable than jewels or gold, according to my father."

Red Tiberius walked across the quarterdeck. He had obviously just emerged from his cabin, immediately below where Suriya and Diran were crouching.

He strode over to the rail and watched as the visitors were escorted to the wooden stairway that led up from the main deck. Suriya had seen him greet other visitors before, but this time was different. Usually, he stayed in his cabin if he was more important than them, letting them come to him, or he went down to the main deck and welcomed them on board personally in the rare event that they were more important than him. Now he seemed to be hovering somewhere in between, uncertain of his status. Or perhaps of theirs.

There was no bowing, or florid greetings. Instead, Red Tiberius made a curious gesture with his hands, which the three visitors returned. He led them into his cabin.

Suriya glanced at Diran, then down at the quarterdeck. She thought furiously for a moment. She knew that the windows in her father's cabin would be open to cool it down. There was a chance that she could hear what was being said, if she moved closer.

She scuttled across the poop deck, keeping her head down so that none of the crew down below could see her. After a few seconds Diran moved across to join her.

"We shouldn't do this!" he protested, terrified.

"It's a small ship," she said, shushing him with a gesture. "If they didn't want to be overheard, then they should have met on the island."

She lay down on the deck and twisted so that her head and shoulders were between two of the rails. Below her she could see the open window of her father's cabin, and below that the waves lapping against the ship's rudder and stern.

"Greetings," her father said. "Welcome to my ship."

"You are late," one of the visitors said. No greetings, no small talk.

Her father didn't respond to the criticism. Instead, he said: "Why was I summoned here?"

Summoned? Her father had been summoned? She was stunned. Who could possibly do that?

"Your last shipment was half the size of the one before," the same voice answered, "and that shipment was half the size of the one before that. Doctor Mors is concerned, and has communicated his concerns to us. You must procure more, and quickly."

Her father's voice was uncharacteristically edgy when he finally replied. "The thing that you want only grows under special circumstances, and in remote places," he said. "It is difficult to find. The demands you are making on it mean that supplies are running low. Perhaps if Doctor Mors used less of it . . ."

He trailed off, and it was a voice with an English accent that spoke next—perhaps the old man? "We need more and more," he said gently. "If we are to expand, if our powers are to grow, then we cannot use less."

"You must find another source for us," the first man said. His voice was harsh in comparison. "And quickly. There must be other islands with the right conditions!"

A sudden noise below made Suriya turn her head to look. A hand—her father's hand; she recognized the rings—had emerged from the window and was pulling it closed.

She sighed, and slid back on the deck. Diran was staring at her. "What was that all about?"

"I have no idea," she said. "But I think we're going to be exploring for a while. Whether my father tells the crew that or not is another question."

CRUSOE WAS BATTERED, bloodied, and exhausted by the time he arrived back at the Globe. His muscles ached and he felt as if he hadn't slept for a week, but it was the thought of Friday in the hands of the Circle of Thirteen that made his heart hang heavy. He had to find a way to get her back, and quickly. He kept thinking about what might be happening to her, and then tried desperately not to.

The Increment guards at the entrance waved him through. They looked almost as bad as he felt. Some of them had cuts and bruises on their faces or hands; others were wearing make-shift bandages. The attack on the bridge had obviously caused casualties.

Sir William, Defoe, and John Caiaphas were all in Sir William's office, overlooking the central area of the Globe. John Caiaphas had also been injured: a dirty white cloth had been bound around his head, and judging by the blood soaking through it, the top of his ear had been sliced off. That, Crusoe thought, was the thing he admired about Caiaphas—he didn't just stay on the sidelines, issuing orders. He actually led his men from the front.

Sir William's expression was thunderous. He watched as Crusoe entered. He didn't wave at a seat, but then again he didn't tell Crusoe to get out. Assuming that he was tolerated, if not actually appreciated, Crusoe slid into a seat.

Defoe smiled at him in greeting. That was something, at least.

"John was just reporting on the raid," Defoe said. "I'm sure you can add to the facts we have, but I suggest that we wait until he has finished."

As Crusoe nodded, Caiaphas cleared his throat and continued. "In total, four of my men are dead or missing, compared with fif-teen of the Circle's people. Eight more of my men have injuries, which means they are unsuitable for duties now, and possibly for some time to come."

"Make sure that the families of the dead men are compensated, and that the injured men are given the best medical treatment possible," Sir William instructed.

"I think it is fair to say," Defoe interjected, "that the level of resistance we encountered was higher than expected."

Caiaphas nodded reluctantly. "We had assumed—erroneously—that this was just an outpost, perhaps one house or one shop that was being used as a place where messages could be left and instructions picked up. Instead, we appear to have found a major base of operations for the Circle of Thirteen. When we blockaded the ends of the bridge and moved to search the buildings it was as if we had thrust a stick into a nest of wasps. There were swords, knives, and fists facing us every inch of the way." He grimaced. "My estimate is that at least two-thirds of the people on the bridge were working for the Circle in some way."

"At least they didn't have any of those strange weapons that were used against us down on the Isle of Thanet," Defoe murmured to Sir William. "The ones that fired those razor-edged discs."

"To think," Sir William muttered, shaking his head, "that such a place could exist so close to the king, and the royal palace."

"And to us!" Defoe added. He glanced back at Caiaphas and continued: "How many enemy combatants have been taken into custody?"

"Sixty-two, including the Countess of Lichfield, who we recaptured while she was trying to sneak away." Caiaphas shrugged. "Although I suspect that some of them will have to be released after they have been questioned, and after inquiries have been made. I think that some people were fighting just because they could, rather than because they had to."

"Sailors . . . ," Defoe murmured, and flashed a conspiratorial smile at Crusoe.

Caiaphas also glanced at Crusoe. His expression was apologetic. "We didn't find your girlfriend," he said. "I'm sorry, son: I don't know where she is. She led us to the bridge, but then she vanished."

Crusoe opened his mouth, ready to tell them about what he and Friday had discovered and what had happened to Friday, but the sudden mention of the word *girlfriend* made him hesitate, surprised, and Sir William spoke first.

"What of the Circle's leaders?" Sir William questioned. "Did you take anyone who appeared to be in charge? Anyone who might know more about the Circle than its guards and its soldiers?"

Caiaphas shook his head. "It is possible that the leaders might be hiding among the rabble that we have locked up, but my feeling is that they weren't there to begin with—"

Crusoe found himself interrupting before he could stop himself. "The Leaders of the Circle *were* there! Including Red Tiberius! They escaped through a tunnel beneath the bridge."

"A tunnel?" Caiaphas frowned. "We found no tunnel."

"Friday found it from the bridge and I found it from outside. We met inside it and saw a group of people in robes and hoods leaving in a hurry. They looked like they were in charge."

All three men straightened up and stared at Crusoe.

"You were *on* the bridge?" Sir William exclaimed. "Against my direct orders?"

"I was *inside* it," Crusoe confirmed. "Later on I was in one of the buildings, in a room that looked like a meeting room. There were papers and books scattered around. One thing, like a map, looked particularly important."

"You will show us where that room, and that tunnel, are." Anger and curiosity were fighting for control of Sir William's expression.

"Indeed." Defoe seemed to notice the cuts and bruises scattered across Crusoe's face and hands. "I think our young friend here has a story of his own to tell us."

Caiaphas frowned. "I had reports of two boats that were traveling up the Thames, treating the ice as though it was simple water. There were reports of explosions as well, and significant confusion and damage to property. Was that something to do with you?"

Crusoe nodded. "They took Friday. I gave chase, but I lost them." He gazed directly at Sir William. "We need to get Friday back," he said firmly.

Sir William leaned back in his chair. He said nothing for a while. His gaze was fixed on Crusoe, and the expression on his face suggested that he was thinking things through, perhaps balancing Crusoe's failure to follow orders against the new information Crusoe had provided. "If we can, we will," he said eventually, "but our priority now is, as it has always been, to protect the Crown from external threats. We have suffered losses, and the resources we have left will need to be dedicated to questioning our prisoners and evaluating what we have found on the bridge. You will go with John and Daniel, and show them this meeting room and these tunnels." As Crusoe opened his mouth to protest, Sir William raised a hand to stop him. "It is possible that there may be information in this meeting room that tells us where the Circle's leaders have taken young Miss Friday. If so, we will follow it up, but we cannot fritter our resources away in a fruitless attempt to trace one boat going up the Thames."

"Surely we could just follow the grooves cut into the ice by the blades that the boat was traveling on! That would lead us to another Circle base!"

It was John Caiaphas who pointed out the flaw in Crusoe's thinking. "Any grooves cut into the ice by their boat will be easily confused with the grooves cut by the blades of skaters on the ice. Also, they will abandon the boat at some stage, and take to carriages. We will never find them that way."

"You realize," Crusoe said quietly, "that Friday's father might actually be one of the Circle's leaders."

"I do," Sir William said.

"And he may have her captive now."

Sir William nodded slightly. "That, too."

"And those facts don't alter your decision?"

"They do not."

And that, Crusoe could see from Sir William's face, was it.

A dark thought had wormed its way into Crusoe's mind. He let it sit there, twisting, for a few moments, wondering whether to say anything. Eventually, he decided that he had no choice.

"What about the scrying orb?" he asked.

There was silence around the table. Eventually, Sir William broke it.

"The scrying orb is not for . . . such uses," he said firmly. "We have barely started scratching the surface of what it can do. Certainly Dr. Dee, who was allegedly given the orb by his Angelic friends, believed that it provided a connection between this world and others—"

"Exactly," Crusoe interrupted eagerly. "Dr. Dee believed that the orbs can be used to tell the future, and the Circle of Thirteen believes the same. If we have such an orb—and we do—then why do we not use it to determine matters of significance—such as, where Friday has been taken?"

"For the same reason," Sir William continued smoothly, but with a frown that indicated he was not used to being interrupted, "that a man does not use a lion as a guard dog. Not only is it a vastly disproportionate use of a powerful thing, but it is *dangerous*."

"I think we need to—" Crusoe started to say, but he was stopped by Sir William's hand slapping down on the table.

"Enough debate," Sir William announced. "The orb stays where it is—in a locked cabinet in my office. There will be no more discussion on this matter."

CHAPTER SEVEN

I saac Newton's rooms at Imperial College were as cluttered, as odorous, and as fascinating as Crusoe remembered. Stuffed animals hung from chains on the ceiling, colored chemicals bubbled in glass retorts above burning candles, and piles of faded manuscripts and cracked leather books were piled haphazardly in every corner.

While Defoe and Crusoe looked for Newton among the confusion, John Caiaphas directed his men to clear a space on one of the tables and fill it with the material they had removed from the Council of Thirteen meeting room on the bridge.

"Isaac?" Defoe called. "It's Daniel—Daniel Defoe and Robinson Crusoe!"

Newton's head rose up from behind a tangle of glass tubes and flasks. "Daniel—I wasn't expecting you. Was I expecting you?" He frowned. "Perhaps I *was* expecting you. What day is it?"

"We've brought the material from—" Defoe glanced around before continuing. Presumably, he was worried that someone else might be in the room, but it was almost impossible to tell.

"We're alone," Newton said, guessing what Defoe was worried about. Crusoe looked around and wondered how exactly he could be sure.

"—from the raid on the Circle of Thirteen base," Defoe finished in a quieter voice. "You heard about that?"

Newton nodded. "London is buzzing with the news that one of the bridges was blockaded and fights broke out. It's all the servants here are talking about. Nobody seems to know if it was the army, a group of armed wardens and watchmen, or someone else who was responsible." He smiled, and the expression transformed his face. "Some people are even saying it's the Dutch again, making another raid up the river and penetrating right into the heart of London this time, but I discounted that explanation. I assumed that this was the work of Segment W."

"Indeed it was," Defoe said. He gestured to where Caiaphas's men had just finished stacking the papers. "We . . . confiscated, I suppose . . . a lot of written material. It's all over there."

"My dear Defoe," Newton said, "flattered as I am, I'm afraid I have other work to attend to. I cannot just put everything down and read some papers because neither you nor Sir William can be bothered. It is a waste of my time and my brain."

"I've glanced briefly through them," Defoe continued as if Newton hadn't spoken, "but the Circle seems to have put all of their writings in code. I can't read any of it. Frankly, Isaac, you're our only hope."

"There's one in particular," Crusoe said encouragingly, "that looks like it's a map of somewhere, or maybe the routes between different places, but if it is, then the place-names are not obvious."

Newton shook his head. "I'm sorry, but I have more important investigations to which I must attend."

Defoe glanced at Crusoe and winked. "Ah, well," he said. "Perhaps someone else from the Royal Society, then. . . ."

"No need to consult anyone else," Newton snapped, moving out from behind the bench. "I'm perfectly capable of working out what it means."

Caiaphas nodded to Defoe, then turned to his men. With quick, wordless gestures he directed them to stand guard outside. He followed them out.

As Newton moved toward Crusoe and Defoe, he passed a scarecrow held up by ropes. Crusoe stared at it, bemused. What was Isaac Newton doing with a scarecrow?

Newton stopped when he saw where Crusoe was looking. He smiled and pointed to a crossbow set up on a nearby table, clamped to a stand so that it could fire across the room at the scarecrow without shifting position. Beside it were several bows, bowstrings, and stocks of various designs and constructed out of various materials. Some of the stocks had complicated devices built into them: levers, cogs, and ratchets, and other things that Crusoe didn't recognize. The whole tabletop was scattered with parchment on which various diagrams had been sketched. It looked as if Newton was trying to improve upon the basic crossbow design. Either that or he was trying to create something that was half crossbow and half clock, but that would have been foolish.

"What are you working on?" Defoe asked, noting where Crusoe had been looking.

"Do you recall those strange weapons that the Circle of Thirteen used in the fort on the Isle of Thanet? The ones that fired sharpened discs of metal?" When Defoe nodded, Newton continued: "They gave the Circle a considerable tactical advantage over the Increment, and I have been trying to come up with something similar that would redress the balance."

"But this is just a crossbow," Crusoe pointed out, looking at the device strapped to the table.

Newton nodded. "Indeed. The weapons that the Circle was using had the obvious advantage that they can be reloaded and recocked with just a pull on a sprung lever, but the *dis*advantage is that their penetration is relatively low. Like arrows from a longbow, they go through skin and cloth with ease, but not armor. A crossbow, by contrast, has enough power to send its bolt through armor, but it cannot be reloaded easily—the string has to be drawn back by a winding mechanism of some kind, and that takes both time and energy. Pistols and rifles have the twin disadvantages that they take too long to reload and they are prone to explode for no reason." He pointed to another table, where Crusoe noticed that a long-barreled flintlock pistol sat on a stand. Its stock seemed to have been modified with various levers. "I have been looking at modifying a pistol to speed up the process, but it is still in the ex-perimental phase." Turning back to the modified crossbow, he went on: "I have been investigating how to modify a crossbow to fire many bolts in quick succession. That way we would have the pene-tration *and* the ability to fire many bolts within a few seconds." He shook his head. "I was hoping to use some of the energy of the de-parting bolt to somehow push the string partially back, but I have hit a dead end there—it requires so much energy that the bolt itself becomes almost powerless. I am beginning to think that the only solution is to have a series of metal bows one above the other in some kind of rack, with multiple triggers. The trick will be to make such a weapon still portable." He frowned. "I might just have to go back to the Circle's weapons and try to improve the penetration of the discs by making them out of a different material, or increasing the power of the firing mechanism. Or . . . hmm, perhaps the at-tractive power of a lodestone might be employed in a crossbow design. . . ." He reached for a piece of parchment and a quill, and was about to start sketching something when Defoe interrupted.

"I'm sure your intellect is up to the task, Isaac, but we need you to take a look at these documents that were taken from the Circle's base."

"Are they here?" Newton asked, as he was only just catching up with the previous conversation. "Can I see them?"

Defoe pointed to the table where the papers were piled up. "Have at it, sir," he said.

As Newton began to sift through the pile, Defoe gently drew his attention back to the item on top—the strange map made up of lines joining dots in patterns like constellations, with scrawled words beside the points where the lines met. "Sir William believes that this diagram in particular may be the key to understanding the Circle's intentions. He asked that you conduct your analysis on this first."

"No," Crusoe said before he could stop himself. "We need to find out where the Circle's other bases are. We need to find where they have taken Friday." He looked at Newton and gestured to the pile on the table. "You need to look through everything first, to see if there is a list of places they consider safe."

"I'm sorry, Robin," Defoe said firmly, "but Sir William's instructions were very clear. Yes, it is a tragedy that Miss Friday has been taken by the Circle, but there are bigger issues at stake here. We need to know what the Circle's next move might be. Only then can we worry about your friend."

Crusoe wanted to argue, but he could tell from the look on Defoe's face that there was no point. Defoe might privately agree with him that Friday had to be rescued first, and the motives of the Circle worried about later, but he had been given his orders and he wasn't going to go against them—not even for Friday.

If Crusoe was going to do anything to help his friend, then he was going to have to do it alone.

Newton was looking from Defoe to Crusoe and back again, aware that something was wrong but unsure what it was. "Young Miss Friday—you say she has been taken by the Circle? That's terrible! She was a brave child."

"She sacrificed herself to save me," Crusoe said, feeling the same dead weight in his heart that he had felt when he heard Friday convincing the Circle's ruffians that he had already gone out of the window. "And she *is* brave. We haven't lost her yet."

Newton nodded sympathetically. "If I find anything that might indicate where she has been taken, then I will tell you straight away, I promise." He turned toward the pile of papers, then turned back. "If it is any consolation," he said, "then they will almost certainly keep her alive rather than kill her out of hand. They'll want to get her to talk about Segment W's plans, manpower, and strengths."

"She won't tell them anything," Crusoe said angrily.

"Not straight away," Newton pointed out in the same gentle tone. "They'll obviously have to torture her to get the information out of her, and that will take a while."

"Isaac—" Defoe said warningly.

"What?" Newton suddenly realized what he had said. "Oh, yes. Well, perhaps it won't come to that." Guiltily, he turned back to the papers and started examining the map of lines on top.

Defoe gazed at Crusoe. "She *is* brave, and she's intelligent. If anyone can find a way to escape from the Circle, then it is she. Try to suppress your concerns and give her the credit she deserves."

Crusoe shook his head. "You don't understand," he said quietly. "We've been together for so long that being apart is . . . difficult. I feel as if a part of myself is missing."

"Wherever she is," Defoe said, equally quietly, "she will be fighting to get back to you."

"I hope so, Crusoe murmured, "I truly hope so." He paused. "Isaac . . . ," he started to say.

Defoe cast him a warning glance.

Newton glanced over at Crusoe. His face was calm, but there was a wary expression in his eyes. "I know what you are going to ask," he said. "The orb."

Crusoe nodded. He felt bad about asking Newton this, but he didn't feel he had any choice. "It may be the only way to find out where the Circle has taken Friday," he said. He could hear the plea in his voice, and he didn't like it, but he went on: "She might die at their hands before we can find her otherwise."

Newton glanced down at the floor and sighed, then looked up again. "There are . . . things . . . in the scrying orb," he said quietly. "I have seen them watching me, when I have been gazing into it. Just from the corner of my eye, you understand. They move, and when I try to focus on them, they are gone. Disappeared." He paused momentarily. "They burn," he said. "I don't know how I know that, but I do."

"I thought Dr. Dee was given the scrying orb by the angels," Crusoe said. "Surely such a thing cannot be . . . evil?"

"Satan was an angel once," Newton pointed out, "and his demons are merely his attempt to make his own angels." He sighed again. "If it is the only way . . . ," he said, trailing off. Crusoe could see fear in his eyes, and it was an unsettling thing. He had always thought that Newton was somehow above fear.

"No," Defoe said loudly. "I forbid it. More importantly, Sir William forbids it. The scrying orb is locked away for a very good reason. It is dangerous, and Isaac here is an important member of Sector W." He glanced at Newton, and there was a strange expression in his eyes. "As well as being a personal friend," he added. "We will not place Isaac at risk in this way on the basis of something that almost certainly will not work."

Newton nodded. He seemed relieved, but also guilty. "I'm sorry," he said to Crusoe, holding his hands up.

Crusoe nodded reluctantly. It was clear that he would have to find another way. The only problem was—he wasn't sure what. . . .

* * *

THE CORRIDOR STRETCHED ahead of Friday, filled with shadows and echoes. She moved silently along, keeping against the wall and slipping in and out of the alcoves next to the doors in case anybody suddenly appeared.

Most of the doors she passed were closed, but one or two had been left open. She checked each open room, but this floor of the hospital seemed to be largely deserted. Some of the rooms held furniture—crude metal beds, rough wooden chairs. Perhaps, she thought, this was where the Sisters and the Brothers slept—a bit like the bunks that she and Robin had used back at Segment W's former base. They had put her into a dormitory area.

Maybe the rooms with the doors shut were being used. Maybe there were people sleeping in them right now. She had better be as quiet as she could.

It occurred to her that she hadn't looked out of a window yet. Perhaps there was some clue outside that would tell her where she was. She didn't want to go into any of the rooms along the corridor, even if they seemed empty, but when she got to the end of the corridor, directly above the entrance hall, she noticed a window looking out over the main doors. She crossed quickly over to it and gazed out.

The view outside was of a green lawn extending away to a line of trees in the distance. There were no other buildings, nothing to break the monotony. The hospital appeared completely isolated.

Friday turned around and gazed across the circular space. A door across the other side probably gave access to a larger room, like the one she had seen briefly into downstairs—the one with the white-gowned man who, she assumed, was Doctor Mors—the same Doctor Mors she had heard her father discussing back on his ship. She crossed the space to see if the door was unlocked.

It was, and after checking for sounds from within, she slipped inside.

She was in a library. Bookcases lined the walls and also stood in the center of the room. Many of the volumes she could see looked like collections of paper that had been roughly bound together between leather covers. A table near the room's main window had open volumes on it. She crossed the room to take a look—and found herself recoiling in surprise. What she saw were detailed diagrams of human bodies that had been opened up to show the muscles, the organs, and the blood vessels inside. They were medical textbooks.

Friday scanned the shelves quickly and checked a few of the books on them, but they were the same thing—medical textbooks in German or Latin, with diagrams. If the Circle of Thirteen had any secrets in this room, then they weren't obvious. Maybe this place was just what it appeared to be—a hospital.

A hospital run by a woman who was happy to hit patients hard across the face.

A second table near the window held a series of glass vials in a wooden case. Friday moved closer. The vials were in rows, and each row was a different color—green, red, brown . . . One vial had been removed from the case and stood alone on the table. Its contents were yellow. Friday picked it up and shook it. The contents moved like oil. Odd, she thought. This had to be important, but she wasn't sure how.

Friday heard voices. She was about to dive beneath the table when she realized that they were coming from outside the window. One of the panes was cracked, with some glass missing, and that was where the sound came from.

She sidled up to the window and peeked out. The back of the house gave out onto a formal garden, with an iced-over pond directly beneath the window, geometrically planted lines of bushes farther away, and a glass greenhouse with a high, pointed roof in the distance. Below her she could see the edge of a flagstone terrace.

"It has been agreed," a soft male voice said. The voice sounded strangely muffled, as if there was something covering the man's mouth. "She must be killed. Red Tiberius has given the order."

Friday felt a shiver of fear. She? Were they talking about her? Would her father have so casually ordered her death?

"Is it certain that she has betrayed us?" That was Sister Berenice.

Friday felt herself relax slightly. There was no way that her actions could have possibly been described as a "betrayal." They must be talking about someone else.

"The attack on the bridge occurred just after she arrived. Either she led Segment W there deliberately or she did so accidentally. That means she is either a traitor or a fool, and there is no room in the Circle for either."

They were talking about the Countess of Lichfield, then. Friday smiled grimly. She had never liked the countess, and she wouldn't lose any sleep if the trust between her and the Circle of Thirteen had been broken.

A pause, then Sister Berenice said in a worried tone: "Is it possible that she might betray our location here? Do we have to prepare for an attack?"

"Don't concern yourself. The countess was never trusted with the location of this place."

"I take it," Sister Berenice said, "that she will be . . . dealt with?"

"The cost of betrayal or stupidity is the same. Death will catch up with her soon." The man's voice became more businesslike. "And what of the girl?"

"She is secured upstairs."

"Does she know what we are planning to do with her? What her father has agreed?"

A snort of derision from Sister Berenice. "She has no idea."

"Good. Send the pirate Mohir to me." The man's voice grew fainter, and Friday heard footsteps as he moved away. "I wish to see the girl. It is necessary to check her state of health before we start."

She needed to get back to her room as soon as she could, but Mors was saying something else. She leaned against the window, trying to get into a better position to hear his words.

The wooden window frame moved as she pressed on the glass, grating against the brickwork. It was loose—years of rain and frost must have weakened the mortar. She pulled her hands back quickly, but it was too late. Mors had heard.

"What was that?" she heard him say.

"It is probably your creatures," Sister Berenice replied. "They have been getting restless recently."

"They have to be starved, you know that." Mors's voice was still as gentle as ever. "Otherwise they will not do what is needed when the time comes. Now—the girl."

Friday felt a sinking sensation inside her chest as she started back toward her room. She didn't know what Mors's plan was, or what his creatures were, but she didn't like the sound of it. She hoped that wherever Robin was, he was in a better position than she was. And she hoped he was coming to help her soon.

CRUSOE RODE BACK to the Globe with John Caiaphas, Isaac Newton, and Defoe. Caiaphas's Increment personnel had been left behind to guard the material from the bridge just in case the Circle of Thirteen tried to take it back.

Inside the carriage, John Caiaphas was holding the experimental flintlock design that he had managed to persuade Isaac Newton to lend him for evaluation. Instead of being reloaded with balls from the front of the barrel and gunpowder from a hole in the top, both ball and charge were pushed into place from separate magazines using a series of springs. Caiaphas was holding it the way a man might hold a baby—carefully but lovingly.

Crusoe's mood was bleak. He had not only gone against Sir William's orders but had also allowed agents of the Circle to escape with Friday. And still he was no closer to finding her.

Except . . .

Except there was still the scrying orb.

He was struggling with his conscience, trying to decide whether to go against direct instruction or abandon any thought of using the orb to find Friday, when he noticed that Defoe was craning his head out of the carriage's window.

"What's going on?" he asked.

"It's the king's carriage," Defoe called back, his voice muffled by the fact that he was half in and half out of the carriage. "He must have left the theater and is heading back for the palace."

Crusoe frowned, trying to work out when he had left. "But he was there hours ago," he said.

"He was at *a* theater hours ago," Defoe pointed out, "but that doesn't mean anything. Sometimes he spends all day there, with the manager desperately calling in acts to keep him and his companions entertained, or sometimes he moves from theater to theater, seeking some kind of perpetual distraction. I've heard of them spending days on entertainments, with food being brought from the palace to wherever they happen to be. Sleep is the only thing that pulls the king back to the palace, and that infrequently."

Their carriage started to turn a corner, taking them away from the king's procession and toward the Globe. It meant that for a few moments Defoe lost his view and Crusoe had a clear sight of both the royal carriage—an ornate conveyance decorated in gold leaf and pulled by four pure white horses—and the king's surrounding guard of several helmeted and mounted soldiers. It also meant that he had a perfect view when the attack began.

Several people suddenly stepped forward from the crowd that lined the route and alternately cheered or heckled the king. They were holding canvas sacks, and they abruptly plunged their hands inside and started throwing things in front of the horses. Crusoe thought for a second they might be fruits, but they were hard and metallic and covered with spikes. Whichever way they fell they stuck to the icy surface of the road with several spikes still pointing upward. And there were enough of them that the horses' hooves couldn't avoid them.

"Something's happening—" Crusoe began to shout, just as the first hoof came down on one of the objects. The spikes must have gone through the hard hoof and into the soft flesh underneath. The horse suddenly reared up, neighing in panic and pain, sending its military rider falling to the icy ground. Within a few seconds half of the horses in the procession were on their rear legs, pawing at the air. The sound of the crowd was drowned out by the piteous cries of the horses.

"Damn me, it's an attack!" John Caiaphas said, pushing Crusoe out of the way so that he could look. He opened the door and leaped out, even as the carriage was completing its turn. He called out over his shoulder: "Crusoe—with me! Defoe—alert Sir William!"

The king's procession had halted in confusion now, with horses leaping around in pain and panic and riders falling backward or trying to regain control of their beasts. Two of the horses pulling the king's carriage were fighting to escape their reins, and the carriage itself leaned over on two wheels, looking almost ready to fall sideways.

Crusoe followed Caiaphas out of their carriage and ran toward the scene of chaos ahead. Caiaphas, he noticed, was still holding the experimental flintlock that Newton had given him. Crusoe was trying to pull his sword from his scabbard while he sprinted, which was proving difficult.

They were halfway across the intervening ground when something emerged from a narrow alleyway opposite the king's carriage. It took Crusoe a moment to work out that it was a narrow, streamlined hull, like a long, thin boat turned upside down and given wheels, with a sharpened metal spike jutting forward menacingly from the bow. Its sides were covered with riveted metal plates. It was like some bizarre mechanical mixture of shark and eagle, and as it emerged fully from the alley Crusoe saw that the back end was on fire.

No—the fire was *inside* the hollow hull. Somehow it worked like a huge firework—flame and smoke pushing the terrifying thing forward at an increasing speed.

Directly toward the king's teetering carriage.

Two of the men who had thrown the spikes saw Caiaphas and Crusoe approaching. It wasn't hard to spot them—everyone else was fleeing in panic. They dropped their empty canvas sacks and drew swords, moving to intercept.

"Damn," Caiaphas snapped. He stopped running, turned, and threw his flintlock to Crusoe. "Stop that thing!" he shouted. "I'll cover you!"

As Crusoe snatched the flintlock from the air, he saw Caiaphas whirl around, pull his sword from its sheath, and engage the two men in combat. His blade flickered back and forth so fast it was just a blur. Under the pressure of his attack the men started to back away, but more of their colleagues were running to join the fight.

Crusoe raised the flintlock to his shoulder. No time to check how it worked: he just had to trust to Newton's ingenuity that it would be simple and to Caiaphas's fiddling that it would be charged and loaded. He aimed at the front wheel of the moving battering ram and pulled the trigger.

Nothing happened.

It wasn't loaded or charged. He pulled desperately at the twin levers on the stock. They resisted for a moment, then he heard a double click.

The battering ram was speeding up now, halfway toward the king's carriage.

Crusoe aimed again and pulled the trigger.

The weapon bucked in his hand, discharging a plume of smoke and fire. Less than a second later something struck the front wheel of the battering ram. The wood splintered and the hub disintegrated. The bizarre contraption lurched to one side, hitting the ground and plowing through the ice. The gunpowder charge at the back kept pushing it, but it slewed around in a circle. People leaped desperately out of the way.

The men who began the attack were now retreating in confusion. John Caiaphas had dispatched two of his opponents, and the third one turned and ran.

Pushed by the gunpowder charge, the battering ram finally crashed into a shop front.

As the king's carriage finally fell back onto four wheels, Crusoe turned to John Caiaphas and said breathlessly, "What was *that?*"

"That," Caiaphas said grimly, "was the Circle of Thirteen's response to our attack on their base. Rushed, and badly executed, but it very nearly worked. Sir William will be furious."

"So will the king," Crusoe pointed out starkly.

CHAPTER EIGHT

Friday ran quietly back along the corridor to her room. The corridor was empty—hopefully that meant Sister Berenice was still trying to locate Mohir. That gave Friday time to heave the door back onto its hinges and catch her breath.

It occurred to her that she could just run—try to get away from the house and find her way back to the Globe Theater, but this wasn't the time. If this mysterious Doctor Mors was coming to see her, then the alarm would be raised if she wasn't there. If she was going to escape, then the best time was when she would have several hours before they checked on her again—maybe overnight.

She lay on the hard bed and closed her eyes, trying to compose herself. There were too many unanswered questions here. She wished she knew what was going on.

She wished that Robin was with her.

It was a while later that she heard noises in the corridor, followed by the sound of the door being unlocked. For a moment she was worried that it might fall off its hinges when it opened, but good fortune was smiling on her—she had managed to put it back successfully. It swept open, revealing a tall man in the doorway. He was the same man she had seen briefly in the room downstairs. He wore white robes that reached all the way to the ground and white gloves. Bizarrely, he also wore a mask made of white leather, twisted into the shape of a bird's head. Below the dark eye sockets the mask protruded into a beak shape that curved down to a point in front of the man's chest.

He stepped into the room, accompanied by the distinct scent of flowers.

"You will forgive my rather strange appearance," he said in the same calm, gentle voice that Friday had heard earlier. "This place is a hospital, where those who are sick or injured can be treated. I am the head doctor here. This mask"—and he tapped the protruding beak"—is filled with dried leaves and petals from various medicinal plants. They purify the air that I breathe, otherwise I would be at risk of catching the same diseases from which my patients suffer. I hope you understand—I know the effect can be rather frightening. Now—my name is Doctor Mors, and you are the daughter of Red Tiberius."

She stared at him without answering. There was no point in making this any easier for him.

He cocked his head to one side as he waited for her answer, curiously, like a bird eyeing a worm.

"You are scared," he said eventually. "I understand. No harm will come to you here, I promise you that. The only thing that will happen is that you will, in a few days, join the Circle of Thirteen as a junior recruit, a minor agent. It is my task, and my honor, to manage that process."

In the doorway behind Doctor Mors, a dark figure appeared. He stepped forward into the light, but Friday already knew with a sick feeling in her stomach who it was.

Mohir grinned at her. He had lost several more teeth since the last time she had seen him, back on the island, and gained a few extra scars. His right ear had been partially ripped off as well.

"I believe you are already acquainted with Mister Mohir," Doctor Mors said. He turned his head slightly to address the pirate. "Does she look well to you? How does she compare with the last time you saw her?"

"She is taller," Mohir replied in the same deep, accented voice she remembered. "I see no injuries on her." His gaze ranged up and down her body. "She is just as beautiful as I remember."

"Be careful," Mors said. "She has been given to me to work on, not to you."

"My captain, her father, decides what happens to her," Mohir said, suddenly scowling. "He is in charge here, not you."

Mors pulled his right glove off and reached out for Friday with a thin, white hand. Friday pulled her head back.

"Do not worry," he said in a kindly tone. "I mean you no harm. I merely wish to check your temperature." He laid his hand on her forehead. His fingers were cold. Before she could react, he put a finger on the skin beneath her right eye and pulled the eyelid down. "Please—open your mouth." When Friday failed to act quickly enough he took hold of her jaw and, gently but firmly, pulled her mouth open. With his gloved left hand he tilted her head back while he gazed inside. He released her chin and stepped back. "All of the bodily humors appear to be in balance," he mused. "I see no obvious reason why we shouldn't be able to safely proceed with her initiation into the Circle. You may inform your master."

"I will tell him," Mohir growled, "but he promised her to me!"

"That was on a different island, and besides—the girl is ours now. Your master has given different orders."

"I will never join you," she said defiantly, deciding that she needed to test Doctor Mors's authority. "You can't make me."

He stared down at her, the dark holes in his birdlike mask giving him a grotesque, ghostly appearance, then turned his head to address Mohir. "Tell Sister Berenice to meet me in my office. We must prepare for the girl's initiation."

Mohir backed out of the room, but he kept his gaze fixed on Friday's face. There was something in his expression that told Friday he wasn't happy with the decision. He obviously still wanted her for his wife, despite the Circle of Thirteen's instructions. Given the choice between him or Doctor Mors, she wasn't sure which one was worse.

As she heard the bolt slide across the door outside, she knew she had to find a third choice, and quickly.

THE STEPS THAT led from the side of the stage down to the warren of tunnels beneath were dirt, covered with rough wooden boards. Crusoe trod them carefully, trying not to make much noise. He wasn't exactly sneaking around, but he *felt* as if he was.

A few yards ahead, the tunnel turned right. Around the corner, a door was guarded by one of John Caiaphas's men. He glanced at Crusoe, hand on his sword hilt.

"Sir William has given me permission to interrogate the countess," Crusoe said, trying to control the nervousness in his voice.

The man considered this for a moment, but Crusoe had seen him around before and he obviously recognized Crusoe's face. He nodded and stepped to one side.

Taking a deep breath, Crusoe pushed the door open. Sir William knew nothing about this, and when he found out, he was going to be very angry. Hopefully, by then, Crusoe would be long gone.

The Countess of Lichfield sat demurely on a rough chair in the center of the bare room. Her hands were clutched in her lap.

Crusoe had forgotten just how beautiful she was. Her pointed chin, her high cheekbones, and the deep blue of her eyes combined with her tight bodice and flowing dress to form a picture that made his breath catch in his throat.

Crusoe's attention had been distracted by his thoughts, and he felt a jolt when he suddenly realized that the countess was staring directly at him.

"Master Crusoe," she said. Her voice was still as sweet and as smooth as honey. "I wasn't expecting you. Are you here to . . . question . . . me?"

"I only want the answer to one question," he said, keeping his voice level and quiet. "Where might the Circle have retreated to now that the bridge has fallen?"

The countess gazed up at him. Instead of answering, she stood carefully. "Tell me, Master Crusoe," she said, "does the king know that I am here?"

"I'm not privy to that information," he said. "Tell me what other bases the Circle has."

She took a couple of small steps toward him. "Perhaps some . . . accommodation could be reached, Mr. Crusoe." Her voice had become deeper, throatier, and her eyes were wide and sparkling as she gazed intently at him. "Perhaps you and I could come to an arrangement which would allow me to leave here with my dignity intact and you with the information you seek."

"Leave so you can continue to work against the king with your friends in the Circle of Thirteen?" he asked. He was shocked to hear a tremor in his voice. "So you can continue to betray your father?"

She was close enough now that he could reach out and touch her. "I lost my friends, as you call them, when I led Segment W to the bridge. They won't trust me now, which means that my life is at risk. I have no friends now, Master Crusoe—or can I call you Robin? Would you let me do that? I have no friends, Robin, unless . . . unless you wanted to be my friend, and to help me. I need protecting."

It took all of Crusoe's willpower to stop himself from stepping backward, away from her, or stepping forward, close enough that he could put his arms around her. Part of him did want to protect her from the Circle and the Segment and everyone who might want to hurt her, but another part remembered Friday's face, and the way she sometimes looked at him when she thought he wasn't paying attention. It was like a cold shower of common sense overcoming whatever force of will the countess was exerting upon him.

"Tell me where the Circle has retreated to," he said. "Tell me where they might take a prisoner."

She was still gazing deeply into his eyes, but suddenly he could see past the surface, past the beauty and the warmth and the vulnerability that she was so desperately trying to project, and into her soul. And he saw the cold, hard marble that was her real personality beneath the soft velvet mask.

"It's the girl, isn't it?" she asked. She was close enough now that he could feel her breath on his cheek. "The Circle has her. That is why you are here—to find out where they have taken her, because you love her and you want her back safe." She narrowed her eyes as she considered. "And you are here alone, without Segment W, because you haven't told Sir William that you are here. What is it, Robin—did Sir William tell you there were more important priorities than rescuing one girl?"

"If you want to be kept here to suffer the justice of the king, then that wish can easily be satisfied."

"But you are prepared to let me go if I tell you where the Circle might be holding your friend?"

He nodded, reluctantly. "Segment W could get you to tell them, I am sure, but that would take some time and some effort on their part, and you might be . . . hurt . . . in the process."

She smiled, and raised an eyebrow. "I doubt the king would allow that to happen."

"I doubt the king would be told," Crusoe countered. "At least, not immediately, and not before a full confession had been extracted from your lips."

"That's treason, surely?" she said, smiling.

"That's politics, apparently."

She seemed to be weighing her options. "I will tell you," she said, "but only when I am safely delivered to a ship leaving this country. I will shout the information down to you from the deck."

Crusoe stared into her eyes. He tried to think of her not as a beautiful young woman staring challengingly up at him, but as a dangerous wild animal whose actions he was trying to predict. There had been times, back on the island, when he had unexpectedly come across a wild boar emerging from the undergrowth, and he'd had to make an instant calculation on each occasion, based on the way it was holding its body and the look in its eyes, over whether it was going to attack or retreat. Similarly, he now had to calculate whether the countess was telling the truth, or lying.

He stared deeply, challengingly, into her eyes.

She stared back.

She was bluffing. He didn't know how he knew it. He just knew that she was desperately trying to make a bargain using information she didn't have. And that meant he was no closer to finding Friday.

"You don't know where they've taken her," he said. He tried to sound confident, but he could detect an undercurrent of hopelessness in his voice. He only hoped that the countess hadn't picked up on it.

She closed her eyes for a long moment, and she let out a breath that he didn't know she had been holding. She suddenly seemed smaller. "You're right, Master Crusoe. Information is carefully controlled within the Circle of Thirteen. Nobody knows everything, and I hardly know anything." She opened her eyes and looked up at him, and this time the pleading in her expression and her voice seemed genuine. "You know what will happen to me at the hands of Segment W. Please—spare me that. Give me an hour's head start, I beg you."

"I cannot."

She nodded reluctantly. A thought seemed to strike her. "There is one thing I know that I don't believe Segment W is aware of. What if I told you that? Would you at least put a good word in for me with Sir William and my . . . and the king?"

"What is it?"

"The true identity of Lord Sebastos. At the theater, Sir William told the king that he was still trying to find out who Lord Sebastos really was. What if I gave that information to you?"

"How would that help me?" he demanded.

"Because the Circle hasn't yet had time to search his house. There may be something there that will tell you where the other Circle bases are." She laughed bitterly. "Lord Sebastos was careless that way. He had less regard for secrecy than most of the others in the Circle."

"Tell me."

"And you will speak in my defense?"

He nodded without saying anything.

"His true name was Count Ferenc Rákóczi. He was a Hungarian nobleman, but a minor one. His house in England is at Richmond, overlooking the Thames."

"Thank you."

She shrugged: a slight movement of her thin shoulders. "We do what we must. You know, of course, that after the attack on the bridge the Circle will be looking to destroy any possible link to them. Whatever is at the house will not last long."

Crusoe nodded. "I know," he said, and turned to go.

He had passed through the doorway and was about to head back down the tunnel when the countess said: "Master Crusoe?"

He turned back.

"The Circle of Thirteen is so called because thirteen people control it. Each one of those thirteen has a color, and an animal. Lord Sebastos's color was black, and his animal was the wolf." She paused for a moment, then went on: "You have, I believe, already met the one whose color is red and whose animal is the shark. This information I give you for free."

"Thank you." He nodded to her and smiled slightly.

She seemed to melt at his smile. "One more thing—Lord Sebastos had . . . pets. They may still be alive. Be careful of them."

"Wolves?" he asked.

She shook her head. "Much rarer and more dangerous than that."

There were stables near the Globe that had been taken over by Segment W to house their own horses. Crusoe crossed to the stables, nodded at the man in charge, and began to pick out his saddle and reins. He tried to look as if he was on an important mission, rather than effectively stealing a horse and its associated tack. Fortunately, the man knew Crusoe by sight and assumed that he had permission to be there. Crusoe managed to saddle the horse, lead it outside, and mount it without being challenged.

Just as he was about to start off, the man called to him.

"Lad—stop there!"

Crusoe cursed inwardly. He knew it had been too good to be true. "What is it?" he called, trying to sound casual.

"Streets are slippery with the ice. If you intend going out without binding some cloth around your horse's hooves you're liable for a fall, and believe me, the last thing you want in this life is to have a horse fall while you're riding it. You're liable to end up underneath it, and we'll be scraping you off a street somewhere."

"Good point." Crusoe sighed in relief. "I'll do that."

"Faster if I do it for you," the man said. He grabbed some spare cloth from a hook in the stables and walked over. Within less than a minute the horse's hooves were tightly bound. The horse didn't seem to mind.

Just as he was about to climb back into the saddle he heard footsteps behind him. Instinctively, he knew who it was from the rhythm and sound. Daniel.

The footsteps stopped a few feet away, and there was silence apart from the *chink* of the metal tack as the horses in the stable shifted position.

"Sir William is furious," Defoe said eventually.

"We saved the king," Crusoe pointed out, hoping that Defoe was talking about the attack and not his visit to the countess's cell.

"He shouldn't have needed saving. John Caiaphas is in trouble for not anticipating that the Circle might respond to our attack on them with an attack of their own. Sir William has dedicated all of Segment W's resources to protecting the king—and that," he added pointedly, "includes you."

"I'm going to go and get her back," Crusoe said.

Defoe sighed. "I know you want to—"

"I *have* to," Crusoe interrupted.

"Very well—I know you *have* to, but you're better off working with us than without us. Segment W can call upon resources that, frankly, you just don't have."

"Resources that are useless if I can't actually use them."

Defoe was silent for a moment. "Sir William will help," he said eventually. "He just has . . . other priorities at the moment."

"My only priority is finding Friday." Crusoe could hear the anger and the frustration in his voice. He knew it wasn't fair to take it out on Defoe, but he couldn't help himself. Inside he felt like everything was boiling and bubbling. It took all of his strength to just stand still.

"And Sir William's overriding priority is protecting the king. He cannot compromise that in order to help you. He will help as soon as things calm down."

"But that's never going to happen," Crusoe pointed out. "There will always be threats to the Crown, and if John Caiaphas manages to extract some usable information from his captives or Newton discovers something in those documents, then Sir William will have to act on it. Don't you realize—there will always be something else to do, some clue to follow up, some base to raid, some threat to counter. It will never end. For as long as there is a Crown there will be threats to the Crown. I have to act by myself before . . ." He trailed off into silence, not wanting to put into words what was weighing on his mind. *Before Friday is tortured by the Circle of Thirteen for whatever information she might possess.*

"There's a bigger picture than just you here, Crusoe," Defoe said eventually. "What if we dedicate ourselves to finding Friday but miss a chance to disrupt the Circle and prevent an assassination attempt directed against King Charles?"

"What if," Crusoe countered, "by finding Friday we also find another Circle base and bring all of their plans crashing down?"

"There are too many possibilities." Defoe sighed. "I'm sorry, but I think Sir William is correct. We deal with the big problems first and then the smaller problems later."

"So Friday being kidnapped is a small problem?"

"In the scheme of things, yes." There was a pause before Defoe went on: "Sir William has asked that you come back to the Globe. He wants to place you on the king's bodyguard detail."

"I don't work for Sir William," Crusoe snarled.

"For as long as you sleep in a Segment W base and eat Segment W food, then yes, you *do* work for Sir William."

Crusoe had expected Defoe's response. He had hoped it wouldn't come to this, but he had known it almost certainly would. "I'm not coming back," he said softly.

"I know."

"I'm going after Friday."

"With no clues, no evidence, and no way of knowing where she is?"

Crusoe was silent.

Defoe sucked his breath in through his teeth. "So—what did she tell you, then?"

Crusoe stared at his friend. Defoe had a slight smile on his face. How did he know? Was he guessing?

"The countess obviously likes you," Defoe went on, "and you know that. A man desperate to rescue his friend might take advantage of that fact to extract information from her—"

"She has no feelings for me," Crusoe protested, "and even if she did, I wouldn't take advantage of her like that."

"Then you are the only person in London who wouldn't, my friend."

"She gave me the true identity of Lord Sebastos," Crusoe explained, "and where he lives."

Defoe nodded. "And who is he? Or was he, I should say?"

"A minor nobleman named Rákóczi. Count Ferenc Rákóczi. Do you know of him?"

Defoe shook his head. "There are more foreign noblemen in Europe than a sane man can keep track of. Sometimes it seems that the various kings and queens hand out titles for Christmas presents. So—I presume we are going to check this Count Rákóczi's house?"

"Do you know where Richmond is?"

"West of London, near the river. We can be there in an hour if we take it carefully, or half an hour if we risk our lives."

"We?"

"Sir William will be furious with you for riding off and ignoring his orders. If I don't go along to protect you he'll be incandescent." He smiled. "And besides, what are friends for if not to risk their lives for each other?"

Within a few minutes Defoe had saddled a horse and they were mounted and riding.

FRIDAY GAVE DOCTOR Mors and Mohir enough time to get to the stairs, and then she quickly lifted the door up and off its hinges, careful to make no noise. It was much easier this time.

She poked her head out into the corridor—low, close to the ground, where any observers would be less likely to notice it. She glanced right, and saw them. They were almost at the central hall that joined the two wings of the building. As she watched, they vanished around the slight angle, heading toward the other wing rather than going to the library. As soon as they were out of sight she sprinted down the corridor toward the hall.

Friday was still torn between the idea of escaping and the possibility that she might be able to get some vital information on the aims and the methods of the Circle. The conversation with Doctor Mors had made her uneasy. She might not have much time. If she saw an unguarded and unlocked door to the outside or an open and unbarred window, then she would have to go for it.

The hall was empty. She sprinted silently across and paused at the edge of the second wing. Doctor Mors, in his white robes and white mask, was unmistakable about halfway down. He was standing in front of a door. Mohir was walking away from him, heading for the stairs that Friday suspected were at the far end, if that wing was the mirror image of the one she had already explored.

Doctor Mors waited until Mohir had vanished into the stairwell, and then he unbolted the door and stepped inside. Friday heard his voice—he was talking to someone. Perhaps it was another prisoner like her. She had to know.

She ran down the corridor, keeping close to the wall. As she got closer she could make out Mors's gentle voice and replies from someone else. The voice was young—and male.

Was it Robin? She felt her heart miss a beat as the thought struck her. Was he a prisoner, too? She had been waiting for him to come and rescue her, but maybe *he* needed her to rescue *him*.

A momentary pause in the conversation alerted Friday to the fact that something was happening. A flash of white material in the doorway told her that Mors was leaving the room. She glanced left and right, looking for somewhere to hide. The hallway between the wings was too far back to get to before he was in the corridor.

Fortunately, Mors paused and turned back.

"It will not be long now," he said quietly. "Soon you will join the Circle, and your suffering will be at an end." He pulled the door closed and bolted it.

The best chance Friday had was the nearest door. The bolt wasn't slid across, and in fact the door was open a few inches. She was going to have to take the risk that the room it led to was empty.

It was late now—later than she had thought. The room was dark, illuminated by the weak light of the moon outside, but she couldn't hear anything apart from the sound of the wind outside. After a few moments she saw Doctor Mors sweep past. He was pulling his white gloves off.

Less than a minute later she heard a nearby door open and close. Mors had gone inside the library.

Friday was about to leave, but before she could move she heard a choking cough from the darkness behind her. She felt her skin crawl. There was someone in the room.

Slowly, she turned. If someone was asleep, then she didn't want to startle them.

Her eyes were used to the darkness now. She saw what she had missed before—the two rows of beds, one on each side of the room running up to the barred window. Each bed had someone in it. Unlike the rooms downstairs, where the patients had been crying and moaning and screaming in pain, these people were all lying quietly. The hiss of their breathing was the noise she had mistaken for the wind outside.

Drawn by some impulse that she couldn't explain, Friday began to walk quietly down the central row between the beds. There were men and women there, all fast asleep, all lying on their backs with their faces upturned to the ceiling. Their eyes were closed, but their faces were twisted into expressions of suffering—not pain, exactly, but more like a kind of spiritual or moral torment.

Friday moved toward the closest of the sleeping figures.

It was a woman not much older than Friday.

Her face was disfigured by a blue blotch, just like the ones that Friday had seen on the skin of Circle of Thirteen members. It stretched from her jaw entirely across one cheek and up, past her eye, to her forehead.

Were all of these people agents of the Circle, too? How did they all come to be marked in the same way?

She felt like she had discovered more questions than answers, and her time was running out.

What was going on in this place?

CHAPTER NINE

One Year Before the Escape

The sound of an explosion broke Suriya's concentration. She was reading a book she'd taken from one of the ships the Dark Nebula had recently attacked. She loved reading. It broke the monotony of the time they spent under sail, but she could also learn things about other lands, other places. Things that might come in useful one day. She also tried to learn languages, in a halting fashion—something she practiced whenever she went ashore.

The sound came again, sending a tremor through the timbers of the ship.

She scrambled out of her hammock. She tried to pull the door to her small cabin open but the ship chose that moment to suddenly tip over a wave. For a moment she was pulling upon something that felt more like a trapdoor rather than an exit, but then the ship lurched back again and she hauled it open enough to brace herself against the frame.

Her father stood on the quarterdeck, holding on to the rail that overlooked the main deck. Behind him the pirate manning the wheel was desperately straining to stop it spinning in his hands. Her father half-turned and yelled: "Keep a straight course or I'll have your feet cut off and sewn on backward!" He caught sight of Suriya, clinging to the frame of her door, and scowled. "Get yourself out of the way, girl. This is man's work!"

There was smoke and sea spray drifting across the deck. The acrid odor of gunpowder made her nose twitch and her eyes water. She glanced upward, to the top of the main mast. The pirate flag was flying proudly there—a crude picture of a skeletal hand with a gold ring around the forefinger.

The small Indian boy—Diran—was crouched down beside her father, ready to carry out any order he was given. He looked terrified. He glanced back toward Suriya and she could see him shaking. She wished she could run over to comfort him, but the way the ship was bucking in the waves and with the cannon fire she might just lose her footing and topple over the side. Instead, she tried to reassure him with a smile, but it felt more like a grimace. This wasn't a situation that encouraged smiles.

Crewmembers were crisscrossing the deck of the Dark Nebula. *Their expressions ranged from scared to exultant. Some were rushing around, holding their cutlasses and the short swords that were known as hangars. Some were carrying the small cannons that could be fastened to the side of the ship and pointed wherever they were needed.*

Mohir was down on the main deck, striding around and lashing out with a length of rope to encourage the crew to move faster. Something was going on, and it was big.

Glancing to port, Suriya suddenly realized what it was.

There was another ship out there. A merchantman, by the look of her. The Dark Nebula *was a brigantine, which meant that she had* extra sails and a lighter, narrower design. That in turn meant that the pirate ship had been able to easily catch up with its prey, despite the fact that the merchantman's captain had clearly loaded on all the sails his masts would take. The pirate ship was nearly parallel with the merchantman now, and Red Tiberius had ordered a broadside from his cannons. There was already a hole in the other ship's side, through which Suriya could see smashed timbers, injured men, and a lake of blood.

The Dark Nebula's cannons fired again with a thunderous roar, knocking the pirate ship sideways and jerking Suriya into the door frame. This time the cannons were aimed higher, for the deck, and the charge was grapeshot rather than cannonballs. Suriya had often seen the canvas bags piled down on the gun deck when she'd been exploring the ship. They'd looked so innocuous there, but the bags burst when fired from a cannon, sending a cloud of metal sweeping across the deck. Over on the merchantman crewmembers were scythed down in a fog of blood and flesh. It was ghastly to watch.

And her father had ordered it. Her father.

The merchantman's captain was visible on the quarterdeck of his vessel. Even at that distance Suriya could see the shock on his face. He shouted an order at his crew. Within a few moments the sails and colors were coming down and a white flag was fluttering in their place. Surrender.

Suriya knew it was his only realistic option. The Dark Nebula could easily keep pace with him, and he either had no weapons on his ship or his crew was reluctant to anger the pirates more by firing on them. Her father's next action would have been to send chain-shot whirling above the deck—cannonballs linked by chains that would tear through the spars and sails like a knife through a loaf of bread. If the captain surrendered now, then he might just be allowed to keep his ship and his crew, after his cargo had been looted.

If he resisted, then Red Tiberius might well slaughter them all and sink the ship, just for putting him to extra trouble. She'd seen him do it before.

As Suriya watched, the two ships gradually slowed until they were maintaining a steady pace parallel from each other. The pirates threw hooked ropes across the gap. The hooks caught on the rails of the merchantman, and the pirates hauled on the ropes to bring the ships closer together. Eventually, gangplanks were laid from rail to rail and tied down so they didn't slide away. Led by Mohir, the pirates swarmed across the gap.

The merchantman's captain was forced at sword point to make the perilous crossing from his ship to the Dark Nebula. *As he walked across, Suriya thought from his expression that he was considering throwing himself over the side and into the sea. In the end, however, he jumped onto the* Dark Nebula's *deck with Mohir behind him.*

Red Tiberius gazed imperiously down from the rail of the quarter-deck. The merchantman's captain gazed up, fury and terror fighting for space on his face, and Suriya felt the last vestige of respect that she had for her father wither and die.

FRIDAY STARED AT the figure lying in bed. Even though she wasn't moving—none of the patients were moving—she felt her skin crawling. There was something unnatural about the way they were so perfectly still.

And then there was the blue mark on the woman's face. It must mean this woman was an agent of the Circle of Thirteen. She already knew that the injured Circle personnel from the bridge had been brought here for treatment—but this woman didn't look like she was injured. She looked like she was ill, and close to death. Had these agents all caught some kind of disease?

She moved to the next bed. The man in it was older, probably in his fifties. His eyes were closed, too, and his arms were outside the blanket. His face was clear of any blue markings, but Friday could see the mottled edges of a blue mark on his chest, just peeking out from beneath the edge of the blanket.

She crossed the room and checked another bed. This patient was a lad in his twenties. There was no obvious sign of a blue mark on his skin, but when Friday gently pulled the blanket downward she saw one on his bare stomach. It was small—no larger than a guinea coin—but it was easily recognizable.

So, it looked like all of the patients here were Circle personnel, and all of them were suffering from the same disease. Had they all caught it in the same place? Were they contagious?

She shook her head. She didn't have enough information to answer any of her questions. She was collecting facts, but she didn't know what to make of them.

Maybe it was time to get out of there.

She moved silently back to the door and slipped out into the corridor. She needed to see who was in the room down the corridor. From the way Mors had spoken to them it was either Robin or it was someone who might be an ally.

The door was still closed and bolted. She tapped lightly on the wood with her fingernails, using a code that she and Robin had developed back on the island. There they had pretended to be wild boar, making messages out of the grunts. Here she could just use simple knocks.

There was no response, but she could sense an interest, a watchfulness, from within. She tapped again.

"Hello?" It wasn't Robin's voice, but whoever was in there sounded young. He also sounded hesitant, wary. "Is there anybody there?"

She took a deep breath, then unbolted the door and pushed it open.

The room was like hers—not as deep as the ones where the patients were lying in their beds, but with two partitioned areas filling up the space between the door and the far wall. A young man was sitting on the bed inside. His eyes, from what she could see in the light from the lamp on the wall, were a pale blue, and it took her a second to recognize him. It was the Increment guard from the bridge—Paul Shadrach.

"Miss Friday?" His eyes widened, and he stood up. "They captured you, too?"

She nodded. "Are you all right?"

"Some scratches and some bruises. Nothing serious." He looked embarrassed. "I was in a sword fight and I tried to step backward, but there was someone on the ground behind me and I fell. I must have hit my head. I woke up here a little while ago." He frowned. "You got out of your room? How did you do that?"

Friday stepped into the room and pushed the door closed. She pointed at the hinges. "You can push those up, if you have the right tools, then you can open the door the wrong way, using the bolt as a hinge."

He softly clapped his hands together three times. "Bravo. I would never have thought of that." He paused for a minute, staring at her. "Are they talking about getting you to join the Circle, too?"

"That's what Doctor Mors said." Friday frowned. "That's the bit I don't understand. What do they mean, 'join'? It's not like they've actually asked us. It's more like they expect us to somehow come around to their way of thinking."

Paul nodded. "I know. It's confusing. I have no intention of joining them, but that doesn't seem to worry them in the slightest." He moved to stand by her side. "You're not like the other girls I know."

"I should hope not." She shrugged. "I'm not from this country."

"You speak very good English," he pointed out.

"I was well taught."

"By Mr. Crusoe?"

She nodded.

"Is he in here, too?"

"No—he's on the outside somewhere, looking for me. When he gets here he's going to help us escape."

Paul smiled. "I don't need his help. Now that you've shown me the trick with the door, it's my job to get us both out of here."

THE HORSES' HOOVES hitting the frozen ground sent vibrations through Crusoe's and Defoe's bodies. Crusoe had expected the horses to slip on the patches of ice covering every road, but the horses managed to keep their footing. Everywhere they rode there were fires on the street corners, fed by wood that people were actually pulling from their houses. Smoke hung over everything like a low, dark rain cloud.

Defoe led the ride. He knew London better than Crusoe. At times, they galloped down wide roads. At others, they moved through winding alleys, but always they were heading south and west. Eventually, the houses began to thin, separated by fields and patches of common ground where cows and sheep tried to lick the ice from the grass so they could eat.

There was something about the landscape and the houses that triggered a faint memory in Crusoe. Things were familiar to the point that he knew what he was going to see farther down the road, before they got there. He had been here before, he thought—when he was much younger. Had he lived here? Had his *family* lived here?

The feeling of familiarity was so strong that his hand moved to his throat, to where he used to wear the medallion given to him by his father on his twelfth birthday—a metal shape, about the size of a sovereign, that had a smooth side and a jagged side as if it had been broken off something larger. These days he kept it back in his room at the Globe so that he didn't lose it, but the sudden flash of memory had been so unexpected that for a moment he had felt the weight of the medallion pulling on its leather thong against his neck.

The feeling faded after a few minutes, leaving him unsettled. He made a mental note to return at some later time—once this was all over. There was still so much he didn't remember about his father or where his family came from. His return to England hadn't given him the answers he'd once thought it would.

Eventually, they arrived in Richmond. Defoe stopped at a tavern to ask the way to Count Rákóczi's house. When he came back he was scowling.

"The count is not well liked around here," he called as he mounted his horse. "I almost had to fight three men just for asking where he lived. I only got out of it by saying I was a bailiff sent to confiscate and sell his possessions."

The house was another ten minutes' ride away. It was a building of red stone and dark wood sprawled over several acres at the edge of the river. It looked to Crusoe as if the ice was thin here. Nobody was out on the surface. He suspected that a little way upstream it was still running water—although it would be nearly as cold as ice if a person fell in.

They tied their horses to a gatepost and approached the house. With the low moon behind it, the place presented a dark and forbidding appearance, seeming to glower down at them from a position of power.

"No lights," Defoe noted. "And no smoke from a fire, either. I think we can assume that the place is deserted."

The house had clearly been abandoned for some time. The main door stood open, and the heavy rains of winter combined with the sudden freeze meant that the entire entrance hall was a sheet of ice. Crusoe and Defoe had to bind their boots with cloth, like the revelers on the Thames, before they could negotiate a way across.

Consumed with worry about Friday, Crusoe led the way inside. He could only hope they would find something useful that would lead them to where Friday was being kept.

There were no lamps apart from the two lanterns that Defoe had brought with them. The flickering flames illuminated a place of dark wooden panels and darker curtains, of floors covered with black rugs, and paintings depicting scenes of fire and storm. The cold and the rain had caused cracks to start forming in the wooden panels and the plaster ceilings, and the paint on the walls to start peeling. Spiders had already started spinning webs in the corners of the rooms and the corridors. Soon enough they would be so heavy with dust that they would look like curtains in their own right. The house seemed to perfectly reflect its former owner, Lord Sebastos: dark, brooding, and intense.

It seemed to Crusoe that there was something more at work in the house. Things should not be falling apart that quickly, surely? It was as if the house already knew that its master was dead and had started to decay along with him.

Quickly, Crusoe and Defoe checked the obvious rooms—the study, the library, and what was clearly the master bedroom. They found nothing. Either Lord Sebastos had not kept any papers or documents in his house or someone had removed them all. Certainly, nobody had been left behind to guard the place.

The next room they entered was a ballroom. Now there were dried leaves piled in drifts in the corners, and a thin rime of frost over the velvet upholstery of the chairs that lined the wall like reluctant dancers.

Defoe stomped in, glanced around, and then headed back toward the door. "There's nothing here," he said. "Lord Sebastos wouldn't hide his secrets in a ballroom."

"You might be surprised," Crusoe said. He was looking at the vaulted ceiling, which was painted a dark blue and scattered with stars. It was obviously meant to give people the impression that they were outside, under a summer sky. Yet there was something familiar about those stars, and the thin tracery of lines that linked some of them together. "I'm reasonably sure that picture on the ceiling has the same patterns as the one on the parchment Friday and I found in the Circle's meeting room."

Defoe stared upward, frowning. "Are you sure? It just looks like a pretty picture to me."

Crusoe nodded. "The more I look at it, the more sure I am. It's the same diagram."

"That might just mean," Defoe pointed out, "that the diagram you found was the painter's early plan for the painting, and that it found its way into the meeting room by accident."

"Or," Crusoe responded, "that it was important enough to Lord Sebastos that he wanted to be able to look at it whenever he wanted."

Defoe was still staring up at it. "Those constellations don't make any sense," he said. "I've never seen anything like them before."

"That's the point," Crusoe said. "I think we need to bring Isaac Newton to see this. He needs to compare this painting with the parchment."

Defoe nodded. "Agreed, but let's search the rest of the house in case we find something more useful than a massive piece of decoration."

Crusoe found himself shivering as he moved from room to room. Partly it was because most of the windows in the house were broken, letting a chill wind blow through them, but partly it was because he was scared about what might be happening to Friday. His imagination kept flashing pictures in his mind of her chained up, or being beaten, or even being tortured as Isaac Newton had suggested. The thoughts chased one another around in his head, distracting him from what he was doing.

As he shoved yet another drawer closed, Crusoe cursed under his breath. "This is useless," he called to Defoe. "There's nothing here."

Defoe had been moving the paintings, looking for any secret cupboards underneath. "I'm afraid you're right," he replied. "Unless something is hidden so well here that we cannot find it, I have to believe that there is nothing to find." He thought for a moment. "Have you seen any stairs leading downward?" he asked. "It occurs to me that we haven't found a way into the cellars."

Crusoe shook his head. "Maybe there are no cellars."

"Then where would he keep his wine?"

Between them they searched the ground floor of the house, looking for any entrance to the cellars, but they found nothing. Defoe eventually had to admit that Crusoe was right—there *were* no cellars.

They also went in the other direction, checking the attic space, but apart from more dust, more cobwebs, and a few empty boxes and trunks, there was nothing.

Despite his words, Defoe seemed willing to stay in the house, searching, for as long as Crusoe wanted. Eventually, it was Crusoe himself who led the way regretfully to the door.

"Let's check some of the outbuildings," Defoe suggested. "Lord Sebastos might have converted the stables or a greenhouse into an office. There might be some evidence there that would help us." His expression brightened slightly. "As the house is on the edge of the Thames, there must be a boathouse. We should check there as well."

Crusoe nodded wearily. He didn't hold out much hope that they would find anything, but Defoe was right—they had to exhaust all of the possibilities before they gave up.

The outbuildings were between the back of the house and the river. Defoe led the way toward the nearest ones.

As he walked along the side of the house, over frost-covered stones, Crusoe thought he felt the ground give way slightly beneath his boots. He stopped, intrigued. Defoe turned around to see what had happened. Crusoe brought his heel down experimentally. He heard a dull noise, not like the sound of stone being hit but the sound of wood.

"I think there's some kind of hatch or trapdoor here," he said excitedly.

Defoe nodded. He bounced up and down. The ground flexed beneath him, springing back a little as his weight shifted. "And here, too. Well spotted." He bent down and scraped at the frost. "Yes—it's wood." Measuring the distance between him and Crusoe with his eye, he added: "This is a large trapdoor. It's far bigger than one would need to deliver coal—or wine—to a cellar."

"Perhaps there are secret passages beneath the house," Crusoe suggested.

The two of them marked out the extent of the wooden section by walking around and banging with their feet. Defoe was right—it was huge.

"The hinges will be close to the house," Defoe said after a few minutes. "That means any handles or locks will be farthest away."

There were indeed several padlocks and handles set in a line parallel to the walls of the house.

"We don't have the keys," Crusoe pointed out. "How do we open this up?"

"Break through the wood?" Defoe suggested.

"It's so thick it'll take us hours. We could set fire to it."

"I think there's an easier way. Wait here for a moment." Defoe strode away. Crusoe stood there, looking down at the exposed edges of the trapdoor and trying not to think of what might be happening to Friday.

By the time Defoe returned, Crusoe was in a black mood.

Defoe held up a hammer. "I checked the servants' quarters and found this."

Crusoe looked from the hammer to the trapdoor and back. "I'm not sure that is going to help," he said.

"Isaac Newton showed me that when metal becomes very cold, it also becomes very brittle. That's probably something you never experienced on the island."

"No cold," Crusoe pointed out, "and no metal to speak of."

Defoe knelt down and hefted the hammer. He struck the first padlock hard. The sound of metal on metal rang out like a bell in the night air, but the padlock remained intact. Defoe grimaced and tried again, shifting his grip slightly. This time the sound was different, more discordant, and the curved section of padlock cracked in two.

"*Et voilà!*" Defoe said, grinning.

Crusoe reached out for the hammer. "Let me have a go."

Within a few minutes all of the broken padlocks lay to the side. They used the material from their shoes to wrap their hands up instead. They each took hold of a corner bracket—the heat still being sucked from their skin by the metal despite their makeshift gloves—and heaved.

The trapdoor creaked upward. With a mighty effort they raised the edge of the trapdoor above their heads and pushed it so that it fell back against the wall of the house with a crash.

Instead of stone steps, Crusoe saw that a stone ramp led downward into the shadows.

"A coal chute?" he ventured.

Defoe shook his head. "Why so wide? No, this is meant to facilitate the arrival of something big, but I have no idea what." He gestured to the sloping surface. "Shall we?"

Together they sat on the edge, legs extended downward, and exchanged a glance.

"For King and Country," Defoe murmured.

"For Friday," Crusoe countered.

They pushed themselves off and slid down the icy stone.

Their lanterns illuminated brick walls and a brick ceiling as they moved. Within a few seconds their feet hit the stone floor with a jolt.

Crusoe got up and looked around.

They were indeed in the cellars—a wide arched passage extended into the darkness in front of them. Arches in the walls gave access to other passages and probably rooms as well.

Something snapped beneath Crusoe's boot as he stepped forward. He looked at the ground expecting to find a twig or a stick, but instead he saw a bone—a long white bone that had been broken in two when he stepped on it. The bone was too large to belong to any animal that was likely to live in a cellar. Crusoe had a sinking feeling in his chest that told him it might just be human. Probably a thigh bone. A man had died here—or, at least, a man's body had been left to rot here—and the bones had been scattered by feral predators like rats and foxes.

He held his lantern up and looked around. There were several white bones near the wall. Some were tiny—fingers and toes, perhaps. Some were curved, and he thought they might be ribs. And finally, half-caught in shadow, he saw a skull lying on its side. The jawbone had fallen off, and was lying nearby.

Thin wisps of hair were still attached to the skull.

"Daniel," Crusoe called.

Defoe came over to join him. He gazed levelly down at the body. "Male," he said eventually. "Probably of early middle age." He noticed Crusoe's quizzical look and added, "My father was a butcher and a tallow maker. I have been around bones for as long as I can remember."

"Not human bones, surely?" Crusoe asked.

Defoe shrugged. "Dismembering a cow or a pig and dismembering a man—they require the same skills. Life was not easy and not pretty when I was growing up. I have seen death, and I have seen it covered up." He leaned closer and picked up a rib. "This has been crushed. In fact, a lot of these bones are broken or crushed. This man did not die easily." He frowned and knelt down on one knee beside the skull. Reaching out, he picked up one of the bones and examined it closely.

"What is it?" Crusoe asked.

Defoe held the bone up. Crusoe saw that it held a ring, still on the finger. It was gold, and at the front, instead of a stone, there was an incised golden coat of arms.

"It's the seal of the Duke of Wimbourne," Defoe said, standing up. His face was grim in the flickering lantern light. "He disappeared six months ago, before you arrived in England. Segment W was tasked by the king to look for him, but we had no success." He glanced down at the skull. "At least we now know where he is, even if we don't know exactly what happened to him."

"Then what we need to do now is tell Segment W," Crusoe said. He gestured into the shadows of the tunnel. "Shall we try to find a way into the house, or shall we climb back up to the grounds?"

In the end, it wasn't hard. The cellars beneath the house were extensive, but the tunnel they were in was straight and it led them directly to a large stone chamber with a door set high up in the wall. A wooden staircase led up the stone to the door.

In the center of the room, however, was another corpse.

This one wasn't human, but it had died a lot more recently than the Duke of Wimbourne—by the look of it, maybe a week ago. It was an animal, but not like any animal Crusoe had seen before. Its skin was gray and hung loosely down around its barrel-shaped body. The folds had wart-like bumps along them as well, as if the thick skin had actually been riveted onto its body rather than just grown there. It was about the size of a horse, but its legs were shorter and thicker and its body far wider. Its massive head slumped onto the ground as if it was too heavy for the creature to carry around properly. That head looked like a massive stone gargoyle, staring down from the tower of a church, but the things that Crusoe found himself unable to look away from were the horns on its head. They were viciously pointed, and curved backward, a bit like overgrown shark teeth. Given the way that the creature's head was held so low to the ground, Crusoe suspected that its main method of attack was to get those horns beneath whatever it was fighting and then use them to tear through its victim and toss it in the air. Its hooves were heavy, and seemingly clawed. In total, it looked like someone had taken a pig, massively enlarged it, and given it both horns and armor plating.

"Have you ever seen anything like this before?" Crusoe asked in a hushed voice.

Defoe shook his head. "Seen, no, but I think I recognize it from the descriptions of travelers to Africa and the Orient. I believe it is called a 'rhinoceros.' I have to say that this one looks thinner than I would have expected."

"It probably starved to death," Crusoe suggested. "If the house has been empty ever since Lord Sebastos died, then this thing has been wandering around down here with no food apart from what it might have been left with."

"Most of the nobility content themselves with dogs and horses." Defoe laughed, but it sounded more like a snort. "I can only wish that Lord Sebastos had followed their example." He stood and gestured toward the steps. "Come on—let's get out of this charnel house."

They emerged through a door disguised in the back of a dusty cupboard into an abandoned pantry.

Crusoe sniffed. "This house *is* deserted, isn't it?"

"Indeed. Why?"

"Because I can smell smoke."

Defoe moved to the door of the pantry and pushed it open against something that had fallen on the other side. He looked out, then turned to face Crusoe urgently.

"I don't want to worry you," he said, "but I think the house is on fire!"

CHAPTER TEN

Friday checked outside the door. The corridor was clear.

Paul moved up behind her. She could sense him, close but not touching.

"Anything?" he whispered.

"Nothing," she said. "Come on."

They moved out of the room and into the corridor. When she realized that he wasn't keeping up, Friday turned to see what the problem was.

Paul was limping, and grimacing.

"Did you hurt your leg in the fight?" she asked.

He frowned. "No, I've got a pain running right up it. Feels like the bone is on fire."

"It's probably a cramp. You've been lying motionless on that bed for too long.

"Let's hope," he said, hobbling to catch up.

"What's your plan?" she asked.

"Look for a back door into the gardens. If it's unguarded we go straight out. If it's guarded, then I knock the guard unconscious and *then* we go straight out. Head for the nearest village, get two horses, and ride for London."

"I've got a better idea," Friday said. "The doors are too obvious—we'll be caught straight away—but there's a loose window in the library down the corridor. We can get out of the window without being seen, climb down, and run for it." She turned her head and winced apologetically. "Limp for it, anyway."

"You just make sure you can keep up," he murmured.

They were halfway along the corridor by now, heading for the library. Suddenly, behind them, Friday heard a door being pushed open, squealing on its hinges. She thought it was the door at the end of the corridor—the one that led to the stairs.

They were just passing the room she'd been in before—the one with the people who all seemed to be asleep.

"Quick!" he said quietly. Grabbing her arm, he pulled her toward the door and pushed it open. He quickly scanned the room, noting the beds and their comatose occupants. "Get beneath a bed. We'll wait until things are clear again and get out."

She dived for the nearest bed, the one containing the woman with the blue marking on her face, and rolled underneath. Seconds later, Paul scrambled into the space beneath the next bed.

The door opened.

From underneath the bed, Friday could see the white robes of Doctor Mors sweeping across the floor toward her. Behind him were the hobnailed boots of two of the Brothers, and the more delicate white robes of one of the Sisters.

Mors swept past where she and Paul were hiding. He stopped at a bed farther down.

"Is this the one?" he asked.

"It is," the Sister said. Friday recognized the voice as Sister Berenice. "He is quiet now, but he was moving around earlier on. His fists were clenching, and he cried out once or twice."

"This was in your presence? You weren't told about it by another Sister or a Brother?"

"No, I saw it and heard it for myself."

"Then he is coming out of his trance. That is good. Have him taken to the recovery ward. I will monitor him there."

Friday heard the Brothers pick the patient up and carry him down the aisle toward the door. Doctor Mors and Sister Berenice followed, but they stopped beside the bed that Friday was hiding beneath.

"This one," Doctor Mors said. "The marking has developed on her face. That is unfortunate. I had intended her to be an under-cover agent within Sector W, but they would spot her straight away."

"Will you have her killed?" Sister Berenice asked calmly.

A moment, and then Mors replied: "No—she can become a Sister, working here. Her face will not matter then."

Mors began to walk toward the door, but Sister Berenice said: "May I ask . . . a question?"

He turned back. "Of course," he said gently. "You have my permission."

"The girl—Friday. Are you intent on converting her to our cause?"

A sudden chill ran through Friday's body.

"Those are the wishes of the Circle."

"Not all of the Circle . . . ," she said.

"Ah." Mors's voice was amused. "Red Tiberius's man, Mohir, has been trying to influence you, then."

She sounded defensive. "He believes that he has some kind of prior claim on her."

"The needs and the wishes of the Circle take precedence over ev-erything," Mors explained patiently. "And Red Tiberius is the voice of the Circle here. The girl will join us, and *she* will be our agent on the inside of Segment W." He turned and headed for the door. "Pre-pare the treatment for the girl," he called back over his shoulder. "I want her to be back inside Segment W and reporting to us as soon as possible."

Friday lay there for another moment after they had gone. So many thoughts were spinning around in her brain. There seemed to be some kind of process going on here. These people weren't just sick—something was being done to them. Something unnatural. And she was apparently next on the list to be "treated." Did that mean she would come out the other side as a Circle agent, fully believing in their aims?

Paul scrambled out from underneath his bed. He extended a hand toward her. "Come on—we need to go."

Friday reached out to take his hand. She shivered. The thought of having her own beliefs somehow replaced by those of the Circle—it was like being taken over by an evil spirit against her will. She couldn't let herself go through it. She would rather die.

One Year Before the Escape

Surrounded by pirates with weapons drawn, the merchantman's captain stared up at Red Tiberius. His face was calm, but it was an illusion, like the mirage of a distant island that should have been beyond sight. His hands were clenched, and his eyes were narrowed in frustrated anger.

Mohir struck the captain between his shoulder blades. He fell to his knees with a cry. Mohir stood back and folded his arms. His eyes moved up to where Suriya was standing, and he stared at her with a half smile on his face.

Suriya felt his gaze like heat on her skin. She looked away, back to the merchantman's captain, but she was still aware of him. Looking and smiling.

"You were wise to surrender," her father called from where he stood at the rail of the quarterdeck. "Things would have gone badly for you if you had not." His voice was pitched perfectly to carry to every part of the ship without it sounding like he was shouting. Suriya knew he had a natural authority that, along with his intelligence and brutality, kept him in charge of the Dark Nebula. He could be kind—to her, sometimes—but he was first and foremost a leader of men.

The merchantman's captain bowed his head briefly. "My life is in your hands," he said. He spoke in what Suriya thought was a Dutch accent. "As are the lives of my crew. I only ask that you treat them with consideration."

"What cargo do you carry?" Red Tiberius asked. Suriya noticed that the pirate crew was listening closely. Under the terms of the Charter of the Coast, which all pirates signed or put their mark on when they joined a crew, they were entitled to a share of any takings.

"I carry sandalwood and cedarwood," the captain replied, "along with many barrels of sweet white wine from Portugal." He hesitated. "And swords from Toledo," he added, knowing that they would have been discovered eventually.

"And passengers?" Red Tiberius asked.

"Five."

"How many are women?"

The captain winced. "Three. I ask—no, I implore you to treat them in a Christian manner. Let them stay with me, on my ship. Take my cargo, all of it, but leave them. Let us go on our way, lighter but still alive and unharmed."

Red Tiberius nodded imperiously. "They shall indeed remain with you, but their jewelry and possessions shall be taken." He paused for a moment. "Each member of your crew will be offered the chance to join us as pirates. If they take that offer, then they will swear their *fealty to me over crossed swords and sign the Charter of the Coast with their mark. These are my demands. Your navigator and any carpenters in your crew will join us whether they choose to or not, as will any members of your crew who know how to set a bone or bind a wound properly. Do you understand this?"*

The merchantman's captain nodded slowly. "I thank you," he said.

Red Tiberius stared at him for a few moments. It was at this point, Suriya knew from previous attacks on ships, that her father would send his crew across to ransack the captured ship, but there seemed to be something else on his mind.

Suriya glanced quickly at Mohir. He was frowning. He was clearly confused about the delay.

"You are Dutch?" Red Tiberius asked eventually.

The captain nodded.

"Then I have a question to ask you," Red Tiberius said in that language. Mohir looked surprised. He obviously didn't speak Dutch, although Suriya did—taught by her father, along with the other languages he spoke, during long sea voyages. "I would take you into my cabin to speak, but that would make us equals in the eyes of my crew and I would lose authority. Do you understand?"

The captain nodded again. "There is something you wish to find out, but you don't want your crew to know," he replied, also in Dutch.

"If you answer me straight, and do not hide information from me, then I will let you keep your navigator. Do you understand this?"

"I do."

"Have you heard of a type of plant, a mushroom of sorts, that is the color of a starless night, with a head that looks like a ball?" His hands came together to form a sphere. "About this size? It is much prized by some. A treasure, if plants can be a treasure."

The captain looked confused. "A mushroom? Is this some kind of delicacy?"

Red Tiberius didn't answer.

"A black mushroom?" The captain thought for a moment. "I do not believe that I have."

Red Tiberius nodded. Looking at him from her position off to one side, Suriya thought he was frustrated. Whatever it was that he was looking for, he hadn't found it. "Return to your ship. Question your passengers and your crew. I will . . . reward . . . any information they have." He looked at Mohir. Switching back to French, he said: "Take this man back to his ship. Bring the cargo here. Seek out the carpenters and anybody with knowledge of medicine and bring them here as well."

Mohir nodded, but the way he looked at Red Tiberius suggested, for a second, that his captain had lost some authority in his eyes. Suriya felt a chill prickle her skin despite the hot sunshine. Her father had already resisted several challenges to his authority, but one day he would be too old or too slow, and there would be a new captain of the Dark Nebula. *If that new captain was Mohir, then Suriya was afraid. She would rather die with her father than be on a ship with Mohir in charge. She wasn't entirely sure why, but there was something in the way he looked at her that made her feel sick.*

FROM A CRACK in the door Friday and Paul watched as Doctor Mors, Sister Berenice, and the two Brothers walked away down the corridor. They stopped at a room farther down—one that Friday hadn't investigated yet. They were in there for a few minutes, then Doctor Mors and the two Brothers reappeared and walked off toward the stairs.

Once they were gone, Friday and Paul emerged into the corridor. He turned toward the library, but Friday hesitated.

"What is it?" he asked. "We need to get out of here quickly!"

"I know," she said, irritated at the way he was automatically taking command. "We do, but I'm curious to see where that man has been taken, and what's happening to him."

Paul frowned. "That isn't as important as us getting to freedom."

"It might be. Remember that you and I are scheduled for recruitment," she pointed out. "That man's just about to go through it himself. I want to find out what it entails."

"There's no point," Paul said firmly. "Our duty is to escape."

"Our duty is to collect as much information as we can, and *then* escape," Friday said, thinking of her father's long-ago advice. If she could return to Segment W with some solid information about how the Circle of Thirteen recruited their members, then getting herself captured would have been worth it.

She started off down the corridor, whispering over her shoulder, "I'll meet you in the library in five minutes. If I don't make it, then push out the window frame—remember, it's already loose, and you should be able to get out and climb down to the ground." She was startled when she realized that he was walking along beside her, rather than following her instructions. "What are you doing?" she hissed.

"Protecting you," he snapped.

"I don't need protecting!"

"That's not your decision."

As they approached the door to the room, Friday bit back an angry retort. She didn't want to alienate Paul, but she was used to taking care of herself. With Robin, it was a partnership of equals. Here, Paul was treating her like an inferior.

Like most of the rooms in the hospital, it was unguarded. The Circle of Thirteen obviously believed that if nobody from the outside world knew about it, then they were safe. Obviously, they weren't expecting people inside the hospital to move about freely.

The door was closed, but unbolted. Friday listened for a moment. From inside she thought she heard the sound of people talking. Taking a risk, she pushed the door open slightly and, while Paul watched the corridor, she put her eye up to the crack.

The arrangement inside the room was similar to the others on this floor—two rows of beds, one on either side of a central aisle—but where the patients in the beds of the last room had been comatose, the patients in this room were all jerking against leather straps that held them down—all except for the patient who had just been brought in. He was being strapped down by the two Brothers, but even he was showing signs of disturbance.

The man in the bed closest to the door was straining against his straps so hard that the tendons in his neck were standing starkly out. Strangely, his eyes were closed, and although his mouth was open, he was screaming soundlessly. The noise that Friday had heard coming from inside the room was from white-clad Sisters who sat at the head of each bed. They each held a book in their hands and were reading aloud. For a moment Friday assumed they were reading biblical passages, but the few snatches that she heard suggested she was wrong.

". . . for the will of the Circle is paramount above all things . . . "

". . . and those who serve the Circle have power above and over all others, and they will rule the Earth . . ."

". . . the enemies of the Circle will be cut down as wheat is cut down . . ."

". . . it has been prophesied that although the Circle of Thirteen will be opposed by those who do not believe, all opposition will be swept aside like dust . . ."

". . . the fire that burns the hottest cleanses the best . . ."

The Sisters were reading in calm, measured voices, and their voices all seemed to join together into a pleasant drone that formed a bizarre background to the soundless protest of the patients.

As she watched, the two Brothers moved away and Sister Berenice sat down at the newcomer's bed. He was twitching and beginning to pull against his restraints. She reached out, took a book
from the table by his head, and began to read. Friday could just
make out her calm, unhurried words: "In the beginning the Circle
of Thirteen was formed to lead and to guide mankind. For many
years the Circle ruled wisely and well, but the actions of men led
to their overthrow. The time is coming when the Circle will retake
their preeminent position. Kings and dignitaries will crumble and
fall before the forces of the Circle, and you are an important part
of that . . ."

The two Brothers were heading toward the door, so Friday
pulled it closed and backed down the corridor, leading Paul back to
the room they had recently left. They hid in the recessed doorway,
prepared to slip inside if the Brothers came their way, but the two
men headed off in the opposite direction, toward the stairs.

"What are they doing?" Paul asked, intrigued despite himself.

"I'm beginning to work it out," Friday whispered. "When the
people in this room begin to show signs of moving, they are taken
down the corridor, to a room where they are read to. Their heads
are filled with the Circle's aims while they're waking from their
unnatural sleep and vulnerable. Presumably, that's how the Circle
can rely on its people—they've been somehow persuaded that they
all believe—but how do they get into this room? What does the
Doctor do to them that sends them into that deep sleep in the first
place?"

She looked at Paul. He shook his head.

"Don't ask me," he said. He took her upper arm and pulled.
"Come on—we need to get out of here. I think we've seen enough."

* * *

CRUSOE PUSHED PAST his friend to see what was on the other side of the pantry door. He was met with smoke, backlit by flickering yellow and orange light, drifting along the corridor toward what he guessed was the kitchen.

"You're right," he said grimly. "The house is on fire, and I don't think it was an accident."

Defoe shook his head. "The only two things that can set a deserted house on fire are lightning and arson, and I don't think this current cold snap is conducive to thunderstorms."

"It's the Circle," Crusoe said. "They're cleaning up after themselves. They must have realized that the only things the Countess of Lichfield could tell us were the real name of Lord Sebastos and where he lived. They must have known we would investigate."

"And by setting the place on fire they've confirmed that there's something here for us to find." Defoe glanced through the doorway again. "We need to get out of here, and quickly."

Crusoe glanced toward the cellars. "I don't know about you, but I don't particularly fancy going back."

"Agreed. Forward it is, then."

They moved along the corridor. The smoke grew thicker, and Crusoe could feel it clawing at the back of his throat and stinging his eyes. The heat grew more intense as well. Given the weather outside, a decent fire was a welcome thing, but this was too intense, too dangerous.

From somewhere up ahead he heard the crack of timber splitting in the heat.

The kitchen was a large room lined with dusty, empty shelves and rectangular porcelain sinks. Defoe was halfway across to a doorway on their left that, Crusoe reckoned, led out into the garden, when Crusoe called him back.

"Daniel! Look!" he coughed.

He pointed to a bucket filled with water. A thin rime of ice on top was already melting away. The water looked brackish and stale, but Crusoe had no intention of drinking it. Instead, he tore at the sleeve of his jacket. When the seams ripped he dipped the material in the water, then tied it around his head so that it covered his mouth. Breathing was difficult through the wet cloth, but the water absorbed the smoke, meaning that at least breathing was an option.

Defoe nodded. Quickly, he did the same.

The two of them moved to the garden door, but when Defoe tried the handle it was locked. He put his shoulder against it and pushed, then took a few steps back and made a run at it, but all he got in return was a bruised shoulder. Crusoe tried kicking it, but the door didn't even shift slightly.

"There's something up against it on the other side," Defoe said, his voice muffled by the wet cloth.

"Let's hope it's just a pile of rubbish, rather than a deliberate attempt by the Circle's agents to trap us," Crusoe replied.

He glanced around. Through the thickening smoke he noticed another door directly opposite. It probably led back into the house. He caught Defoe's shoulder and pointed. Defoe nodded, but what Crusoe could see of his face above the cloth was grim. He knew, like Crusoe knew, that the bulk of the fire was through there as well. They would be risking their lives, but if they didn't go to the fire, then the fire would surely come to them.

The moment Crusoe opened the door a wall of hot air and smoke pushed it fully open. Through the doorway he could see orange and yellow tongues of flame licking across the ceiling of the corridor. The plaster cracked as he watched, almost like ice on a lake, and the varnish on the woodwork crisped and turned black.

Together they ran into the fire.

The heat mauled them like some rabid beast, and the smoke was so thick that it was impossible to see more than a few feet ahead.

Sparks drifted lazily past, borne on the breeze they had created just by opening the door. He and Defoe automatically reached out and grabbed at each other's jacket so they could stay together. Crusoe could even feel the terrible warmth coming up through the soles of his boots—that, and the vibration of falling timbers from somewhere deep in the house. He had a sudden vision of the ballroom in flames, and the star-field painting peeling and vanishing. If there had been any clues there, they were liable to be lost to the conflagration.

Defoe stumbled and tripped. His grip, hard on Crusoe's jacket, pulled Crusoe down as well. As soon as his hands touched the floor he could feel blisters forming. He rolled onto his back, letting the material of his jacket absorb the heat, but he and Defoe rolled in opposite directions, and suddenly a curtain of smoke hung between them.

"Daniel!" Crusoe yelled, pulling the wet cloth from his mouth for a moment, but the crashing of timbers and the crackling of the fire was too loud. If Defoe was calling him, then he couldn't hear the man's voice.

The cloth itself was almost bone-dry now, and the smoke coated his mouth and nostrils with the bitter taste of soot. He could even feel his eyes drying out in the heat.

He looked around desperately, either for his friend or for a way out, but there was nothing but shifting smoke all around him. He took a few steps and then stopped. What if he was heading directly into the heart of the fire? He tried to work out whether one side of his face was hotter than the other, but they were both burning. It was like the sunburn he'd had back on the island before he'd learned to tie a cloth over his head. He was afraid that his clothes and hair might suddenly catch fire, the way that he'd heard hay-stacks could spontaneously combust in high summer.

A shadow loomed up through the smoke and the sparks. He thought for a second that it was Defoe, but it was too big. A hand reached out for him. It took him a few moments to realize that it was John Caiaphas. Segment W's head of security grabbed his shoulder and pulled him roughly away. A rope was tied around Caiaphas's waist, and someone out of sight was pulling it taut, showing them the way back to safety.

"Daniel's in here!" he shouted into Caiaphas's ear, but he could hardly hear the words himself.

Caiaphas nodded. *Got him already!* he mouthed.

The journey out seemed to take forever, and by the time they got outside the mansion Crusoe's eyes felt like twin coals set into his eye sockets. His clothes were smoldering, and he thought his hair probably was as well. The coolness of the night was shocking.

Defoe was already outside, being looked after by several other Increment personnel. His face was dark with soot. Wordlessly, he passed him a cup of water.

Crusoe turned around and looked at the house. One wing was already consumed, its timbers black and skeletal against the hungry flames, but the other wing was so far almost untouched. And, if he had his bearings properly, that was the wing with the ballroom.

"We need to get you out of here," Caiaphas said, pulling at Crusoe's shoulder.

"No," Crusoe said firmly, suppressing a cough. "We need to rescue that half of the house. There are clues left behind there that we need to retrieve."

Caiaphas stared at him for a few moments. "Are you sure, lad?"

"I'm sure."

"Good enough." The big man turned to his men. "Get buckets and anything else that will hold water. The Thames is just down at the end of the gardens. If the fire hasn't melted the edge, then get burning timbers and move them onto the ice. Bring as much water as possible and *put that fire out!*"

* * *

THEY GOT TO the library without being noticed.

Friday was still bothered by what she had seen. She felt like she had bits and pieces of the story, but she couldn't work out how to put them together to form a coherent whole. Somewhere in there, however, was the secret that cut to the heart of what the Council of Thirteen was doing.

She glanced at the multicolored oils on the table by the window. They had to be important as well, but she wasn't sure how they fit in.

Paul pushed past her to take a look out of the window. He put his hands up to the frame and pressed slightly—not enough to push it out, but enough to make it move an inch or so. "It looks like the weather over the years has weakened the plaster," he said thoughtfully. "There must have been a hole somewhere for the rain to seep in."

"We mustn't let the frame and the glass fall into the garden. Someone will hear it."

He nodded. "I'll try to push it out at the top; you get your hand around the frame and hold it."

It only took a few pushes to weaken the grip of the mortar. The frame began to topple outward, and Paul quickly slid his hand through the widening gap and caught it. Friday did the same on the other side. Together they managed to work the window back and forth until the bottom edge loosened. Finally, they were able to pull the frame inside the room and rest it on the floor.

"Well done," he said admiringly.

Friday glanced out the window, checking to see if anyone was in the garden. She already knew it was night—it was some kind of legacy of living on the island that she could always tell what time it was, even if she couldn't see the sun. The air was cold but clear. A few clouds scudded across the sky, illuminated by a half-moon.

She didn't spot anybody outside. She leaned out farther and checked the outside of the house—there seemed to be a lot of projecting ledges and decorative features that they could use to climb down.

"Are you ready for this?" she challenged.

He raised an eyebrow. "Of course I am—I'm trained for this."

Friday threw one leg over the edge and then twisted her body around until she was facing back into the room. She took a deep breath and clamped her hands on the bottom of the window frame, then brought her other leg over and let herself be pulled downward. Within moments she was searching for finger- and footholds as she climbed down toward the garden.

Glancing up, she could see that Paul was following her. He did seem to know what he was doing.

In under a minute Friday was on the ground. Still there was nobody there to see them. She looked around the garden, trying to form a mental map. There was an iced-over ornamental pond a few feet away, and a high-roofed greenhouse over to her right, about a hundred yards away. If they sprinted over there, they could take shelter and take stock.

Paul jumped the last few feet. He landed lightly by her side.

They both started to run across the formal gardens toward the greenhouse. Friday became aware that Paul was trying to get ahead of her. He was turning this into a race! She drew on her reserves of energy and pulled ahead, getting to the building just a fraction of a second ahead of him. They took shelter in its shadow and waited. There was no hue and cry from behind them. They hadn't been seen.

The building's windows had been whitewashed so there was no looking in or out. Friday led the way around the corner, so they were out of sight of the house. There was a closed door near where they stood.

Friday looked back at the house. It was the first time she had actually seen it from the outside—an impressive white stone building with two wings extending from a central circular hub, a bell tower and cloisters running along the sides. There was no sign to say what it was, or anything to suggest where it was. The two of them would have to go a lot farther to find that out.

She assumed that there would be some kind of wall around the grounds of the building, and a guard at the main gate. This was, after all, a Circle of Thirteen base. That meant she and Paul would have to go over the wall, but first they would have to find it.

Before she could decide on a direction, Paul caught her wrist and pulled her away from the shelter of the whitewashed building. He sprinted across the ground, away from the house. She pulled herself free from his grip, but he didn't falter. He just kept running, assuming that she was behind him. Furiously, she followed.

There was a line of trees ahead, and when Paul was a few feet inside their cover he stopped and turned around. He barely seemed to be breathing heavily.

"What the hell do you think you're doing?" Friday hissed as she came to a halt, panting.

"Trying to get away from the house," he said. "That's the plan."

"You were just running blindly! You didn't know which direction the wall was in!"

He shrugged. "The house is in the center of the grounds. The wall will run around the grounds. If you run away from the house you're running toward the wall. It's not difficult."

"Robin would have done some reconnaissance first," she said darkly.

"Then Robin would have been wasting his time."

Friday opened her mouth to say something cutting in defense of her friend, but before she could form the words a bell began ringing back in the house.

"They've spotted our absence." Paul's face was grim. "We need to move quickly, before they can send out search parties."

Before Friday could come up with any counterplan, he began to run through the trees. Suppressing a curse, she followed.

The frozen roots of the trees seemed to clutch at her feet as she moved, and her breath streamed out behind her in a misty cloud. She could hear shouts, as well as the mournful pealing of the bell. Up ahead, through the trees, there was nothing but darkness. Darkness that soon resolved itself into a stone wall, about ten feet high, on the other side of a cleared area of ground.

Paul was about to dash across the open ground without stopping when Friday caught his arm and pulled him back. He almost slipped on the icy spears of grass.

"What the—?" he snapped, but Friday punched him in the stomach. He folded up with a surprised *"Whoof!"*

Moments later the sound of people running toward them, and of metal slapping against leather, came from both left and right.

Paul's face twisted in annoyance. "So close!" he hissed.

Friday looked to where the Brothers were approaching from, and then at the wall. "I'll pull them away," she said, the words coming barely after the thought. "You get over that wall and get a message to Segment W. Tell them where I am."

"I can't do that! My job is to protect you!"

"We can't both get out! One of us has to stay behind!"

"Then I'll stay and distract them," he said urgently.

The sound of their pursuers was getting closer now.

Friday shook her head. "If I escape and you stay, then my father will do anything to get me back. If *you* escape and *I* stay, then he's less likely to send anyone after you." She smiled up at him. "He may not even notice."

Paul stared down at her, then glanced at the wall. He obviously knew she was right, but he didn't want to admit it. After a few long moments he nodded abruptly. "You're brave. I hate abandoning you."

"Then make it up to me by bringing back a rescue party."

"All right. I'll come back—I promise."

Before either he or she could change their mind, Friday stepped out deliberately into the open space between the trees and the wall.

"There she is!" The shout was instant.

Friday glanced to both sides as if startled. She turned and ran quickly back into the trees, noticing as she did so that Paul had vanished.

Friday sprinted as fast as she could away from the wall. Within a few seconds she could hear the Brothers chasing after her.

She hoped that they were so intent on capturing her that they didn't bother leaving anyone behind. If they did, then Paul might not be able to get over the wall, and if he didn't, then how would Robin ever know where she was?

CHAPTER ELEVEN

When they got back to the Globe, Crusoe pleaded tiredness and hunger and went off to the refectory rather than join the others in briefing Sir William. Daniel Defoe waved him off with a casual "I shall see you later." Crusoe suspected, from the look that Defoe gave him, that his friend knew Crusoe wanted to avoid seeing Sir William for a while.

He did as he had said—went to the refectory and grabbed some food—but he didn't intend to go to bed afterward. Instead, while he sat by a window and ate a plate of stew that he hardly tasted, he watched and listened. Eventually, after an hour or so, there was a sudden flurry of activity outside. A coach pulled up. Crusoe couldn't see who climbed in, but he assumed that it was Sir William, undoubtedly on his way to brief the king on what had been discovered. Within moments it had clattered away.

And that gave Crusoe the opportunity he needed.

He left the refectory and crossed the central space of the Globe, heading for the stairway that led up to Sir William's office. There were no guards—if you were inside the Globe, then it was assumed that you were permitted to go anywhere. He glanced around casually. Nobody was watching. Quickly, he climbed the stairs and walked around the curved corridor to the audience box that now served as Sir William's office. Crusoe knocked on the door, just in case Defoe, John Caiaphas, or Isaac Newton were still in there talking. There was no response. He quickly slipped inside and closed the door behind him.

Sir William kept his desk and meeting table almost fanatically neat, but what Crusoe wanted was in an ornate case on a stand in a corner. The case was locked, but that posed little challenge to Crusoe. He and Friday had both learned a lot from John Caiaphas's men over the past few months.

He stood before the case for a long moment, feeling the conflict in his heart. He knew that the thing it contained might be his only hope of saving Friday, but he also knew that if he opened that case, then he would be crossing a line. He had gotten very close to that line already, by disobeying Sir William's orders not to go onto the bridge and by going to question the Countess of Lichfield. Perhaps he had even stepped briefly across it. If he opened that case, however, then he would be making a straight choice. He would be throwing away everything that Segment W had given him for the vague possibility that he might see something inside the orb. There would be no going back.

He was being torn in two. On the one hand he wanted— *needed*—to do something to save Friday himself, but on the other hand the resources of Segment W might just be the best chance she had. Should he go it alone, or should he depend on his friends?

Eventually, he took a deep breath—and stepped backward. Sighing, he turned toward the door.

"I was hoping you would make the right decision," a voice said.

Crusoe took a startled breath as Sir William stepped out of the shadows by the door.

"I didn't—I mean, I *wouldn't*—" He frowned. "The carriage—it wasn't you?"

"I sent Daniel in my place," Sir William said. His voice was calm where Crusoe had expected it to be angry. He stared curiously at Crusoe for a moment. "You want to save your friend. I understand that. I have had friends myself, and they have sometimes found themselves in serious trouble." A shadow seemed to cross his face. "I have *lost* friends that way—lost them forever. Believe me, I understand your feelings on this. I understand your need to do *something*, no matter how disruptive or foolish." He walked across the room and sat down heavily at his desk. "But I cannot run an organization, an executive arm of the State, in which my agents are allowed to ignore orders and go off alone. We stand together, or we fall apart. I have given you enough rope, young Mr. Crusoe, and I have watched carefully as you have deliberately formed a noose from it for your own neck. I hoped that you would refrain from putting your head through the noose. Am I right? Are you with the Segment? Will you follow my orders from now on, even if they seem to go against your own personal desires?"

Crusoe nodded once, abruptly. His heart still burned with the desire to rescue Friday, but he knew now that he would have more chance of doing that as part of Segment W than he would alone. It was a bitter pill to swallow for someone who had come to rely on his own resources—and those of his friend—for so long, but perhaps he needed to accept now that, for the first time in a long time, he had more than one friend.

"Then let us see what we can do to get Miss Friday back from wherever the Circle of Thirteen has taken her."

"How do we do that?" Crusoe asked.

"By trying to understand what it is that they are trying to achieve." Sir William nodded decisively. "I understand that John Caiaphas's men have secured at least some of that ceiling painting

you were so concerned about. Let us see whether Isaac Newton has
discovered anything from it."

"And quickly," Crusoe said. "Please."

THE SOUND OF frozen twigs and branches breaking underfoot
echoed through the woods with every step Friday took. She could
hear the sounds of pursuit behind her, and they were getting
closer.

That was good, on the one hand. It meant she was pulling attention away from Paul's escape. On the other hand, she would rather
not get recaptured herself, if she could help it.

She realized unhappily that circumstances meant the choice
was being taken out of her hands.

Friday stepped out of the shadow of a tree, and something
ahead of her suddenly moved. She froze in place. For a second she
thought—no, she *knew*—that they had found her. She took a slow
step backward, into the shelter of the tree's shade. . . .

A twig snapped beneath her heel.

Up ahead, a deer suddenly bolted, startled by her presence.
Friday felt herself relax slightly, knowing it wasn't her pursuers,
but the sudden flurry of activity as the deer ran away that alerted
the Brothers that something was amiss. They started shouting and
running—not toward Friday, but after the deer.

Friday waited until the sounds of their pursuit faded, and then
she moved in the opposite direction.

After a few minutes she emerged from the trees near the
building with the whitewashed windows—the one that looked
like a greenhouse. She glanced around carefully, but there was
nobody else in sight. Beyond the single-story building, the hospital sat in pure white splendor, but Friday certainly wasn't

going back there. She might, however, take refuge in the nearer building.

Approaching quietly and cautiously, she pushed the door open. It was mercifully silent. She slipped inside, closing the door slowly behind her.

Despite the coldness outside, the greenhouse was warm. Uncomfortably warm, and humid as well. It reminded Friday of the island. As she moved farther away from the door, she realized the windows were blacked out, shrouding the greenhouse in complete darkness as well.

Standing in the black, Friday's other senses came into play. She could smell something sharp and unpleasant in the air. Whatever it was, it made her nose tingle. It smelled a bit like Isaac Newton's laboratory. Were chemical experiments going on in here? She could also hear a vague rustling noise, like wind in dry leaves or vines hanging in the high roof. The problem was, she couldn't feel any wind.

Her instincts told her that it was more dangerous inside the greenhouse than it was outside, but it was too late. She had made her choice.

Above the rustling she could hear footsteps outside crunching on the gravel path as they got closer. She moved farther into the warm embrace of the darkness, just in case whoever it was decided to check inside.

It occurred to her that her eyes should have adjusted to the darkness by now, but she still couldn't see anything. There wasn't even a scrap of light coming in from outside.

Something made a noise, directly above her head. It sounded like cloth flapping in the breeze, but there was still no wind.

She moved closer to where she thought the center of the room was, but suddenly felt she was walking on something slippery and sticky at the same time.

The sharp, horrible smell was getting worse, making her eyes water.

Suddenly, the background rustle in the room intensified a hundredfold. All around her she could hear the same abrupt flapping noises coming from up high near the roof and she thought she knew what they were. Wings. The sound of wings being stretched and exercised. That meant the stuff that she was stepping in was . . . well, she hardly liked to think.

But what birds would be kept in the dark?

The stretching of wings above her suddenly turned into an explosion of noise as whatever it was up there decided to take flight. Friday didn't know whether it was a few of them or all of them— she didn't even know what they were—but within moments the air around her was full of flying objects, all heading in different directions but somehow managing to miss one another and her as well.

Friday tried to move, but she was moving over the sticky stuff and she didn't want to fall. She was struggling to keep her footing when something brushed against her hair. She jerked away instinctively, but something else touched her cheek for a second—not feathers, but something warm and soft, like velvet.

She felt as if she were at the center of a tornado. Bodies whirled around her in a dense cloud, and she could feel the breeze from their wings stirring up the unpleasant atmosphere.

Abruptly, she was hit in the chest and sent staggering backward. Her heel slid on whatever was covering the floor, and she almost fell. She just managed to catch her balance, but whatever was on her chest started buffeting her with its wings. The blows came thick and fast against her ribs, her neck, her head. She could hardly even think, it was so disorienting. Instinctively, she grabbed for whatever was attached to her, and her fingers closed around a warm body covered with matted fur, about the size of a cat. She could feel its ribs, and the rapid flutter of its heart, but it wasn't crying out, or growling, or making any noise that she could hear apart from the fluttering of its wings. She got her thumbs underneath it and pushed it away. It flashed past her face, just catching her forehead with . . . with what? A finger? A claw? She didn't know.

Friday could feel panic unexpectedly fluttering inside her own chest, nearly matching the fluttering of the beast's heart when she touched it. She took a deep breath and held it in, pushing down on the panic until she could move once more.

She stepped forward gingerly, cursing under her breath. She had completely lost track of which way she was facing, or how far into the greenhouse she had gone. She had to try to reach the door, but she risked walking farther and farther into the greenhouse, and into the dark heart of whatever was living in there.

She didn't know what to do. She wished again for Robin—the two of them together seemed to be able to work things out instinctively. Now it was just her, and she felt the loss.

Light suddenly washed over her as the door to the greenhouse burst open. The moonlight outside was thin, but it almost blinded her. She thought she saw bulky shapes in the doorway.

"Get her out of there," a calm, gentle voice said. "Try not to get scratched or bitten—there is nothing I can do for you if that happens, apart from killing you quickly and mercifully."

The bulky shapes plunged into the greenhouse and toward Friday. Rough hands grabbed her and manhandled her back to the brightly lit opening. As they got closer to the moonlit gardens, she turned her head and stared into the darkness, trying to get one last glimpse of whatever it was they had disturbed.

For less than a second, something flashed through the wedge of light cast across the greenhouse floor. It was gray-black in color, and it had thin, leathery wings that, at full stretch, would have been wider than John Caiaphas was tall. Its face was wrinkled, like a screwed-up ball of black paper, and its ears were the same size as its head. Its mouth was a mass of needle-like teeth.

It was a bat, but larger than any bat that Friday had seen on the island. There the bats had been the size of mice, and timid. These creatures were huge, and vicious.

The two men threw Friday onto the ground outside. The greenhouse door slammed behind them.

"Stand still," Doctor Mors's voice said. She could see him as a hunched shadow with an elongated beak, like some bizarre bird. "Let me see your faces and your hands. Now—turn around." After a moment he went on: "You are safe. There are no cuts or scratches. Now, pick the girl up and let me examine her."

Large hands pulled Friday to her feet. She felt a gloved hand take her chin and move her head left and right. As her eyes grew more accustomed to the moonlight, she saw the dark holes of Mors's mask staring down at her.

"You are fortunate," he said. "You, too, are unhurt. One bite or scratch from my tropical friends in there and you would be sentenced to an unpleasant death. They are carnivorous, and they carry a poison in their mouths that is invariably fatal." He let go of her. "It seems that luck is on your side. Well—relatively speaking. You will still go through the recruitment process into the Circle, and that is not pleasant. Also, your father would like to talk to you before your recruitment begins." He gestured to the two Brothers. "One of you take her back to her room, and this time chain her to her bed." He paused. "The other will go back inside. The boy must still be in there. Find him."

The two Brothers shared an uneasy glance. "But, Doctor Mors—"

"You would disobey my instruction?" His voice was calm, but Friday could feel the implacable force of his will in his tone.

"No, Doctor Mors." The two men shook their heads, looking at the ground like disobedient children.

"I shall let you choose which one takes the girl and which one goes inside," he said. "Oh, and if any of my little beauties are harmed in any way, then I shall let them feast on *both* of you."

A Month Before the Escape

The sun was hot and the horizon was just an indistinct line sepa-rating two similar shades of blue when Suriya heard a man begging for his life.

The retreating tide left pools behind in the rocks, and small crabs and fishes had taken up habitation there until the tide came in again. This was the fifth island that the Dark Nebula *had dropped anchor at in the past ten days, and she had persuaded Diran to accompany her on shore, knowing that the ship would be here at least until the next day. They were perhaps an hour away from the ship when they heard sounds coming from the other side of a rocky ridge. Quickly, they climbed to the top and looked over, keeping their heads low.*

They saw a gang of three pirates pushing a fourth one along the sand. His hands and feet were bound with ropes, and every time he fell they either kicked him until he got up again or dragged him along by the ropes until he screamed for them to stop. He was bleeding from scrapes and scratches all over his body, and he looked fright-ened. No, Suriya thought, he looked terrified.

She thought she recognized him as Delahey—a sailor from Brus-sels who had joined up with Red Tiberius's crew after the pirates raided his merchant ship. That had been five years ago, and he had been a faithful crewmember ever since. Until now, it seemed.

"It must be a punishment," Suriya whispered to Diran, "but what's he done wrong?"

Diran shook his head. "I don't know."

The leader of the pirate gang was Mohir. The other two pirates were particular favorites of her father. One of them had thin mustaches hanging down on each side of his mouth and an equally thin beard hanging between them, while the other was a mute with a vivid scar running through his useless left eye. They were both carrying spades.

On the beach below, Mohir and his two companions pushed their captive to the ground. He lay there, panting and staring up at the sky as if it might be the last thing he ever saw.

Mohir said something to the other two. They began to dig a hole in the sand, choosing an area wetted by the tide a few hours before so it was easily dug out and the sides of the hole didn't crumble in. Closer toward Suriya and Diran, the sand was dry and it was almost impossible to dig a hole of any size.

"They're burying him?" Diran murmured. "Alive or dead?"

"Alive to start with, I think," Suriya said quietly. "Do you think we should do something?"

"Is there anything we can do?"

She frowned. "My father is the captain of the Dark Nebula. If I tell them to stop, then they might listen to me."

"Possibly," Diran admitted, "but why?"

"To save his life. He's always been nice to me. He gives me sweet-meats sometimes, if he's been ashore at port."

"He's nice to you because you're the captain's daughter. He's trying to buy favor with the captain. I've seen some of the things he's done to captives, and even to women ashore when the rest of the crew are enjoying some time on land. He's an animal. If he dies, I won't cry." Diran gestured to the men down on the sand. "And neither will they, apparently."

Suriya gazed at him for a long moment. There was real hatred and bitterness in his voice. What, she wondered, had Delahey done to Diran to make him react like this?

It took the pirates a while to dig a hole deep enough to take their prisoner standing up. All the time they dug, he pleaded with them, prayed to whatever gods pirates had, and sobbed to himself. All the time, they said nothing in return. By the time they finished the sun was low in the sky.

Finally, Mohir gestured to Delahey to get into the hole. He refused, shaking his head violently and babbling. The pirates picked him up and dropped him in. Before he could climb out they started shoveling sand back into the hole around him, blinding and choking him so that he couldn't escape. Not that there was anywhere to escape to.

When they finished the sand was up to his neck. Only his head emerged above it.

"At least give me a quick death!" Delahey screamed. "Five years I've spent on that ship, working for Red Tiberius. Doesn't that earn me something?"

"You disobeyed the captain's orders," Mohir said finally. His voice was deep and grating, like rocks grinding together. "That earns you death."

"I only went into a cave, for the Lord's sake! A cave! It's not like I killed a shipmate or stole some booty!"

"You went into the cave on top of the hill here—the cave that the captain's been searching for, for months now. That earns you a bad death. Nobody goes into that cave but the captain—that's what he said."

"I thought there was treasure in there!" Delahey cried. "I just wanted a few gold coins to spend the next time we go ashore, but there weren't no treasure—just mushrooms growin' everywhere. Black mushrooms, like nothin' I'd ever want to eat. I dunno what the captain wants wiv 'em, I honestly don't!"

Mohir took a small jar out of his leather vest. It looked almost delicate in his hands. He pulled a cork out of the top, then poured something out of it onto Delahey's head. The buried man began to sob as Mohir walked away, making a trail that led up toward the rocks of the hillside. Fortunately, it wasn't in the direction of Suriya and Diran.

Mohir vanished for several minutes. The other two pirates passed the time by kicking sand into Delahey's face and watching him choke.

When Mohir came back he didn't have the jar anymore. Without saying anything he began to walk off. The two other pirates called after him. They seemed to want him to stay and watch, but he just gestured for them to follow. Reluctantly, and with protests, they left.

The buried Delahey called after them plaintively, but they didn't turn around or come back. Eventually, they were out of sight.

Suriya stared at the trail of liquid leading into the rocks. She had a terrible feeling that she knew what was going to happen. "That's honey, isn't it? Or something like honey?"

Diran didn't reply. His face was grim.

The edge of the trail, where it vanished into the rocks, had changed color. It was red now, and it seemed to ripple.

"Those are ants, aren't they?" she said.

"Soldier ants," Diran said. Despite the fact that the pirates had left, he kept his voice to a whisper. Perhaps he didn't want Delahey to hear them, and beg them to dig him up.

"They bite," she said.

"They bite," he agreed.

The swarm of ants was almost halfway toward Delahey now. He knew something was happening because he kept trying to turn his head around, but he couldn't twist it that far.

"Despite what he's done in the past," Suriya whispered, "we can't just let him be . . . eaten! Not for just finding a cave full of mushrooms!" She made as if to get up, but Diran put his hand on her arm, pushing her down again.

"If your father does this to a man who went inside a cave when he wasn't supposed to, then how do you think he'll feel about us freeing a man he sentenced to death?"

"He wouldn't hurt me," Suriya said, shocked.

"No," Diran said quietly, "he wouldn't hurt you."

She thought fast. "We could tell him to run into the island. He could live here secretly."

"Your father will send someone back to check that he's dead. Your father is very careful about checking things. He leaves nothing to chance." Diran sighed and closed his eyes for a moment. "If you really want to help him, then get a stone and bash his brains out before the ants get to him. If not, we either watch or we leave him to it."

In the end, Suriya decided to watch. Perhaps the only thing worse than dying badly was dying badly alone. If the only thing she could do was to bear witness, then that's what she would do.

It took several hours before the sky was so dark that they couldn't see the pirate captive anymore, and another hour before his screams stopped. When they returned in darkness to the Dark Nebula it seemed not only that nobody had missed them but also that nobody mentioned Delahey's name. Not ever again.

CHAPTER TWELVE

C rusoe and Sir William found Isaac Newton standing on a pile of crates in the center of the Globe. He balanced precariously atop them while staring at the stage. All around him, Increment personnel and other Segment W employees stared curiously.

The ceiling from the deserted manor house had been painstakingly reassembled on the stage—set on its side so that it was visible from the auditorium. Chunks of masonry were missing, and others were charred or blistered, but John Caiaphas's men had saved a fair percentage of it.

Newton was making notes with a piece of charcoal in a small notebook. His gray, unkempt hair stuck out all around his head.

"Isaac," Sir William called. "A moment of your time, if you please."

Newton seemed not to hear for a moment, but then glanced down. With a series of leaps and slides that reminded Crusoe of the goats back on the island climbing down steep hills, he descended from the crates to the ground.

"You were correct, young man," he said, nodding toward Crusoe. "The painting on the ceiling matches very closely the diagram we found in the meeting room on the bridge."

"But does that allow you to decrypt it?" Sir William asked.

Newton nodded. "I had mostly broken the code already, but I was stuck on certain important elements." His face was grim. "The painting here has given me enough additional information to understand what the Circle of Thirteen wants and, more importantly, how they intend to achieve it."

His words hung in the cold air like the chimes of struck bells.

"Is there," Crusoe asked, "any hint as to where the Circle may have taken Friday?"

Newton shook his head sadly. "Not directly, no. I'm sorry."

Sir William glanced around. "Leave us!" he called, his voice cutting through the air of the theater like an actor proclaiming from the stage. The various Segment W personnel stopped what they were doing, turned around, and left without a word. Turning back to Newton, Sir William said, more softly, "Tell us."

"You will remember," Newton said, falling into what Crusoe recognized as his "lecturing" mode, "that where the painting above our heads shows stars, joined together in constellations that are unfamiliar to our eyes, the parchment contained words. The words are actually names, in a biliteral code." He shrugged. "The code was already known to me. A man named Francis Bacon developed it, some fifty years ago." His expression was grim. "What I have determined is that the coded words on the parchment are actually the names of *people*. Some of the names were familiar to me and others not, but I have discovered that some of them are nobility and some commoners, some are English and some foreign, but most importantly that some are dead, and they died under strange circumstances."

"The Duke of Wimbourne?" Crusoe said quietly, remembering the bones they found in the cellars, and the ducal seal on the ring.

"Indeed." Newton gazed at Crusoe with some interest. "I have also discovered that the lines that join the names indicate the order in which they have died or will die." He paused dramatically. "The diagram on the parchment and"—he pointed at the reconstructed sideways ceiling—"this painting are either predictions of, or plans for, murder."

"There are several different lines joining the names, or the stars," Sir William pointed out. "If these things are death lists, then surely there should be just the one line?"

"Not so," Newton replied. "I believe there are alternative paths. Let us say that, for instance, the death of one Giles Farnaby, gentleman, has to be followed by the death of the Duke of Wimbourne, but the death of the Duke of Wimbourne could be followed *either* by the death of a lady named Jane Willmer *or* the death of a man named Pierre Leblanc. Either would be an acceptable route through the constellation. I do not know who most of these people are, but these are names that I have decoded from the diagram."

From behind Crusoe, John Caiaphas's voice snorted. "This makes no sense. If you have a reason for killing someone, you kill them. You don't either kill one person or another person depending on, what? The wind direction? Whether or not the sun is shining? Assassination is a means to an end, not a multiple-choice questionnaire!"

"A good point," Newton said, rubbing his chin thoughtfully. "And this is where we find a link to Dr. John Dee's scrying orbs— of which we have one and the Circle has, I suspect, several. Dee wrote about ancient Babylonian prophecies, carved into the bases of statues of their gods. He also wrote that the orbs helped him translate these prophecies. They apparently say—although nobody apart from Dee ever managed to translate them—that if the stars can be 'made right' in some way, then great power will be bestowed on the person or people who achieved it. They will, for all practical purposes, rule the world and everyone in it. They will be made higher than kings or emperors."

"Absolutely ridiculous," John Caiaphas growled.

Sir William held up a hand to mollify him. "It doesn't matter whether it's ridiculous or not—it merely matters whether the Circle of Thirteen believes it. If this Babylonian prophecy is what is driving their actions, then we need to understand it." He waved to Newton to continue.

"I believe," Newton explained, "that the Circle of Thirteen, using esoteric calculations and obscure philosophies, has equated particular stars in the sky with particular people on the earth. They believe these people are actual embodiments, or representatives, of these stars. If they kill these people in the correct order, they believe they can change the stars and the constellations, and thus become all-powerful."

Crusoe glanced across at John Caiaphas. He seemed on the verge of bursting with anger.

There was silence as the four of them tried to come to terms with what Newton was saying.

"This is just an extension of astrology, surely?" Sir William observed. "Astrology tells us that the movements of the stars influence events on the earth. That implies if you change the stars, you can change events."

"And you change the stars by changing the people who embody those stars," Crusoe went on. He looked at the other three. "If you believe in all of this."

"It is astrology, yes, but not as we know it," Newton said. "The patterns here and on the parchment—they aren't the constellations we are familiar with, or the astrological signs that we know— Aries, Taurus, and so on. There have been many other astrological systems. The one being used by the Circle of Thirteen, you won't be surprised to find out, dates back to the Babylonians and the Chaldeans. Instead of animals such as the Ram and the Bull, they used other animals—real and legendary—that were more familiar to them."

"Such as . . . ?" Caiaphas asked.

"Hornets . . . snakes . . . bats . . ."

"Rhinoceroses?" Crusoe glanced at Sir William meaningfully.

Newton nodded. "Yes, I know of several ancient astrological systems that used rhinoceroses—which, to them, would have been mythical animals."

John Caiaphas suddenly frowned. "Giles Farnaby. Stung to death by hornets on a ship moored at Rotherhithe, seven months ago. I remember, because you asked me to investigate whether there was any threat to the *Great Equatorial* from hornets' nests in the area. Do you remember, Sir William? I didn't find any, which made me wonder about the death of Mr. Farnaby."

Sir William nodded grimly. "I do remember."

Another silence, broken by Crusoe. "Death by hornet sting and death under the hooves of a rhinoceros. That can't be a coincidence."

Newton nodded. "It would seem," he said, "that the Circle of Thirteen not only is using ancient Babylonian and Chaldean astrological charts to predict who to kill and in what order, so as to gain this mystical power that has been prophesied, but they are also using the creatures in those charts to *carry out* the deaths—no matter how difficult."

Crusoe cleared his throat. "I remember Friday telling me about something she saw on the island—the pirates using honey to attract ants to a man they wanted to torture. The ants followed the trail of honey and stung him to death." He felt a shiver run through him. "There are probably other things, known to the Circle of Thirteen, that can be used in the same way to attract hornets, or bats, to a person they want to kill."

Newton nodded, and opened his mouth to say something, but just then a man ran into the auditorium and toward them.

"I apologize," he called to Sir William as he ran, "but I thought you would want to know right away. One of the Increment has escaped from the Circle's clutches. He stole a horse and rode here, nearly killing the horse. He says that the girl—Miss Friday—is still there!"

"Assemble an attack force," Sir William snapped to Caiaphas. "As many men as you can spare from the king's protection. Get there as soon as possible." He turned to Crusoe. "Saddle two horses. Ride to the palace and intercept Daniel, then the two of you ride ahead of the force. Time is of the essence. If you can save your friend, then do so."

"Thank you," Crusoe gasped, and ran.

THE MANACLES WERE heavy on Friday's wrists, and they chafed her skin as she shifted, trying to get comfortable on the bed. The chains that fastened her to the bed frame added to the weight. Her mattress was as thin as her thumb, and she could feel the metal slats beneath it digging into her through the stuffing. Whichever way she turned, it hurt. That, she thought wearily, was probably the point.

She sighed, and tried to relax. Slowly, she breathed out, then back in. She did her best to clear her mind, setting the pain in her wrists and her back to one side: noticeable, but unimportant. Setting aside the anger at having been recaptured, the concern about what was happening to Paul Shadrach, and the worry about where Robin was proved more difficult, but she persevered. It wasn't as if she had much else to occupy her mind.

The noise of the bolt on her door sliding open broke her concentration. She opened her eyes just as the door swung open.

The shadow blocking the light from outside stood there for a few moments, watching her. Before it moved into the room she knew who it was.

Her father.

As he moved into the room—the *cell* she reminded herself—the light from the lantern on the wall caught his face. He looked older. Time had lined his face and added gray to his hair. He still looked like a pirate captain, however. It wasn't necessarily the gold chains around his neck, the gold rings on his fingers, or the gold earrings, although they helped. It was more the scars on his forehead and his cheeks.

He wore long red robes, covering his usual brocade jacket, black silk trousers, and heavy leather boots. The hood hung down behind him. His ponytail of hair hung down almost as far.

She stared at him, meeting his gaze and refusing to look abashed, or frightened. In fact, she found that she was amazingly calm inside. The possibility of this meeting happening had tormented her for so long that the actuality of its occurrence was almost a relief. Almost.

"Many years have gone past since you decided that life with me was not what you wanted," he said. His voice was as guttural as she remembered. The trace of an accent still tinged his words. "You shamed me by denying my wish that you marry Mohir, you shamed me by refusing the fatherly love that I offered, you shamed me by leaving my ship and my protection, you shamed me by replacing me—and Mohir—with another man, one not of my choosing, and you shamed me by fighting against me, hurting my crew and damaging my ship and my authority." His mouth twisted in anger, and his voice dropped even deeper. "And then, as if shaming me five times was not enough, you compounded your crimes by joining my enemies and setting yourself against the Circle of Thirteen." He closed his eyes momentarily as if to calm himself, but when he opened them again there was a spark of rage burning in them. "People who shame me once die but quickly. People who shame me twice die slowly and only after I have inflicted so much agony on them that they beg me to kill them." His voice was louder now, and more shrill, but the rage in his eyes seemed to fade over the course of a few seconds, replaced with . . . some emotion she couldn't identify. Love, perhaps? Or just uncertainty. "And yet you are my daughter. What would you have me do, Suriya? Tell me that, at least."

"My name is not Suriya—it is Friday," she said.

"What do you *want*, Suriya?"

"Let me live my life and choose my name," she said as calmly as she could. "Let me go. It's not a lot to ask."

"It is everything," he replied. "I have many powers. I have men standing by to satisfy my slightest order. My reach extends around the world. And yet, there are some things even I cannot do. That is one of them."

"Then what is the point of you being my father, or me being your daughter?" she asked softly. "Father, I made my choice. I live by it, or . . ."

"I gave you to Mohir, to be his wife," he said. "He could have made you happy. He could have given you riches."

"You gave me to him like you would give a silver chain or a gold bracelet," she cried. "I was a possession, to be exchanged to reward his loyalty!"

"Loyalty is rewarded," he pointed out. "Disloyalty is punished. That is what being a leader is all about."

"I didn't want riches," she said. Tears were stinging her eyes—tears she hadn't felt for years. She had thought all this was behind her. "I just wanted choices. Father, do whatever you have to. Do whatever you need to. But don't pretend that this is my fault, or that I have brought it down on myself. Whatever happens, it is your choice, not mine."

"This boy you travel with." Red Tiberius sounded genuinely curious. "Is he worth all of this?"

"Yes," she said firmly, "he is."

"Then where is he?"

"Robin will come for me," she said with certainty.

"Then Robin will die."

"We will die together."

Red Tiberius shook his head. "You will not die. The Circle of Thirteen has decided that you are more valuable alive, working for them. You will return to our enemies and you will report their secrets to the Circle. When it suits the Circle's purposes you will kill them, or anybody else whose death they require. The matter is out of my hands."

Friday shook her head violently. "I will never join the Circle. Nothing will make me!"

"You have no choice," he replied. "You will understand the Circle's aims and you will support its plans. If the Circle orders you to give your life to further its ambitions, then you will do this happily. As I would. As we all would."

"You speak about the Circle of Thirteen as if it is something . . . something separate. Surely you are one of the Thirteen? Robin saw you with the others, leaving the bridge through the tunnels. You rule the organization—you and them."

He shook his head. "You do not understand. The Circle is bigger than us. But you *will* understand, and soon." He made to leave, then turned back briefly. "It will hurt," he added. "I can promise you that—but after it is over you will know with every fiber of your heart that it was worth it." He smiled, for the first time. "It hurt me when I joined, but the fire that burns the hottest cleanses the most." And as he left the room, he threw behind him, almost casually, the words: "You are no longer my daughter, Suriya. I have no daughter."

It was only when the door shut that Friday realized two things: first, that she was sweating so much the mattress beneath her was wet, and second, that she had heard those words before. Not the words about not being his daughter—that was new, and almost a relief. No, it was the words about the fire that burns the hottest cleansing the most. She had heard them read by the Sisters earlier that day to the patients waking from their comatose states.

She'd been right in her conclusion earlier: this was all part of a process to take over peoples' minds, to influence them into becoming slaves of the Circle—and if she didn't escape quickly, then it was going to happen to her. . . .

CRUSOE REACHED DEFOE just as he was stepping out of a carriage in front of the Palace of Westminster. It took just a few moments to explain the situation.

"My apologies to the king!" Defoe shouted to a footman, and mounted the second horse.

Defoe led the way—not crossing the river but heading almost directly south. Their horses soon emerged from the smoky slums of London into bright sunlight and a world of frost-covered fields and hedgerows. Despite the urgency of their mission, Crusoe felt his spirits lift slightly as the cold air tingled in his lungs. They finally had a lead to where Friday was being kept.

The sound of their horses' hooves hitting the iron-hard ground rang out like rapid drumbeats, and the breath from the horses' nostrils drifted back behind them. The landscape flashed past in a series of tableaux: orchards, thatched cottages, copses of trees, the occasional windmill or watermill. A perfect image of England, ignorant of the rot beneath the skin of the apple.

Eventually, just when Crusoe thought they might be riding forever, they arrived in the area known as Tulse Hill. Defoe slowed down, obviously trying to work out where this strange hospital was. There weren't many large houses nearby, but there was one building on the hill itself: made of a white stone that seemed to glow in the early morning sunlight and with a roof of lead tiles. Most of it was hidden by a high wall made of the same stone. As soon as Defoe saw it he urged his horse on and galloped directly across the fields and up the hill, jumping any hedgerows that crossed his path. Crusoe followed, desperately trying to keep up.

At the top of the hill they came up hard against the white wall surrounding the house. It was too high to jump or even to easily climb. Defoe glanced over at Crusoe. "You go left; I'll go right. We need to find the gate."

Crusoe nodded and hauled on his horse's reins.

The trees had been cleared away from the wall for a distance of about thirty feet. There was no way of climbing a tree and getting over. The gate probably was their only option, but if this was a Circle base, then it would be guarded. Fiercely.

Turning a corner, he saw in the distance a gateway framed by two Greek-looking columns. He raced toward it.

The gates were wooden, studded with nails, and they looked thick. There were no gaps in them, no way that anyone could attract the attention of anyone inside. Of course, that meant nobody inside could see Crusoe or Defoe, either.

A bell hung at a height of about six feet above the ground—presumably to alert those inside that someone outside wanted to enter. Crusoe had a feeling, however, that ringing the bell would bring guards and that they would probably want to know what he wanted.

How to get in?

While Crusoe considered this, Defoe cantered up from the other side of the twin pillars. He took in the situation with a glance.

"We could collect branches from the trees, pile them up, and climb over," Crusoe suggested.

Defoe shook his head. "That would take too long. I suggest the direct approach. Follow my lead."

Defoe pulled his horse around until the horse was facing the left-hand gate. Crusoe did the same, so that he was beside Defoe and his horse was facing the right-hand gate.

Defoe twitched his reins, and his horse trotted up to the gate until its head was almost touching the wood. Crusoe was only a second behind him.

They shared a glance. Crusoe realized what Defoe was going to do, and when Defoe hauled back on his reins Crusoe did the same.

Their horses reared up together, pawing at the air. As the horses began to come down again, the two men dug their heels into the horses' sides. The animals lashed out, hitting the wooden gates dead center with their hooves. Instead of bursting open, the gates fell, their hinges pulling right out of the stone pillars. They hit the ground with a thud that Crusoe could feel through the ground.

Together they encouraged their horses to step carefully across the now-flattened gates. They both looked around, but for the moment there was no sign that anybody had heard the gates fall.

Crusoe noticed that his horse had to step down when it got to the far edge of the gate. It seemed that there was something beneath the wood. He glanced down and was shocked to see a hand projecting from underneath. Someone had been standing just inside the gate when it fell.

Defoe was staring down at the hand as well.

"I hope we've got the right place," he said.

The fingers on the hand were clenching and unclenching. Crusoe felt sick, but he couldn't stop to help. He had to find Friday—wherever she was.

They started to ride toward the large stone building. It had a central main section with two wings coming off it on either side. Staring at it now, Crusoe saw that it had the look of a church—there were cloisters running along the walls, a tower in the center that looked like it probably had bells hanging in it, and buttresses running along the sides of the roof, linking it to the main body.

"It looks like it used to be a monastery," Defoe called over his shoulder. "Many of them were taken away from the church by King Henry VIII and turned into hospitals."

Men in black suddenly spilled out of the building's main doors and from around the corners of the wings like ants from a nest. Some of them held crossbows; others held the strange new spring-loaded weapons that Crusoe and Friday had faced at Lord Sebastos's fort in Thanet, the ones that fired saw-edged metal discs. Instead of challenging Crusoe and Defoe, they opened fire straight away. Bolts and spinning discs carved their way through the air toward them.

"That clears up the question of whether or not we're at the right place!" Crusoe shouted.

His mind raced with plans and options. They had caught the element of surprise by bursting through the gates, but they couldn't afford to let the Circle regain the initiative. They had to do something unexpected.

"Head for the main doors!" he yelled. "Follow my lead!"

He raced across the intervening ground. Two Circle guards were in the way. One had a crossbow and was struggling to reload; the other had a disc-gun, but didn't seem sure how to use it. His discs were going wide, posing more of a danger to his friends than to Crusoe and Defoe.

Crusoe rode straight at them, knocking them aside like bowling pins.

He could hear the hoofbeats of Defoe's steed behind him as his own horse galloped up the five broad steps that led to the doors. He could also hear something else. Turning his head, he saw three mounted horses come around the corner of the building. Their riders were carrying wickedly curved swords.

Before he could even react, the riders raised their swords and began to charge.

CHAPTER THIRTEEN

Friday lay on the hard mattress, staring at the cracked ceiling and feeling a heaviness in her heart. She couldn't see a way out of this, short of Doctor Mors bending over her to check that she was still "suitable," whatever that meant, and the key to her padlocks falling out of his pocket and into her hand. Realistically, she couldn't put her faith in that happening, but what else was there to hope for? She wanted desperately to believe that Robin was out there, coming to her rescue, but she knew that he might be dead, and she might be alone.

The sound of the bolt on her door sliding back broke her out of the self-destructive cycle of despair she had fallen into. She raised her head as the door swung open.

Mohir was standing in the doorway. His dark skin, bald head, gold earrings, and gold tooth were unmistakable.

He stared at her for a long while. His expression showed a shifting set of emotions—desire, hatred, confusion, and concern. It was like a mask illuminated by a flickering candle flame, the shadows crawling and jumping across its surface like something alive.

"You've grown," he said. "You're not a girl anymore."

"Running from people who want to kill you will do that," she pointed out. "I had to grow up fast."

"I can save you," he said finally. He glanced over his shoulder, as if he was scared of being overheard.

"I don't need saving," she said.

"Then you don't understand what's going to happen to you."

"Apparently, I'm going to join the Circle of Thirteen," she said.

"No," he responded. "You're going to be *recruited* into the Circle. There is a difference." His English had improved since the last time she had met him.

"Have *you* been recruited?" she asked, suddenly interested. "What happens? What do they do?" When he didn't answer, she went on: "What does it have to do with that blue mark that recruits have on their bodies?"

"I was never recruited," he said eventually. "Your father keeps his crew loyal to him, not to the Circle. He wants to be sure that we will obey his orders above all others." He laughed—a noise that sounded more like a snort. "Even after his recruitment into the Circle, your father is a very intelligent man. He always makes sure he has an escape route. I've noticed that. With some people, the recruitment process doesn't work as well as with others."

"So he *has* been recruited?" she asked.

He looked back along the corridor. "Say you will marry me," he said, voice lowered, "and I will get you out of here. We can run away—wherever you want. Just say you will be mine willingly. Name a country and I will take you there and treat you like a princess."

Friday searched her feelings, but there wasn't even the slightest flicker of desire to agree with him, not even just to get herself out of there. She would stay true to herself, even if it meant death. Or recruitment—whatever that might be.

"No," she said quietly but firmly. "I will never marry you. Whatever happens to me, it will be better than being married to you."

He scowled. "Then damn you to hell. You must live with the consequences of your choice."

He reached out for something on the other side of the door frame. When his hand came back into view it held a dish. Inside the dish was something she initially mistook for a flower but quickly realized was some kind of strange mushroom, of a type she had never seen before. Its black stalk was tall and thin, and the knobbly black head on top was shaped roughly like a ball. Mohir was holding it as if it were made of glass and might shatter if he dropped it.

"What is that for?" she asked.

He turned and reached out with his other hand for the thing the mushroom had been sitting on—a tall, three-legged stool. He walked forward and placed the stool just by the head of her bed, then set the dish and the black mushroom down on it. She could see now that the mushroom was growing out of a layer of dark, wet soil in the dish.

"This is what will recruit you," he said. He stared at her, as if trying to memorize her face for the last time. "This is what will change you." He took a step back into the corridor. "After you have been recruited, if the Circle orders you to be my wife, then you will do it happily. I will ask your father for that, as a reward for my loyalty."

"Then why try to persuade me now?"

He winced—an unexpected expression, and one she had never seen on his face before. "Because," he said, "I wanted you to choose to be with me yourself." He shrugged. "But if I can't have your mind, then I will settle for your body."

He began to close the door, but Friday called out to him. "Mohir—please. Tell me one thing. Just one."

He stood in the doorway, staring at her impassively.

"Diran—the Indian boy. Do you remember him? What happened to him after . . . after I escaped?"

"Of all the things you could ask me, you ask this?"

"He was my friend."

Silently, Mohir shook his head and closed the door.

Friday stared at the mushroom he had left behind. She didn't know what she expected it to do, but it just sat there. Was the ball-like head more swollen than it had been a few moments before? She wasn't sure.

"Have you heard of a type of plant, a mushroom of sorts, that is the color of a starless night, with a head that looks like a ball . . . It is much prized by some. A treasure, if plants can be a treasure." Her father's words drifted back to her from her time on the *Dark Nebula*. Had he known about this thing, even then?

"You went into the cave on top of the hill here—the cave that the captain's been searching for, for months now. That earns you a bad death. Nobody goes into that cave but the captain—that's what he said." Mohir's words, again from long ago. Did these mushrooms grow inside that cave? Was that why Red Tiberius kept going back to the island?

There was shouting from somewhere outside, breaking the hush that usually blanketed the hospital. For a moment she thought it might be Robin, coming to rescue her, and her heart started to beat faster, but then she realized that it was more likely to be a disruptive patient downstairs, someone in pain from an amputation or worse.

She kept staring at the mushroom, trying not to blink. She was scared that if she took her eyes off it, then something would happen. The problem was, she didn't know what. . . .

* * *

GUARDS WERE PUSHING the main doors closed, but Crusoe's horse just shouldered them aside. They fell, smacking their heads hard against the stone floor. Crusoe tried to quickly work out the lay of the building. The central space he'd ridden into was large and circular, with corridors going left and right, but no obvious staircase leading up to the next floor as he would expect. Monasteries obviously had their own design rules.

Defoe's horse clattered into the hall behind him. Crusoe heard the distinctive sound of a sword being pulled from its scabbard. He did the same, holding on to the horse's reins with his left hand.

"Friday!" he shouted as loudly as he could, and again, "Friday!" There was no response, apart from the sound of booted feet on stone and the sight of black-clad guards running at them from all directions. There were white-clad women as well, wearing strange headgear, but they were running away from the entrance.

Which way to go?

A crossbow bolt *swished* past his face. He felt his hair move. Friday was here. He just had to find her.

The Increment boy—Shadrach—had said she was kept in a room upstairs. They had both been. And he'd said that Friday had told him about spiral staircases at the end of the corridors.

A saw-edged disc snagged the shoulder of his jacket before zinging and bouncing off the ceiling. From behind him he heard Defoe's sword clashing against someone else's blade.

"Follow me!" he shouted to Defoe, pulling on his horse's reins to head down the corridor to his left.

As his horse sprang into action, three sharp-edged discs and two crossbow bolts went through the space his body had just occupied.

There were two guards heading down the corridor toward him. He engaged one with his sword, knocking the man backward with the impact, while he kicked the other one in the cheek.

The guard spun around but didn't fall. Crusoe brought his sword over and intercepted the guard's blade, pulling his horse sideways. The horse obediently stepped sideways into the guard, knocking him off his feet with its flank. A hoof came down on the guard's sword arm, and he screamed. Crusoe heard the snap of bone breaking.

This horse was a natural-born warrior, he decided.

The guard he had knocked away with his sword came rushing back, blade swinging down like a man chopping wood with an ax. Crusoe swung his sword up and blocked it. The impact sent painful vibrations through his arm. The guard pulled his blade back and lunged toward Crusoe again, but he was aiming clumsily upward. Crusoe engaged the blade, twisting his arm to bring his opponent's own blade around in a circle and to get in underneath it. He suddenly flicked his sword sideways, taking the guard's blade with it. Before the man could react, Crusoe brought his blade slashing back. It caught the man across his face from cheek to cheek, opening up his nose. He screamed and fell backward.

Crusoe urged his horse forward along the corridor. Defoe followed on.

A door opened beside him. He just had time to see a guard in the doorway holding a sword, and behind him two rows of beds, all apparently occupied by injured patients. Everyone was looking toward the door.

He was past it before he could do anything. Behind him he heard a clatter of hooves as Defoe pulled his horse up, and the unmistakable clash of metal blades striking each other. Despite the fact that he desperately wanted to get to Friday, the corridor was wide enough to turn his horse around, so he pulled on the reins and headed back to help his friend.

Defoe and the guard were engaged in a fierce fight, with the guard trying to cut Defoe's horse's legs out from underneath it and Defoe leaning over dangerously in his saddle, intercepting the slashes as best he could. Defoe was definitely on the defensive. The horse was dancing back and forth in a strangely delicate manner, knowing that something was going on but unsure what to do.

Crusoe rode up behind the guard and brought his sword down, biting deep into the man's shoulder. He screamed and jerked backward, dropping his blade. Crusoe booted him in the head so that he fell, sprawling backward into the room. Crusoe found himself thinking that the man was lucky—he was in the best place for treatment.

Defoe nodded his thanks and urged his horse into a gallop, heading off down the corridor. Crusoe was about to follow but a shadow cast across the ground made him look up.

A rider was thundering toward him, sword extended. The light from the lanterns on the corridor's walls glittered off it menacingly.

He urged his horse toward the approaching rider and raised his sword in response.

The two swords struck as the horses went past each other. Sparks flew in the corridor, falling like fiery rain.

The guard hauled his horse around and slashed at Crusoe again. Crusoe intercepted the blow with his sword. The impact numbed his arm and he nearly dropped the blade. His horse, sensing that its master needed help, lowered its head and rammed itself into the side of the guard's horse, sending it staggering sideways.

Crusoe clenched his fist around the hilt of the sword and brought it quickly upward, just as the guard got his horse under control. The pommel on the end of the hilt struck the guard in the nose. He yelled out in pain and threw his hands up reflexively to protect himself. His sword went flying out of his hand as blood splattered down his chin. Crusoe shoved him with the hand holding the reins. The man fell from his horse, hitting the ground heavily.

Crusoe shot a glance toward the hall and the door. More guards were rushing toward him, three on foot and one behind them on a horse.

He pulled on the reins, pointed the horse toward the end of the corridor, where Defoe had come to a puzzled halt, and dug his heels into the horse's flanks. It sprang into action, bolting along the wide stone floor.

When he got to Defoe he scanned the doors at the end of the corridor. The last door on the right was higher and wider than the others, and the hinges were on a different side. He leaned forward and pushed against it. The door swung open, revealing a stone spiral staircase leading upward.

"You can't be serious!" Defoe said, aghast.

"She's up there," Crusoe insisted. He glanced back, then reached out with his sword hand and used the weapon to unhook the nearest lantern from the wall. It slid down the blade to bang hard against his fingers. With a sudden gesture he flicked his arm up, sending the lantern hurtling away from him. It hit the floor halfway down the corridor, sending hot oil across the stones. Moments later the spilled oil ignited in a sheet of flame.

The approaching guards fell back, arms upraised to protect themselves. The horse, who was almost at the flames, reared up, unseating its rider. He fell, hard.

Defoe laughed, grabbed a lantern, and threw it. The glass and metal shattered against the wall, sending a blanket of fire across one of the doors. The dry wood caught immediately. There were screams from inside the room. Crusoe tried to tell himself that they might well be innocent patients, there for treatment, but he knew he couldn't afford to feel for them. He had a task to complete.

Before he could reconsider, he urged his horse through the door. The horse hung back for a second, then did as Crusoe wanted.

The stairs were wide near the wall but narrow near the central spine of the staircase, and the horse had difficulty finding its footing. Its hooves slipped on the stone, making the animal stagger and threatening to send Crusoe plummeting to the floor, where he might smash his head open. He secured his sword back into its sheath and took tight hold of the reins with both hands. By sheer force of will he forced the nervous horse onward.

Behind him he could hear Defoe's horse clattering uncertainly around the turns of the stairway. There was shouting somewhere below him. He kept pressing on.

At the top of the stairs was a flat area, leading to another door that opened inward. Crusoe had to maneuver himself and his horse carefully so he could open it. Eventually, he managed to get it wide enough for his relieved horse to exit the stairwell. Defoe and his horse followed moments later.

The corridor was mercifully empty of guards. Crusoe galloped along, counting doors, until he was where Shadrach had said Friday was held. Leaping off his horse, he pushed the door open.

She was there, as he knew she had to be. She was chained to a bed, straining to sit as upright as she could. There was some kind of strange flower—no, a mushroom—on a dish by the side of her head. It looked swollen to the point of bursting.

He moved closer to the bed, ready to get her out of the chains.

Her expression changed to one of horror as he moved closer to the mushroom. "Don't touch that thing!"

"What is it?" he asked.

"It's what makes the Circle," she said grimly.

The Escape

Suriya should have realized that everything was going to change. She cursed herself for not anticipating it and preparing better. Mohir gazed at her with a challenging smile on his face. The talks he'd had in her father's cabin. The way the other members of the pirate crew had begun to whisper to one another when she passed by. It all pointed to something, but she'd not seen it. Not until the moment when her father had called her in to speak with him.

They were back at the island again. It was the third trip that the Dark Nebula *had made to the same secluded cove. She knew it was the same island because she recognized the central peak surrounded by smaller hills and the way the jungle seemed to creep up the sides of that peak like attacking armies. It was the same island where Delahey, the Belgian pirate, had been eaten by ants while she watched from hiding.*

In the meantime, they had made several trips back to the floating wooden island of Lemuria. The crew of the Dark Nebula *was getting restless at the lack of spoils from attacking other ships. Red Tiberius had seemed preoccupied—more concerned with returning to the island time and time again, climbing one of the taller hills by himself and spending several hours in a particular cave—a cave off-limits to the rest of his crew, on pain of death—before returning with a sack full of something he had collected. Suriya was pretty sure that he was taking something from the island and giving it to the black-robed people who lived on Lemuria. She guessed it was the mushrooms that Delahey had been shouting about before he was killed, but what were the mushrooms for? Were they something* used for pleasure, like tobacco or strong drink, or some kind of medicine?

She was sitting up at the stern of the ship, staring out over the island, when her father called her. She thought she'd seen a faint wisp of smoke and was wondering whether anyone actually lived there, when his voice interrupted her.

"Suriya—come here. I need to talk to you."

She walked over to the steps and descended to the quarterdeck. Her father wasn't visible, but the door to his cabin was open. There was only darkness within.

She felt a crawling sensation on her skin and stared out over the main deck. Mohir was there, a marlinspike in his hands. He had been in the process of splitting two twisted strands of rope apart, but had now stopped and was watching her closely. He was smiling, but it wasn't a smile of friendship or even of humor. It was a smile of triumph. Of possession.

She shivered, and walked into her father's cabin.

Red Tiberius was standing behind the carved desk he had plundered from a galley some years before. There was a dark stain on the wood where the blood of the galley's captain had soaked in. Sometimes she had seen her father absently running his hands over the stain as if remembering the attack.

Now, however, his back was to her and he stared out the narrow panes of glass that made up the window in the ship's stern.

"Father?" she said submissively.

"I have some news for you," he said.

"Are we leaving the island again?"

He shook his head. "No—not yet, anyway." He paused, as if searching for the right words. "You know that when a woman gets to a certain age it is customary for her to take a husband?"

Her stomach suddenly lurched, as if the ship was in the middle of a violent storm, although the sea outside was calm. She tried to keep her own voice as calm as the sea as she replied: "That is the custom, I know, but—"

"I have decided that Mohir will take you to be his wife. He has been asking me for some time. I have put him off before but . . ." He sighed. "But Mohir's influence over the crew is strong, and there has been little booty recently to keep them, and him, happy."

"You're throwing me to him the way you might throw a bone to a dog to stop it from biting you," she said. She tried to make her voice angry, but she could hear the tremor in it. If she could hear it, then her father could, too.

"Best not to think of it like that," Red Tiberius said. "I am told that the royal houses often marry their children in order to form alliances of blood. This is no different."

"Can you at least turn and look me in the eye as you barter me away?" she said.

He made a small, dismissive movement of his right hand. "Go to Mohir. Make him happy. He is a good man—a loyal man. He will treat you well."

"Is there anything I can say to change your mind?" she pleaded.

He shook his head. "Nothing. The decision is taken."

Suriya took a deep breath. Straightening her back and raising her chin, she turned and walked calmly out of her father's cabin. The glare outside momentarily blinded her, and she stopped. There seemed to be no noise on the Dark Nebula apart from the cries of the seagulls and the albatross circling its masts. Their cries sounded like the last appeals of lost souls.

She realized that Mohir was standing at the top of the stairs that led down to the main deck. He reached out a hand and gestured to her with his fingers. "Come here, woman," he said.

She should have known that this was coming. All of the doubloons, the silver, and the jewels she had managed to take from under the noses of the pirates over the past few years, all the maggot-ridden biscuits and dried meat that she had hidden away—none of it would do her any good now. She was on her own.

She began to run toward the side of the ship closest to the island. Her feet slapped against the wooden planks of the deck. Behind her she could hear Mohir's muffled curse, and the thudding of his boots as he moved to intercept her. She imagined his thick, calloused hands reaching out for her, and the horror that ran through her added speed to her legs. The side of the ship was getting closer. Something tugged at her hair, but she jerked her head free. There was no time to climb over the side, or look for a rope or a ladder. She dived, not even knowing what was on the other side. There might have been rocks, or a spit of sand, but as she cleared the rail and began to fall, arms outstretched in front of her and palms together, she saw that the sea was clear and blue.

Her hands hit the water and it parted before her. She dived deep, bending her back so that her path curved toward the beach that she had briefly seen as she fell. Kicking with her legs, she tried to put as much distance as she could between her and the Dark Nebula before she surfaced again.

Eventually, just as the breath began to burn in her lungs, her head broke the surface and she started to swim. No time to look behind her. She pulled herself through the waves with a powerful overarm stroke. She thought she could hear cries behind her, but she kept going. She didn't know what the island held for her, but there had to be enough game and fruit there for her to survive. Whatever happened, it would be better than the fate that awaited her back on the ship.

She swam until she could feel the drag of the sand beneath her, then struggled to her feet and splashed out onto the beach. Risking a glance over her shoulder, she saw that Mohir and three other pirates had launched one of the Dark Nebula's boats. They were rowing furiously, trying to get to the beach before she vanished into the foliage that paralleled the line of the sea.

She had to decide which way to go, and quickly.

And she had to pray that she found some way of evading them, of hiding, of surviving there on the island by herself.

It would be a harsh life. But still better than being on the Dark Nebula.

She ran toward the foliage, angling in the direction of the smoke she had seen earlier. If there were people on the island, perhaps she could seek sanctuary with them. Perhaps there might be someone there who could protect her from Mohir. . . .

CHAPTER FOURTEEN

F riday stared up at Robin in gratitude and wonder.

"I thought I'd lost you."

"Never," he said reassuringly. He bent down to check the padlocks that held her to the bed. "If I had a bent nail," he said, "I could get these open within a minute."

"There's a bent nail under my collar," she responded.

He smiled. "Of course there is."

True to his word, he undid the padlocks quickly.

"How did you find me?" she asked as he worked.

"One of John Caiaphas's men—I think he was here as well."

"Paul!" She felt a flush of relief. He'd gotten away safely, and that made what she'd been through worthwhile.

She was just rubbing the circulation back into her hands when Daniel Defoe appeared in the doorway. He smiled when he saw that Friday was all right. "Young Crusoe was worried," he said. "I thought I'd better come with him."

"Of course," she said, feeling happier than she had in a long while.

Defoe saw the mushroom by Friday's head and frowned. He stepped closer to it. "I don't think much of the decoration in here," he said, leaning closer.

"Get away from it, Daniel," Friday warned.

He turned to look at her, but he didn't shift position. "Why? What is it?"

"Seriously, Daniel—move away! It's something to do with the Circle. It's what they use to recruit people!"

"Then I'd better remove it," he said. Before she could object, he had picked up the stool and was carrying it through the doorway into the next room.

"We discovered that the Circle has some kind of bizarre plot to kill particular people using strange animals," Robin told her.

"I know," she said. "Or at least, I've seen some of the animals. There's a greenhouse full of carnivorous tropical bats in the back garden." She felt her face twist into a sudden grimace. "Robin— my father is here. And Mohir. My father and Doctor Mors both told me that I was going to be recruited into the Circle whether I wanted to or not . . . but why would they all want me to be exposed to a *mushroom?*"

"Good question," Defoe said, coming back into the room. "I suggest we postpone the answer to another time and get out of here while we still can."

There were two horses standing calmly outside the room. Friday stared at them.

"You brought friends," she said. "Which one is mine?"

"You can ride behind me," Robin said. He moved toward the horse. "We're going to have to fight our way out."

"Then *you'd* better ride behind *me,*" she replied.

THERE WAS NOISE and confusion from back where they had come, suggesting that the Circle guards had made it up the spiral staircase. They couldn't see anyone yet, but it was only a matter of time.

Crusoe glanced left and right. There was a commotion in both directions now. Friday caught his eye. "In the hall there's a library," she said. "The window frame is loose. Paul and I escaped that way earlier. They may have put the window back, but they can't have made it secure—not yet."

He nodded. "Lead the way."

Friday went back toward the central hall. Crusoe mounted his horse, and he and Defoe followed.

They could see guards armed with swords, crossbows, and disc-weapons advancing toward them from the staircase that Crusoe and Defoe had come up. Friday diverted sideways, through a doorway. They followed, dismounting from their horses when they got inside.

The room was a library, as Friday had said, lined with shelves of old books and manuscripts and with freestanding bookcases in the center. Crusoe immediately saw what Friday had meant—the entire window that looked out over the back of the house had been roughly jammed back into the rectangular hole in the wall. It would be the work of seconds to push it out.

Defoe and Crusoe set to work overturning bookcases so that they fell against the door, spilling their contents but ensuring that it couldn't be opened.

"Do we have to climb?" Crusoe called to Friday, where she was busy pulling the window from its frame again. "What about the horses?" He crossed to join her, passing the table on which the vials of mysterious liquid that Friday had noticed earlier still stood.

"I think they're important," Friday said, glancing around. "Isaac might be able to work out what they are. We should take them with us. They have something to do with what the Circle is doing."

Crusoe joined Friday at the window. "I think I know," he said. "It's how the Circle gets their creatures to attack their victims."

"Like drawing ants to honey." She nodded, remembering. "There's an ornamental pond just beneath the window. We'll have to abandon the horses—for the moment, at least."

He could hear a pounding noise from the doorway—a regular banging, indicating that the guards outside were using some kind of battering ram to try to push the door in.

Crusoe joined Friday at the window. Together they each pushed on their side of the window, moving it closer to the edge of the hole in the wall.

"Wait," Friday said. At Crusoe's questioning glance she said, "We have to time this carefully." She waited until the latest and loudest crash from the door, counted to three, and then shouted, "Push!"

They both heaved. The window and the frame came loose and began to fall. Just as they reached the ground there was another crash from the door as the battering ram hit. The noise covered the sound of the frame and the glass smashing on the flagstones.

"Come on," Friday said. "Let's get out of here."

Defoe joined them. He was staring at the wooden case containing the vials of liquid. "We can't carry that case down while we're climbing," he pointed out. "We'd need to lower it down with a rope."

"We haven't got time to search for ropes," Crusoe pointed out.

Defoe pointed upward. "There's a bell tower up there," he said, "from when this building was a monastery." He pointed to a doorway at the side of the room. "And if I have my geography correct, that door over there leads to the stairs up into the bell tower."

Crusoe frowned. "But we can't—oh! The bell ropes!"

"Exactly. Let's hope they weren't removed when this place was converted."

"I'll cut the ropes at the top," Crusoe said, springing into action. "You collect them as they fall and then climb down yourselves. I'll follow on," he said. He grabbed his sword from the scabbard hanging from his horse's saddle and scooped up the vial of yellow liquid that was sitting on the table next to the case. "Just in case we can't get the case lowered," he said, slipping it into his pocket and heading for the small side door. It creaked as he opened it.

He found stairs on the other side of the door, but they were wooden and they went around the square inside of a tower that rose up for several hundred feet. There was another door on the far side of the tower, but fortunately it was bolted. Nobody could get through from outside the library. Up toward the top of the tower Crusoe could see a wooden platform. Luckily, there were ropes hanging down from a square hole in the center of the platform. They ended in braided grips.

He took a deep breath, tucked his sword into his belt for safety, and started to sprint up the stairs.

The square spiral went three times around the inside of the tower, and Crusoe was out of breath, stumbling and supporting his weight with his hands as he approached the top. Thankfully, he hauled himself through the small square hole that led up onto the platform.

Vertical slits in the stone walls encircled the tower, from where the sound of the bells would have escaped to the surrounding countryside. Seven bells hung from the roof, ranging in size from a small child to a medium-sized pony. They were covered in dust, and cobwebs linked them to the tower's walls and its roof. Ropes hung down from complicated wooden mechanisms that enabled them to be rung from far below. Icicles surrounded the rims of the bells like teeth around gaping mouths.

The sound of the Circle guards trying to get into the library was muffled now by distance and by the whistling of the wind around and through the tower.

He got as close to the edge of the central hole as he could, pulled the sword from his belt, and slashed at the nearest bell rope. It fell, coiling as it dropped away like a snake. He heard the sound as it hit the stone floor, and Defoe's shout of, "Got it! Well done!"

He was just about to start down the stairway again when something pushed him from behind. Before he could catch hold of anything he was tumbling helplessly into the center of the bell tower.

FRIDAY MANAGED TO tie one end of the rope that Robin had provided to the wooden case and lower it to the ground while Defoe tied the other end to one leg of the heavy table.

Just as they finished, one of the bells in the tower began to ring.

"Either young Crusoe is in trouble," Defoe said, frowning, "or the Circle's guards are up there ringing the alarm. Either way I should go check. You get out."

She nodded, crossed to the window, and began to climb over. The climb down was easier this time, and within a few seconds she had slithered down the rope to the garden. There were no guards around—they must have all been called into the hospital.

She was just about to move away from the wall when there was a crash and something smashed through the ice of the pond. Water splashed upward. Friday thought that the droplets at the edges of the water were turning into ice even as she watched.

The ringing of the bell was stopping now but, whether or not it had been an alarm, the Circle guards were responding. The black-clad men that Sister Berenice had called Brothers were running across the grounds of the hospital and setting up a defensive line facing out, away from Friday. A few carried something that looked like a cross between a cannon and a very large crossbow. She had no idea what they were. Others set up boxes beside the strange weapons.

Two figures came around the edge of the hospital and sprinted toward a wooden building on the other side of the greenhouse.

It was her father and Doctor Mors.

As Friday watched, they tore off their robes and threw their masks on the ground. They had obviously decided that discretion was the better part of valor. If the alarm was wrong they could always come back.

Her father turned and—

No, she thought, if he has no daughter, then I have no father.

Red Tiberius turned and glanced behind him. He saw Friday standing on the edge of the pond and gestured to the two nearest Brothers who were setting up the strange cannon/crossbow weapons. He pointed to Friday. They immediately swung the device around and aimed it at her. One of them started winding the crank on the metal bow backward while the other one took something from a box and placed it in front of the twisted rope that served as an exaggerated drawstring. At a signal, the first Brother pulled a lever, and the curved metal bow suddenly straightened with a deep, echoing *twang*.

A metal ball, about the size of Friday's head, flew in a low arc across the ground between the weapon and the hospital. For a second or two she thought it was a cannonball, fired by a sprung metal bow and a twisted rope rather than gunpowder, but the ball seemed to be trailing a burning piece of string. It passed to the left of the pond and hit the cloisters running down the side of the hospital. A sudden explosion rent the air, deafening her and almost knocking her off her feet. She looked down the side of the building. A pillar had been smashed into pieces. She looked urgently back to where the two men were reloading the weapon. Somehow they were firing iron balls that actually *contained* gunpowder, rather than using gunpowder to fire the balls themselves. Another Chinese invention adopted by the Circle?

The two Brothers had reloaded by now. They adjusted the position of the weapon, compensating for the way the previous shot had gone.

Red Tiberius and Doctor Mors had reached the wooden building. Friday could see now that it was a stable, and a Brother was saddling horses for them to make their escape.

Without his mask, Doctor Mors was obviously younger than her father. His hair was so blond that it was almost white, but it was his face that made Friday gasp. His skin was pockmarked, ravaged by disease, and his nose was half-eaten away.

She switched her gaze back to the two Brothers with the weapons, just as they fired again.

The ball of gunpowder arced through the air, directly toward where she was standing . . .

. . . And dropped into the pond, smashing some of the fragments of ice that were still left into smaller bits. The fuse fizzled out and the ball sank to the bottom of the pond. Friday heard curses from the direction of the weapon.

She glanced around. Brothers were setting up defensive lines at both ends of the hospital building. There was no escape in those directions.

The weapon fired again. An iron ball filled with gunpowder flew toward her, above the pond, and hit the flagstones, cracking one into pieces. It rolled toward her and stopped a few feet away. Friday could see the fuse burning, vanishing into the metal shell.

A figure pushed past her and threw itself onto the ball.

She recognized him instantly. It was Paul Shadrach. Somehow he'd found his way back into the hospital grounds, looking for her.

Nothing happened. The ball didn't explode.

Paul rolled off the iron sphere and onto the flagstones. He was holding the fuse in his hand. He had pulled it out of the sphere and stopped the burning with his fingers.

"How's that?" he asked.

Friday looked at the iron ball, then at the Brothers, who were winding their bow back for another shot.

"What are you *doing* here?"

"I said I'd be back. The Increment is following on, but I rode ahead."

"You idiot!" She smiled to take the sting out of the words. "Do you have a flint on you?" she asked.

He nodded. "I smoke a pipe sometimes."

She tore a section of her shirt off, bent down, and thrust it into the hole in the ball where Paul had pulled the fuse out. "Light this," she said.

He pulled his flint out of a pocket and struck it. Sparks flew. Within a few seconds the material of her shirt was alight, but because it was longer than the original fuse she had more time. A little more time.

"Stay here," she said. She picked up the ball and started to run around the pond toward the two Brothers and their weapon.

They looked at her, aghast. Quickly, they fired again, but the ball went past her and over the pond. She hoped that Paul had the sense—and the speed—to get out of the way.

The explosion behind her rocked the ground and nearly knocked her off her feet, but she kept running. The Brothers were frantically trying to reload, but they didn't manage it before she threw the iron ball toward them. The cloth fuse was still burning. It hit the grass just in front of the weapon and rolled underneath it.

The Brothers ran just before it went off, blowing the weapon apart.

As Crusoe fell he saw, from the corner of his eye, the bell ropes flashing past. He twisted his body in midair and grabbed for the nearest bell rope with his left hand—the one that wasn't holding his sword. The fibers were icy, and they slid through his fingers. He clenched his fist harder and dug his fingernails in. The nail on the middle finger of his left hand tore, and he almost lost his grip, but he stopped slipping down the rope. Instead, he swayed as it swung to and fro. Above him a bell began to ring—a mournful tone, distorted by the icicles around its edge. As the clapper hit the bell again the icicles dislodged and began to fall around him like tiny white spears.

He glanced back up to where he had been standing. A dark figure stared down at him, hands behind its back.

Mohir.

The pirate was dressed in his usual colorful silks and leathers, with a leather overcoat hanging down to his heavy boots. He was smiling. Gold teeth glinted in the meager winter sunlight.

"You are the boy she prefers over me?" He shook his head. "Ah, you are weak and stupid. She would have done much better had she married me, as her father intended."

"She hates you," Crusoe gasped.

Mohir shrugged. "That doesn't matter. Only her father's wishes and my desires matter." He brought his hands out from behind him. He was holding a crossbow. The drawstring was cocked, and a bolt was ready to fire.

Crusoe desperately looked around for some chance, some possibility, of survival. Hanging there, he was a perfect target. Mohir couldn't miss.

In the belfry above, the bell kept tolling as if signaling his imminent death.

He dropped the sword and grabbed for a different bell rope with his right hand. A second bell began to ring, discordant with the first. More icicles began to fall.

A *twang* echoed around the tower. The bolt flashed past his chest, tearing through the material of his shirt, and he heard it strike the wall behind him and clatter to the stairs.

Somewhere down below, his sword clattered against the stone floor of the tower.

Mohir's face contorted into a vicious snarl. He dropped the nose of the crossbow to the platform, put his foot on the bow, and yanked the drawstring back with both hands until it cocked again with a solid *click*. As Crusoe watched, trying to work out his options, the pirate brought the crossbow back up, took a bolt from his pocket, and slipped it in front of the taut drawstring.

"I've seen the strange weapons used by the Circle's guards," he called, "and I appreciate the speed with which they can be reloaded, but there's something about a crossbow that I find appealing." He hefted the weapon in his hands. "At close range I can shoot this into a man's eye and watch it come out the back of his head. Would you like me to demonstrate?"

He pointed the weapon at Crusoe's face and fired.

Taking advantage of the ice on the rope, Crusoe released his grasp and then immediately tightened it again. He slid a few inches downward—enough that the bolt skimmed across his scalp, drawing a line of pain, but it left him dangling from the cut end. His legs thrashed wildly in midair.

Mohir nodded. "You are quick of mind and quick of body. That is why you evaded us for so long on the island." As he spoke, he was already reloading the crossbow. "There you had plenty of places to hide. Here there is *nowhere*."

As the pirate raised the crossbow once again, Crusoe pulled his knees up, changing his center of balance so that he swung forward, then swung his legs behind him again. As Mohir fired, Crusoe's shifting weight propelled his body backward. The bolt went past his shoulder. He brought his knees forward and up again, and when his body had traveled as far forward as it could he let go of the rope and fell toward the wooden stairway that ran around the side of the tower, hoping to land squarely on it.

He fell short. The edge of the wood slammed into his chest, knocking the wind from him and making his vision go red and fuzzy for a few seconds. The fingers of his hands scrabbled on the stairs for purchase. He could feel them gouging splinters out of the wood. The fingernail that he had ripped just a few moments before tore off, sending a wash of agony all the way through his hand and up his arm. His entire left hand began to spasm.

Above him he heard Mohir's booted steps thudding on the wooden platform. The pirate was running around to the other side, probably reloading as he went.

Crusoe managed to swing himself sideways, bringing his left knee up onto the lower stairs. He hauled himself up and desperately rolled toward the wall of the tower.

A crossbow bolt dug into the wood by his cheek, sending splinters flying in all directions.

Scrambling to his feet, he staggered down the stairs, desperately trying to get to a position below where Mohir was standing. Once he was relatively safe—at least for the moment—he leaned back against the wall. He dragged air into his burning lungs while he tried to ignore the pain from where his chest had slammed across the stairs.

Footsteps above him signaled that Mohir was moving around the platform, trying to get a better position from which to fire again.

Crusoe moved up the stairs, trying to keep Mohir above him. Ice crunched beneath his feet from where the icicles had fallen.

He got to the point where the last stretch of stairs led up to a hole in the platform and stopped. Above him, Mohir stopped as well.

Crusoe knew that if he tried to go any farther up the stairs then, his head would be visible above the edge of the hole and Mohir would fire. If he tried to go any farther down, then Mohir would move to the edge of the platform and fire at him as soon as he was in sight. It was a stalemate.

Somewhere down below, Crusoe heard booted footsteps ascending the stairs. Another Circle ruffian? It seemed likely. He was now caught between two men, each of whom would kill him as soon as they saw him—and his sword was lost.

He shifted position and felt something knocking against his boot. He looked down. It was an icicle, one that had fallen from the ringing bells. This one was large—about the length of his arm, and sharply pointed.

He had one chance, and it depended on how accurately he could throw.

He ripped a piece of material away from the hole that the crossbow bolt had left in his shirt, wrapped it around his fingers, and bent to pick up the icicle. It was heavy but the cloth protected his hand from the cold and stopped the icicle from getting slippery. Quietly, he crept up the stairs toward the hatch.

Below him, heavy footsteps thudded up the stairs.

He only had a moment. Picturing in his mind where Mohir was standing, Crusoe abruptly straightened up through the hole in the platform and turned around. The pirate was standing ten feet away, crossbow raised. His eyes widened in surprise when he saw Crusoe.

Crusoe brought his arm up and threw the icicle.

The shard of ice hit Mohir directly in his left eye. His head

jerked back as he cried out. The crossbow fired, but Mohir's movements had disturbed the aim and the bolt went wide.

The pirate dropped the crossbow and raised his hands to his face.
His fingers explored the icicle in disbelief. As Crusoe watched, he
staggered backward toward one of the slit windows in the belfry.
The backs of his knees hit the stone, and he toppled out. With a
shriek, he fell through the gap and vanished.

Crusoe climbed up onto the platform and staggered over to
where the crossbow lay. He had to load it before whoever was
climbing the stairs reached him.

His fingers fumbled with the crossbow, trying to cock it, while
he tried to remember where the last bolt had gone. Was it still on
the platform, or had it fired low? The rest of the bolts had fallen
with Mohir.

The crossbow cocked with a satisfying *click*, but Crusoe couldn't
see the bolt anywhere. He scanned the platform, wondering if
there was an icicle there he could use instead.

Suddenly, a head appeared through the hole in the platform.

"Looking for this?" Defoe asked, holding a bolt up.

Crusoe slumped against the nearest wall. "I thought—"

"You look like hell," Defoe said, climbing all the way up onto
the platform. He walked toward the slit window that Mohir had
fallen through. Crusoe moved to join him.

They looked out and down. Mohir's body had smashed through
the icy pond and into the black water beneath.

"You should have seen the other fellow," Crusoe muttered.

CHAPTER FIFTEEN

Friday turned to make sure Paul had escaped the previous explosion. For a second she couldn't see him. The place where he had been standing was blown into a mass of stone fragments and churned-up earth. Her heart raced as she imagined him being blown apart by the metal ball as well.

A hand emerged from the pond, then another hand. She watched as a head appeared. . . .

It was Paul. He pulled himself slowly out of the freezing water and lay on his back, breathing heavily. She could see blood in his hair.

She started to move back toward him, but something hit her from behind, knocking her over. As she hit the ground, she rolled sideways, and a horse's hoof came down just where her head had been. If she had tried to roll a moment later she would be dead.

She scrambled to her feet. A horse was standing side-on to her, just a few feet away. Doctor Mors sat in the saddle, his blond hair plastered over his forehead. His right hand was hidden by the horse's body.

He shook his head. "Our plans were so large, and you are so small," he said gently. "How is it that you have managed such devastation?"

"I had help," she said. "And I had right on my side."

Behind Mors she could see her father on a second horse. He seemed to be waiting—either for Mors to join him or for the situation to resolve itself. Perhaps he realized that there was no attack from outside—that all the chaos and confusion was down to Friday, Crusoe, Defoe, and Paul.

Mors brought his right hand up from where it was hidden. He was holding a massively curved blade. It looked like something a farmer might use to thresh crops.

Now Red Tiberius trotted up beside Mors. He gazed down at Friday impassively. There was something about the lack of emotion in his expression, and in Mors's stance, that chilled her to the bone. She couldn't move.

"This is an amputation knife," Mors said in a calm, almost disinterested voice. "I usually use it to remove arms and legs swiftly and cleanly. In your case—and on your father's orders—I intend using it to take off your head."

CRUSOE WATCHED FROM the belfry as Doctor Mors's horse began slowly to approach Friday. She seemed frozen, unable to move.

He desperately scanned the grounds of the hospital, looking for something, anything, he could use to help her. Apart from the crossbow, he had nothing—and the crossbow only had one bolt. One chance to save Friday—but Red Tiberius was there as well, holding back to see what Mors was going to do.

A thought flashed across Crusoe's mind. He reached into his pocket and pulled out the vial of yellow oil. It had survived unscathed, thank heaven. If it was what he *thought* it was—separate from the rest of the oils—it was probably the one that Doctor Mors was going to use next.

Quickly, Crusoe unwrapped the cloth from his hand and used it to tie the vial to the head of the crossbow bolt. It wasn't secure, but it just might work.

He leaned out of the window and aimed the crossbow at Doctor Mors, then aimed slightly up. He was higher than his target, and if he aimed directly at the Doctor, then the bolt would just drop and plow into the ground.

"Friday!" he shouted.

She turned. Even at that distance he could see the desperation in her eyes being replaced with hope.

"The greenhouse!" he called, and fired the crossbow.

The bolt arced downward in a perfect curve. The weight of the tiny vial dragged it down, but he had compensated for that. It was almost perfectly on target. Almost.

The vial missed Doctor Mors but it hit his saddle. The glass smashed, splashing the oil inside over him and Red Tiberius next to him. The two men flinched as the oil soaked them, looking around to see where it had come from.

"The greenhouse!" he yelled again, but Friday was already moving. She scooped up stones from the ground as she ran and threw them at the blacked-out windows, one after another. The glass smashed, tinkling to the ground in sharp shards that reminded him of the icicles.

For a long moment, nothing happened. Friday kept running, kept throwing stones, while Doctor Mors and Red Tiberius stared at her.

Doctor Mors realized first. His face suddenly convulsed in fear and he jabbed his heels into his horse's side, goading it to a gallop, but he was too late. A dark cloud burst from every broken window: hundreds of creatures with leathery wings and gaping jaws lined with needle-like teeth expanding into the sky as if to make their escape, but then looping back, attracted by the adulterated oil. They struck at Doctor Mors, covering him from head to toe in a mass of black fur and wings. His horse panicked. It bucked up on its hind legs, throwing Mors to the ground. Within moments he was hidden by a mass of flying creatures, all voraciously trying to get to his exposed flesh.

Red Tiberius pulled his horse around, his face contorted in a curdled mixture of rage and fear. He galloped away, toward the boundary of the hospital grounds, but the creatures followed him in a massive smokelike trail.

From where she stood in the gardens, Friday looked up at Crusoe. He could feel her warmth and her gratitude.

"Thanks," she called.

"Don't make a habit of it," he called back. "I'm not sure I'll be able to do that again."

The Escape

Suriya crouched behind a rock, scanning the beach for any movement. She couldn't see the pirates, but she didn't think that they had gone back to the Dark Nebula. *Her father's wrath would be like a force of nature, and nobody would want to tell him they had lost track of his daughter. Men had lost ears, eyes, and hands for less than that.*

She closed her eyes for a moment and took a long breath, trying to calm her racing heart. Her actions in jumping off the ship and swimming to shore had been impulsive. She didn't have a plan in mind— she just knew that she couldn't stay on that ship a moment longer. Not if her father really was going to give her in marriage to Mohir.

She had known this day would come. She had tried to persuade herself that things could go on as they always had, with her living alongside the pirates but never being part of the crew, but that had been a dream. Just a dream. Maybe she should have thought things through better. Maybe she should have collected together the various things she had scavenged over the years and left the ship at some port where she could quickly have gotten lost. But that wouldn't have worked, she realized her father always sent two members of the crew with her when she went ashore. She had thought, in her innocence, that it was to keep her safe, but now she knew that it was also to make sure she came back.

The sun was warm on her face and shoulders, and the sky was a deep blue. Seabirds circled over the waves, and often they would pull their wings in and suddenly dive into the sea in search of fish. Judging by the frequency of the dives, there must have been a lot of fish out there, and that was good. If she was going to have to survive on the island by herself, then she was going to need a source of food.

She looked away from the beach, to where the hills rose up toward the blue bowl of the sky. There was a lot of vegetation up there, which meant fruit, and probably some kind of animal that she could hunt and kill for food. There would be caves where she could shelter. All in all, this island wasn't a bad place to live her life. Of course, even if it had been a bleak, black rock it would have been preferable to life married to Mohir.

She felt suddenly dizzy as her body began to relax. She knelt down, the sand rough against her knees. She knew that life on the island would only be possible if her father gave up the search for her, but she also knew that he was under pressure to get those strange mushrooms back to the floating wooden island of Lemuria. At some stage he would have to make the decision to leave her behind.

Suriya felt the tension in her chest easing as the possibilities began to unfold in front of her. Maybe, at some time in the future, another ship would arrive, and she could leave the island and travel elsewhere.

Her lips curved into a smile. Her impulsive action might, accidentally, work out well. Her only regret was leaving Diran behind, but there had been no chance to take him with her and there was no chance now that she could go back for him. But he was clever, and he worked hard. He would survive. He would probably prosper. Perhaps he might even escape one day, on another island, or in some distant port.

A hand clamped around her mouth and pulled her backward.

She fought, biting and scratching, but the hand wouldn't let go. An arm went around her throat and began to choke her.

"Stop fighting, and I will release you."

She felt despair wash through her like a bucket of cold water dumped over her head. It was Mohir's grating voice. The pirates had found her again.

She relaxed in his grip, but only to fool him into thinking she was surrendering. Her fingers closed around a handful of warm, gritty sand. Abruptly, she threw it back, over her shoulder. Mohir cursed as the sand went in his eyes, and the arm that had clamped tightly around her neck loosened a fraction. Suriya threw her weight backward. Surprised, Mohir began to topple. Suriya twisted in his grip and wriggled free. Without looking back, she ran.

She could hear feet pounding the sand behind her. Several sets of feet. She sprinted along the beach, parallel to the waves. She had no plan in mind, no destination. She just had to get away. She just had to survive the next few seconds, then the few seconds after that, and so on until she was free.

A body crashed into her and she fell forward, into the sand. The impact knocked the breath from her body. By the time she knew what was going on she had been pulled to her feet and was being *pushed along by the pirates. They were laughing. They knew there would be a reward for bringing Red Tiberius's daughter back to the ship.*

No. She couldn't allow it to happen. She would rather die.

She was already walking slowly, trying to get her breath back, and she began to deliberately slow down more. Without noticing, Mohir and the other pirates began to slow down with her. Eventually, when she judged they had slowed down enough, she abruptly started to run.

She knew they would catch her again, but she knew that if she angered them enough, then one of them would hit her, or strangle her, and then it would all be over.

As her feet hit the sand so lightly, it felt as if she were flying, and as the warm breeze whistled past her ears and pulled her hair out behind her, she almost managed to resign herself to her fate. She was saying good-bye to everything when she suddenly heard a voice calling: "Here! Quickly!"

She looked up. Ahead of her was a boy, half-hidden by the rocks. She thought he was paler than anyone she had ever seen. She also thought that he was the most handsome thing she had ever seen.

From somewhere inside, new strength flooded her limbs, and she began to speed up, outpacing the pirates.

Perhaps there was hope for a new life after all.

"WHAT'S GOING TO happen with the bats?" Friday asked.

It was the morning of the next day, and they were still at the hospital. Increment personnel had arrived not long after the bats had been released, and they spent the next few hours sorting out who was with the Circle and who was just an ordinary patient in the hospital. Meanwhile Crusoe, Friday, and Daniel had found the kitchens and raided them for an enormous meal they were now eating in the library, despite the missing window and the cold breeze. Crusoe wasn't sure whether it was technically dinner or breakfast, but it was good.

"I suspect they won't survive long in this country," Defoe replied through a mouthful of bread and gravy. "From what Doctor Mors told you they were obtained from the tropics, and that greenhouse was certainly heated to an excessive level to keep them alive. They'll be dead within a few days."

"Let's hope so," Friday said. She had a goblet of water in one hand and a pie crust in the other. "I'm not sure it's part of Segment W's job description to hunt down carnivorous bats."

"Oh, that young man—Shadrach—can do it," Defoe said. "It seems he enjoys that kind of thing."

Crusoe caught Friday's eye. "Speaking of John and carnivorous bats," he said, "he told me a few minutes ago that his men had found Doctor Mors's body a few miles away. There was enough of him left to identify, but only just."

"And . . . Red Tiberius?" she asked quietly.

"No sign." He tried to smile, but he was so tired his face couldn't quite make it. "Perhaps they ate everything."

"Perhaps. But he has a knack for survival. He's even more poisonous than the bats," she said.

"That Increment lad—Shadrach," Crusoe said slowly. "He was imprisoned like Friday was. Is it possible that he was infected by one of the Circle's mushrooms?" Friday frowned at him, and was about to say something when he added: "He was out of your sight for a while. Someone needs to ask the question."

"Someone already has." The voice came from the doorway. Crusoe looked over, surprised, to see Isaac Newton standing there.

His hair was as wild as usual, and his jacket was half-buttoned. "Sir William specifically asked me to keep an eye on him, just in case."

"Do we know anything about that mushroom, and how it works?" Defoe asked. "I've never heard of anything like it before."

"I have." Newton shrugged. "At least, I have been reading up on something similar, in the journals of some explorers in the Royal Institute's library."

Crusoe and Defoe looked at him in surprise.

"There is a particular type of fungus, described by Richard Hakluyt—one of Queen Elizabeth's favorite explorers. He first encountered it on an island in the Caribbean. He described the way it could infect a large species of ant on the island with its seeds. It would grow inside the ant's head, but instead of killing it the fungus would change the ant's behavior. It would make the ant climb the highest tree in the forest, despite all the danger on the way and the chance that birds would see it once it had reached the top. Once it was at the top of the tree, the fungus would spread through the ant's body and burst it open. The seeds would then spread on the wind all over the forest. If the fungus hadn't made the ants climb so high, then when their bodies burst they wouldn't spread the seeds anywhere near as far."

"We've not seen anything like that with the Circle's people," Defoe pointed out. "They haven't got mushrooms growing in their heads—have they?"

Friday shook her head. "I think these mushrooms work differently," she said.

Defoe nodded. "I wouldn't be surprised," he said, "if, as well as making their victims believe what they are told without question, the seeds also make them exhibit arrogant and grandiose behavior, and believe that they were born to rule the world. We've certainly seen Lord Sebastos, Doctor Mors, and Red Tiberius all act that way."

"The mushrooms come from the island." Friday glanced across at Crusoe. "I think that's where my father got them for the Circle. From what I heard on the *Dark Nebula*, it may be the only source."

Newton threw himself heavily into a chair. "I have been trying to determine what the Circle of Thirteen is doing here. They seem to have two different processes at work. On the one hand they want to ensure that the various thugs and ruffians who work for them are loyal to the Circle's beliefs, and won't just run away at the first sign of trouble, so they expose them to the mushrooms very early on in their employment. Once their operatives are exposed, they fall into a trance for a while—during which the unpleasant side effect of the blue rash develops. When the operatives begin to wake they are apparently in a suggestible state, and this is when the Sisters read to them, inculcating them with the Circle's core beliefs." He hesitated for a moment, marshaling his thoughts. "In contrast, if the Circle wishes to 'turn' a member of Segment W, for instance, or perhaps a member of the Royal Court, then they might kidnap that person and expose them to the mushroom seeds while they are imprisoned. The same thing would happen—the person would fall into a trance, and while they were gradually waking up the Sisters would whisper the Circle's beliefs to them. Either way, the Circle ends up with operatives who will apparently fight to the death for the Circle." He frowned. "I almost think that the entire Circle started when one person—I don't know who—was exposed accidentally to the mushrooms while reading some book or manuscript that gave them grandiose ambitions and led them to believe they could take over the globe if they simply killed the right people."

"Perhaps they aren't too far wrong," Defoe observed quietly. "Experience tells us that the Circle isn't doing too badly."

Crusoe glanced between the faces of his friends. "From what you're saying," he pointed out, "the Circle won't stop. They'll keep coming at us, keep killing innocent people, and we don't know how to stop them without killing every single member."

"There is a way," Friday said.

Crusoe turned to stare at her in surprise.

"We have to go back to the island," she said. Her gaze met his, and he could see the steely resolve in her eyes, and beneath that resolve the fear of returning to the place they had struggled to escape. "We have to destroy the mushrooms so that the Circle cannot convert any more operatives to their side."

Crusoe sensed Defoe and Newton holding their breath.

He nodded. "You're right," he said. "We have to go back. It's the only way."

EPILOGUE

D aniel Defoe's rooms in Camden Town were small—
enough for a bed where he slept and a table where he
ate and wrote. He had a family house on the outskirts of
London, but he stayed in these rooms when he needed to be near
Segment W, the palace, his publishers, and his various business in-
terests. At least, that was what Sister Berenice had been told by
the Circle operatives who brought her to London.

She watched from her position in the shadows across the road
as Defoe walked unsteadily down the cobblestones from the tavern
where he had spent the evening. Two of the Circle's operatives had
been there as well, with instructions that if he left before Sister
Berenice had completed her assigned task they were to buy him
drinks and engage him in conversation, stopping him from leaving.
In fact, it hadn't been necessary. Defoe had apparently spent his
time talking to friends, telling tall tales that caused laughter, disbelief, and tears in equal measure. He was, by all accounts, a great
storyteller.

But Sister Berenice had some tales of her own to tell, and she
would be telling them soon.

Once Defoe was asleep and snoring, the warmth of his breath
would cause the black mushroom she had hidden on the floorboards
beneath his bed to start to open. As he unwittingly breathed in the

seeds, he would gradually slip into a deeper sleep—one from which he would not awake for a few days. The Circle operatives in the tavern had heard him tell his friends that he was tired following recent exertions, ones that he mysteriously could not talk about, and that they shouldn't expect to see him for a while. That was all to the good. When she thought he was ready Sister Berenice would slip quietly into his room and begin to read to him from the book she had with her.

And when Defoe's friends saw him again, he would be a different man.

He would be the Circle's man.